SNOW IN SUMMER
THE LANTERN CREEK SERIES, BOOK 2

LAURA KEMP

RAMIREZ & CLARK LLC

PRAISE FOR LAURA KEMP

"Spellbinding, captivating, compelling-- Snow in Summer kept me on the edge of my seat, my heart in my throat, pulse-pounding. There are so many incredible layers to this novel: suspense, paranormal, and time travel all combine with a heartfelt story of love, family, and forgiveness. Justine and Dylan, as well as the rest of the characters, are multi-dimensional and complex. I was completely wrapped up in their personal lives as well as the mysteries and danger that enveloped them. This book is moody and atmospheric, and the setting adds to its allure. Snow in Summer is the sequel to the author's debut novel, Evening in the Yellow Wood. It can be enjoyed as a stand-alone, however, I encourage you to read the first book, so that you can fully appreciate the story and its characters." **Susan Peterson, Sue's Reading Neighborhood.**

"Laura Kemp draws you in from the breath-taking prologue, takes you on a mysterious and intriguing journey, and sets you down at the end, a little shaken, but thrilled. In this compelling follow-up to her genre-bending debut, Ms. Kemp has delivered another winner." **Alison Ragsdale, Bestselling author of *The Art of Remembering*.**

"In Snow in Summer, Laura Kemp weaves a fast-paced, captivating, and intricate story filled with romance, drama, and adventure that's all wrapped up in a hefty dose of the paranormal. With intrigue and secrets galore, readers will be pulled in from the opening pages, no doubt desperate to solve the multiple mysteries in their race to find out who will survive at the end to tell the tale." **-- Hannah Mary McKinnon, internationally bestselling author of *Sister Dear***

"A delightfully creative follow up to the wildly popular, Evening in the Yellow Wood, yet Snow in Summer stands its own in the hierarchy of memorable, edge-of-your seat, plot-twisters, sealing author Laura Kemp's standing among the authors to watch." **Claire Fullerton, author of *Little Tea, Mourning Dove* and others.**

To Scott, I love you more.

"You see it your way, I see it mine, but we both see it slipping away."

—— THE EAGLES

PROLOGUE

Amanda Bennett stood looking over the place where the Great Lakes met the morning sky. The clouds seemed to mix like a charcoal drawing as the sun breached the horizon. A seagull hovered at eye level, and she found herself gazing past it, and then down at the asphalt ribbon that encircled Mackinac Island.

The world was just beginning to awaken with the sound of voices below.

And that was fine, because what she wanted to do did not require secrecy or stealth or privacy, even. She knew what was expected of her. It was not a matter of what was right or wrong, only what she could no longer do.

And who she couldn't live without.

A picket fence surrounded this outcropping of limestone known locally as Robinson's Folly. Legend said that an Ojibwa maiden had jumped to her death from here. She had loved a white fur trapper named Robinson and her father, the chief, would not allow them to marry.

Or maybe the trapper had jumped.

Amanda couldn't remember.

Laughter floated up from below.

She turned from the hovering gull and saw a tandem bike flash silver in the rising sun. A man and woman--lovers perhaps--their voices light as the wind caught hold and lifted them to her perch. There was talk of a party later that night at Horn's bar and a restaurant that served pancakes all day.

Up it came. And vanished.

Amanda took a breath, looked to where the gull had been a moment before but it was gone, having joined a group of birds streaking towards Round Island, its lighthouse as bright as a piece of peppermint candy.

Amanda thought of the birds and wished for their wings.

To go anywhere.

And nowhere.

She gripped the picket fence meant to keep tourists from the same fate as Robinson and his Ojibwa maiden and threw a leg over, then the other, until she stood with her back against the barrier, her fingers gripping wood that was slick with morning dew.

Amanda Bennett breathed in the morning air and smiled, leaned forward until she hovered over nothing.

And let go.

CHAPTER ONE

It was Thursday evening, the sky just calling it quits when my grandmother pulled up outside the bungalow I'd called home for the last ten months. She waved once from behind the windshield of her green Oldsmobile and jumped out with an ease that belied her years.

A few brisk steps carried her across my lawn and when she reached me in my garden she smiled, her eyes reminding me of my father.

She carried my orange tomcat under her arm, having adopted him under the pretense that they could visit occasionally.

So far it had worked. We had started a tradition of gathering in the kitchen of the house my boyfriend and I were renting while he took classes in the neighboring town of Alpena. The past three months we had finally been able to save more than we spent, and I was downright giddy to be making a home with the man I adored.

"Good to see you," she said, her voice full of the familiarity I'd dreamed about while growing up without her. "Joey just came for the catnip."

"Iris," I stood up and dusted my hands on the back of my worn denim jeans. I was unable to call her "Grandma" or "Granny" ...or "Nana," even. Absent from my life for the first twenty-two years, she would remain Iris.

For now.

"Where's Dylan?" she asked, and I smiled, secretly suspecting she liked looking at him as much as I did.

"He picked up an extra shift at the station," I answered. "But he'll be home soon."

"Don't let me keep you," she smiled, dropping Joey in front of me where he did his customary figure eight swish around my legs. "I know this was a surprise."

"It's okay," I assured her, appreciating the congeniality that had helped me regain some normalcy since the summer before, a season in my life my best friend Holly had dubbed "The Strange Occurrence of the Flatlander and the Friggin' Freak."

Holly had only been privy to a portion of the so-called "Strange Occurrence." Dylan, myself, and my younger brother Adam had been the ones forced to combat Henry Younts- an immortal Lutheran preacher hell-bent on revenge. Although his son, a handyman named Jamie or Jonas depending on the century, had grown on me despite the fact he had been driving when his fiancée was killed in a car accident, a woman he thought was me at the time.

But that's another story.

I shook the memory off and tried to smile as Iris surveyed my attempt at a raised garden bed.

"Your radishes look tasty," she said, one finger beneath her chin.

I chuckled. Anyone could grow a radish, and still a compliment from Iris was worth its weight in gold.

"Maybe I can take some home with me."

I nodded, rocked back on my heels and took a deep breath, the evening air reminding me of last summer.

"What are you thinking about?"

I started, unnerved by Iris' uncanny ability to read my mood.

"Hmmm," I said, my laughter light. "Not much."

She touched my shoulder. "You can't fool me, Muffet."

I laughed again, realizing there was no reason to hide my feelings from her.

"Well, it's been a year...exactly."

"A year?" she asked.

"Since I went with Dave and Holly to that karaoke bar out on 68 for dollar Jell-O shots."

"Jell-O shots?"

"And Jamie Stoddard took me home. Or at least I thought he was. But then Dylan pulled us over and I jumped out of the truck because I thought he was going to murder me."

"You did?"

"Which makes it exactly two years since Karen died."

"Karen?"

"Jamie's fiancée, the girl Dylan thought was me."

"He did?"

"Yeah," I said, wondering why some random date on the calendar could throw me off when every other day had played itself out with relative ease. "He was in love with her and then--"

Iris smiled. "He got a load of you."

I bowed my head and grinned, thinking back on all the months and weeks and hours that had passed between now and then. Dylan and I had talked about what had happened to us, but mostly we were trying to move on and live the life of a normal couple who wanted to better themselves by turning one of them into a public educator.

But there were the scars, literal and otherwise, that were impossible to ignore. I looked down at my wrists, slit during my attempt to kill Henry Younts, and knew it hurt Dylan every time he looked at them, remembering the moment he had put his hands around them and willed the bleeding to stop.

"Did I pick the wrong day to stop by?"

I looked up quickly, shook my head.

According to the official police report, I had attempted suicide after an argument with Dylan, and no one who knew different was able to speak up without buying a one-way ticket to the loony bin. Immortality and shamans and girls who were able to break curses with their blood weren't the topic of everyday conversation up here.

Or anywhere, for that matter.

I didn't want to be labeled a nut case, and Dylan was enough of a catch for the story to gain traction among the local girls he'd jilted over the years.

And so, I played along, grateful that others believed my dysfunctional reconciliation story, so I didn't have to explain what had really happened in the woods beyond Ocqueoc Falls.

"Not at all," I said, wiping my brow with the back of my hand. "And if I don't think about it, I can pretend I'm a normal girl who found a quirky northern town to write a book about."

Iris laughed, "You might want to consider a series."

I smiled, led her inside the small bungalow Dylan and I found in the classified section of the *Lantern Creek Lectern* last September. Sure, he had an ancestral lake house gifted to him by his wealthy parents- but that came with "Taking Over the Family Law Firm," written in fine print.

His mother had been furious when he decided to ditch the cushy digs and move in with me. She had been quite vocal regarding her reasoning as well.

Didn't he know that my unstable mental condition would likely repeat itself, and HE might be the next victim? Did he really want to throw away his chance at a healthy relationship and a bright future at the law firm for a woman who was encouraging him to go into public education?

She had moved his terminally ill father to a nursing home shortly afterwards, a passive-aggressive move Dylan believed was meant to punish him.

I pushed the memory of that terrible day aside, tried to focus on Iris as I led her to our customary spots at the kitchen table. Four sunflower place mats I'd bought at the Dollar General adorned the top and I thought of how much I loved having a place to call my own, a place I could share with Dylan; a situation I could never have dreamed up a year ago when I moved to Lantern Creek in search of the father who had vanished before my twelfth birthday.

"Anything new and exciting happen?" Iris asked, and I pressed my lips together, thinking she was a little too formal for my normally blunt grandmother.

"Not really," I answered while pouring us each a glass of iced tea. "Dylan's taking a few classes. How to survive grading papers all weekend and still have a social life or something like that."

She smiled, "That's one class I wouldn't miss."

I chuckled, took a sip of my iced tea.

"You still doing doubles at Huffs?" Iris asked and I nodded. Huff and Puffs was the tavern I'd been bar tending at under the close and often unqualified supervision of a roughneck named Mallard Brauski.

"Yep. But Dylan keeps bugging me to write."

The idea seemed to amuse her. "What do you think about that?"

I shook my head. "Sounds like a good way to go broke."

She smiled, "And beyond the glitz and glamour of the *New York Times* bestseller list?"

I shrugged, touched my glass, and watched my fingerprints appear in the moisture that had gathered there. "Not many jobs are popping up."

"Nothing wrong with working at a place where you make good money."

I took another slow sip, grateful and suspicious by turns.

"How's the commute going?"

I shrugged. Dylan's drive to Alpena was daunting only in the sense that it disturbed the routine we had perfected over the past ten months. And I hated change with a passion reserved only for tarantulas and female authority figures.

"Everything will work out," she seemed to sense my discomfort. "You two are cute as bugs in a rug."

I smiled, still unable to think of myself as an equal contributor to our couple attractiveness quotient.

The room fell silent. Iris took another sip of iced tea and leaned back in her chair. Pleasantries had been dispensed with. Now for the real reason behind her strange demeanor.

"I talked to your mom yesterday," she offered, and I felt myself stiffen. Mom and I had made progress on our strained relationship, but old habits were dying a slow death.

"Hmmm," I said, wondering what she was getting at.

"She's doing good," Iris offered.

"Hmmm," I said again. "I talked to her last week."

Iris paused, and I saw her swallow. "She's met someone."

I almost choked as the iced tea came back into my throat.

"*What?*"

"You're surprised."

I coughed, tried to catch my breath. "You could say that."

"I thought you would be."

I glared at her.

Mom hadn't dated seriously since Dad left us eleven years before. It had always been the two of us--Justine and Brenda, Brenda and Justine. For better or worse. Mostly worse. And now she had met someone? After all the half-baked attempts throughout my formative years?

But it made sense. Since learning that my father had died in the woods past Ocqueoc Falls, I was able to release his memory.

Maybe Mom had done the same.

"She wanted to make sure you were settled before she pursued anything on her own."

I frowned; my irritation piqued by Iris' defense. "Why didn't she tell me?"

She laughed, a bit of my cantankerous grandmother breaking through at last. "She was chicken."

"I need to talk to her," I said, feeling a strange emptiness in my stomach, missing the place where my parents had been.

"She wants you to meet him."

I scrunched up my nose. "Bad timing."

"Never was a good time to meet your mom's boyfriend."

She was right, of course, and as she continued to explain I learned that Mom had met him at a pottery class in Kalamazoo. He was artistic, like Dad had been, and was divorced with two grown children of his own. I twirled a piece of hair around my finger while considering these newfangled kids, wondering if Mom was showering them with the affection she usually reserved for potted plants.

"His daughter lives in Alpena. Maybe you can meet her."

I laughed.

"Paul sounds very nice."

"Ahh," I nodded, assuming Paul was "The Boyfriend," not wanting to talk about it anymore because if Mom wanted to confess to a middle-aged tryst she could damn well call me, not send my grandmother in to smooth the rough waters her ruse had created.

Iris sensed the change in our conversation and set her glass aside. Moments later she was searching for Joey, gathering him up. "It won't change anything, you know."

I laughed. "Don't bet on it."

"Justine--"

"I had one semi-good year."

Iris looked away and I knew my words had spoiled something.

"She deserves this, you know."

I felt the truth of her words hit my heart.

"I never said she didn't."

She looked at me long and hard until I had no choice but to clear my throat.

"Thanks for telling me."

She nodded, knowing I was lying and that I didn't want to meet the guy Mom had met in her pottery class or his two adorable children, both of whom probably filled their father with the pride I'd yet to instill in not only my own parent, but Dylan's as well.

I walked Iris to the door, wishing our visit had been like all the others with her offering me unsolicited gardening advice sandwiched between bites of small-town gossip.

I stood at the kitchen window after she had gone, chewing on my lip while contemplating my next move. If Mom was serious about introducing me to Paul, did that mean she was coming to Lantern Creek, or would I be forced to revisit the town that had always seemed like home before last summer?

I wasn't sure which I preferred, although the thought of introducing Dylan to all the girls who were mean to me in high school held a certain sadistic appeal.

Disconcerted, I sat down on the sofa and spent the rest of the evening scribbling in the journal Dylan had bought me for Christmas. A memory surfaced from the year before centering on a remote lighthouse Dad painted. I'd visited a few times since, the knowledge that it was special to my father comforting me in a way no other place could.

I needed to go there now.

Jumping in the Jeep Dylan gave me when my crappy Honda Civic finally took a dump, I made the short drive in less than twenty minutes.

Once at the lighthouse, I picked my way over rocks that littered the shore. A large boulder offered a smooth spot for sitting, and so I did, the smell of water and wind mixed with pine calming me.

I thought about Mom and her boyfriend, wondering what Dad would think had he been around to offer his opinion. It was hard to judge since he'd had an affair with Adam's mother.

But even now, after everything, I'd begun to think of my father and Pam as part of some omnipotent plan that had given me my brother--a person I couldn't imagine my life without.

We'd been able to talk without saying a word the summer before, and even though we no longer spoke of evil preachers or lovelorn shamans, we remained close, the bond we'd formed spilling over into subjects that seemed mundane but necessary.

I picked up a stone, threw it across the lake and watched it skip four times.

I had been stronger last summer, too. So strong, in fact, that I'd been able to fend off three roughnecks who had tried to cause trouble at Huffs. But as fall wore into winter and winter to spring, the strength that had both terrified and empowered me seemed to fade like a curtain drawn against the sun.

Yep, things were downright boring in Lantern Creek until Mom threw a monkey wrench into my well-oiled mechanism.

I closed my eyes, felt the wind gather and release my hair.

Being at the lighthouse felt good.

Right.

Closer to Dad.

Who had never left me.

I thought of him. Tried to feel what he would want me to do, wanting him to know this new person would never take his place-- the man who had died for my brother and me.

My cell phone rang.

Glancing up, I saw that the sky had darkened, the moon hanging above the lighthouse tower.

"Hello?"

"Hey," Dylan said, obviously relieved that I had answered. "Everything okay?"

"Yeah," I said, loving that he still worried about me even though the most exciting thing I'd done in the past eleven months was locking the Jeep with the keys still inside. "What time is it?"

"Nine-thirty."

I hit my forehead with the palm of my hand. Sure, things were quasi-normal, but it was hard to erase the image of a three-hundred-pound zombie trying to kill your girlfriend- like I couldn't shake the picture of Henry Younts lurking on the other side of the Ocqueoc River, his eyes like flames in the darkness.

And so, we'd made a pact to always check in no matter how neurotic it seemed.

And here I was, reneging on our deal because Mom had hijacked my brain.

"I'm sorry," I said, genuine regret coursing through me. "I'm at the lighthouse."

I could almost hear him smile. "Spending time with your dad?"

My heart warmed.

He got it.

Got me.

Like always.

"Yep."

A slight pause. "I'll be here when you get home."

Which made me want to get there all the faster.

CHAPTER TWO

It must have been the lighthouse because I dreamed of Dad that night. He was standing on a limestone cliff, the sunrise startling the world behind him. I took the setting in as I scanned from left to right, recognizing the scene as a place I'd seen on a postcard but had yet to visit myself.

"Muffet."

"Dad," I returned, grateful we could talk in this way.

"I'm glad you're happy."

I smiled. "You told me to be."

"Doesn't your mom deserve the same?"

I frowned, walked to where he was standing and looked down at a road that hugged the shoreline below. People were riding bikes, pointing up at something behind us. I turned and saw a stone archway silhouetted by the rising sun, a natural wonder that had entranced these tourists below.

"Give her a break," Dad said, his voice drawing me back. "And this time I mean it."

I smiled. He had me there.

"I'll try."

"You'll do better than try," he said. "Because our little bird is about to break her wings."

At first, I thought he was talking about the robin that had flown into our picture window so many years ago. But he wasn't, and so I looked to the awakening sky and saw a girl perched on a ledge not far from us. She was holding onto a picket fence, climbing over, leaning out. Letting go.

I jerked forward, my hands splaying as though I could catch her in the palm of my hand. I saw her hit an outcropping of rock and bounce off in a way that must have shattered her shoulders.

A scream rose in my throat.

"Justine," Dad said, his voice calm. "How can she live if she can't fly?"

I buried my face in my hands, felt him touch my shoulder.

"Can she?"

"I don't know," I said, the dream beginning to crumble around me.

"Find her, Muffet."

"What?" I gasped. "Where?"

"On a bridge that was built backwards."

"A bridge," I repeated, breathless now. "What?"

"Hurry."

"Dad?" I cried, opening my eyes to blackness, arms encircling me in a way that had me straining against them.

"J," the voice had changed. My father was gone. Dylan was here in the bed we shared, trying to calm me. "It's okay, baby. It's just a dream."

I sat up quickly, the covers sliding down to my waist, the sound of the girl's breaking bones fresh in my ears.

"Dylan," I breathed once I realized I was not perched beside a stone archway watching a girl commit suicide. "It was awful."

"I know," he said, his voice soft as he drew me against him. "You were crying."

I put a hand to my throat, searching for the silver necklace that Adam and I had buried beneath the yellow trees.

"It was Dad," I whispered, and he went still, pulled away in the slightest.

"You haven't dreamed of him since last summer."

"I know."

A pause. "What did he say?"

I put a finger to my lips, chewed absentmindedly at a nail.

"Was it bad?" he asked, and I loved how sweet he sounded, how unsure, because he trusted my father and believed in my ability to communicate with him.

"He told me to give Mom a break."

He chuckled, reached over and turned on his bedside lamp.

"And that made you cry?"

I smiled while glancing over at him, adorable with his messy hair and sleepy eyes, the band of his boxer shorts just peaking above the sheets. Yes, sleeping beside Dylan Locke was usually enough to keep the nightmares at bay.

But not tonight.

"He said that a bird was about to break her wings."

"A bird?" he asked. "Like the one I followed in my dreams?"

"No," I said, wanting to comfort him. "It was a girl. She was climbing over a fence, jumping off a ledge. Dad told me to find her."

I watched him tense.

"He said she was on a bridge that was built backwards."

"That doesn't make any sense."

"I know."

The next moment he propped himself up against his pillows, resigned to the fact that we weren't going back to bed anytime soon.

"I can't say dreaming about your dad makes me happy," he finally said. "Things've been quiet for a while."

I nodded while scooting over to snuggle against him. "That's how I like it."

"Me, too," he said, and I felt him trace my wrist with the pad of his thumb. An absentminded habit on his part, but one that spoke volumes to me.

"I'm just upset about Mom," I said while glancing up at him. "It's probably nothing."

"That's not the word I'd use to describe anything involving Robert Cook," he said, ever the pragmatist in our relationship. "We should figure it out."

"Figure it out?" I asked, confused. "I thought you liked things nice and quiet?"

"I do," he said. "But the sooner we realize there's nothing to it the sooner we can move on."

It made sense. Too much sense. And I knew Dylan well enough to recognize when he was shutting his feelings off and going on intellect alone. It was a survival tactic he used when he was worried about something.

And my dream had disturbed him.

"Did the place have any distinguishing features?" he asked, suddenly a cop instead of my boyfriend.

I nodded, tucked a piece of hair behind my ear. "There was a stone archway above the water with a road underneath. People were riding bikes."

He pressed his lips together.

"I've seen it on a postcard." I offered, feeling like I was searching for something in a dark room.

"You have."

I looked into his eyes, which had changed to the color of a stormy sky.

"How do you know?"

He touched my wrist again, his finger lingering on the knotted flesh.

"Because I dreamed about it, too."

AMANDA BENNETT LAY CRUMPLED HALFWAY down the side of Robinson's Folly, her fall broken by a copse of cedar trees that clung supernaturally to the side of the limestone. Blood was running from her nose and out of her left ear. Her collarbone was fractured. Her right arm crushed.

She remained undiscovered for almost twenty minutes before a voice broke free from above. A couple who finished their morning jog along the East Bluff had turned off to admire the view. They had come to the edge, noticed the broken limbs, and followed the trail until they saw a piece of blue fabric.

Then an arm.

Then blood.

The woman cried out as the man pulled out his cell phone. An ambulance was called, and tourists turned to stare at the emergency vehicle, so out of place on an island that only allowed horse and carriage.

Two men from the rescue squad went up to Robinson's Folly and repelled down the side of the cliff. It took them a half hour to reach her and when they did, they secured her to a board that kept her from moving.

One of the rescuers recognized her. Auburn hair with a touch of gold. Brown eyes. Little nose with a smattering of freckles across her cheeks. Pretty in a way that called to mind pirates and mermaids and the wild places of his youth.

She was known on the island because her grandparents owned a mansion behind the Grand Hotel. But Amanda Bennett's mother had been turned out by them. Not acknowledged.

Amanda was not far behind her mother in their affection. Not that they hadn't tried to bring her into the fold--the only child of their dead son.

And now she had shamed them.

If she lived, it would be in humiliation.

After securing her to a backboard, the medics moved her down the cliff and to the boat that would take her to the hospital in St.

Ignace. Once there, the doctors tried to stabilize her condition and stop internal bleeding. Keep the girl from drifting into the clouds she had stood eye to eye with just two hours before.

Meanwhile, the first responder who had recognized her made a phone call. Discreetly.

Twenty minutes later the man he had called burst into the emergency room, asking to see the woman who had fallen from Robinson's Folly.

He was just over six feet tall and broad shouldered, wearing an old tee shirt stained with traces of mud and grease. One glance and the medical staff knew he was a logger, as many of the men who worked north of town were.

His hair was dark, almost black, his eyes green and his hands rough from heavy labor.

"Troy," the first responder called, waving him over. "They won't let you in."

"Like hell they won't," he grunted. "What happened?"

His friend held up a hand, motioned for him to step out of the hallway.

"Troy--"

"Did she try to kill herself?"

"She climbed over a fence."

Troy put a hand to his face, kept it there, and his friend let the moment pass in silence.

"*Shit.*"

"The family will try to keep this quiet."

"I know."

"Lucky I caught you when I did."

"We were taking a break from cutting. Otherwise..." his voice trailed off.

"She's a fighter. Always has been."

Troy looked down the hallway, saw the staff rushing in and out of the ER.

At once there was a commotion at the entrance. A flurry of

activity as three people made their way to the end of the hallway where they stood. Two men and a woman, rushing now, coats flying behind them, their feet leaving hollow heartbeats on the linoleum floor.

Troy drew back, turned into the wall so the younger of the two men wouldn't recognize him.

And still he pushed his shoulder out, bumping the man as he passed, making his expensive shoes squeak. For an instant he turned, ready to confront the stranger who had been so rude, but the others shouted, and he was gone, rushing towards the room Troy was not allowed to enter.

"You should go," his friend offered. "I'll let you know if something changes."

Troy turned again, looked at the younger man as he began barking orders at the nurses who had tried to intercept him in the hallway.

"Bastard--"

"Keep a cool head. This isn't the place."

Troy turned into the wall again and thought of Amanda lying in surgery--bruised and broken and wanting to fly when she had no wings.

He thought of how it would have been better if he'd never taken the job on the Island or met her in the stable yard or danced with her under the soft lights of the harbor deck.

But that was just an excuse to not feel the pain he was in right now.

Because he loved her.

And she was engaged to someone else.

CHAPTER
THREE

I soon discovered that getting to the bottom of our shared dream was going to be harder than Dylan and I realized. First and foremost, there were the summer classes that seemed to be suctioning off his excess brain capacity.

Then there were the hours I was putting in at Huffs to pay for the aforementioned classes, where I now stood with my regulars talking about who had walked off his job on the freighters because "so-and-so" had told him to dump out his beer.

Mallard was there, giving me a hard time as usual- asking me why I didn't get a better job- telling me he didn't know a barmaid who could scrub a better toilet moments later.

Shaw was there, too--a dead-ringer for Santa Claus with a forty-two-ounce bottle of Blatz. I suspected he was sweet on Iris as she was his dog sitter of choice when he went to see his grand kids.

I was leaning against the bar, watching the fryer and Shaw's medium-well hamburger when I finally decided to do some detective work.

Stealing a glance at Mallard, I flipped the burger and said,

"Seems like I heard something about a girl trying to kill herself over on Mackinac Island."

Mallard almost choked on his mouthful of Pabst Blue Ribbon. "You sure know how to kill a buzz, Flats."

"And something about a bridge," I coughed into my fist. "That was built *backwards,* or something."

"What in the hell are you talking about?"

I smiled, flipped the burger again. "Is it true?"

Mallard, who had a head of shaggy hair he always seemed to be scratching, did just that. "I ain't heard shit about shit. But my old lady's cousin don't work at the Hoity-Toity Hotel no more, so I ain't got no inside track and how in the hell do you build a bridge backwards unless you're dead ass drunk?"

"Ahh," I sighed, wondering how to proceed. "Maybe I heard it wrong. Dylan and I were watching the news, but then he started tickling me in my really sensitive spot and I got distracted and--"

Mallard held a hand up. "I don't need no dirty details. Why don't you check the newspaper, or the internet on that smarty-pants phone o' yours?"

I frowned. I'd already done that, and nothing had surfaced aside from a girl who had fallen off a local overlook while chasing her dog.

And my dream was clear- she had jumped on purpose and not in some vain attempt to save Fido.

"Hmm," I frowned again, slid my spatula under the burger and took a quick peek. "Not that it matters or anything. It's just kinda weird and all."

Mallard took another look at me, shook out a cigarette from his pack of Marlboros and lit up. "So's that painting I helped you hang that looks like a dog drug his ass across it."

I frowned. "It's called contemporary art."

"I call it shit."

I sighed in frustration, hoping Dylan and I could chalk this up to mere coincidence and move on. He could get back to learning how to write detailed lesson plans that tied daily objectives to state standards and I could start scribbling down ideas for the great American novel on old bar napkins.

No one could say I hadn't tried, and since a week had passed maybe it was time to stop worrying about Dad and start worrying about Mom's new boyfriend.

"Flip that meat, Flats!" Mallard yelled and I gave him a glazed look as he rushed over to do it himself.

I stepped aside. Not caring. Thinking about my inevitable meeting with Mom's beau and where the gala event was likely to take place.

As if on cue, Shaw said, "I hear your mama has a new fella."

I felt my mouth fall open and quickly closed it.

"Uh--"

"They've been dating about a month, I hear."

"Uh--"

"What the hell, Flats?" Mallard turned on me while slipping the burger into its bun. "You got major life changes happening and I don't know shit about it?"

"Well,"

"Ain't I right?" Shaw asked, stroking his beard, a strange smirk on his face. "Iris said they might be paying you a visit."

"Oh, hey!" I said. "I never heard anything about--"

"I don't get it," Mallard continued while putting the burger in a basket and dropping it in front of Shaw. "You got people visitin' from downstate who surely want to meet the guy who turned you into the barmaid you are today, and I don't get a goddamn minute to spruce this dump up."

My surprise quickly turned to anger. Once again, Iris had been privy to something my mother should have told me herself. And I thought we had been making progress on our crappy relationship. I reached for my cell phone, but instead grabbed a handful of fries Mallard had sitting beside the till and crammed them in my mouth.

"Better slow down," Shaw chuckled. "No tellin' if you'll burn that off this winter."

"Nah," Mallard elbowed my shoulder, the previous affront forgotten. "Don't matter what she shoves down her pie hole, she'll always be a scrawny runt."

Shaw laughed, squeezed a huge glob of ketchup onto his burger and I had a merciful moment to think.

Was Mom really coming up to Lantern Creek, and what happened to my half-concocted trip to Webber and Dylan's grand introduction to the girls I hated and my ability to flee at any given moment?

With Mom here, I would be at her mercy, and she would be in control of everything.

An hour later I was driving home, punching her numbers into my phone and trying to steady my nerves so I didn't drive into Lake Huron.

She answered on the second ring with a lilting rendition of my name.

"Hey," I barely managed. "What's this I hear about you coming to Lantern Creek?"

"Oh," she began, and I heard a voice in the background.

His voice.

I imagined her holding a slender finger up. Calling for silence because she was talking to *the daughter* now.

"I was just thinking it was time for a visit. I haven't seen your new house."

"No biggie," I said, hoping to discourage her. "It's just a rental."

"Rent to own, Justine. There's a difference."

I nodded to myself. There was a difference, but that wasn't the point.

"Did Iris tell you I wanted to come up?" she asked when the silence became uncomfortable.

"No," I said, my voice flat. "Her boyfriend did."

I heard Mom giggle. A strange thing in and of itself but it tipped me off to her mental state.

"I didn't know Iris had a boyfriend but..." she paused. "Everyone deserves a little cream in her coffee."

"Like you?" I asked.

A year ago, I would have felt guilty for talking to her this way, but too much had happened for me to waste time on regret.

"Justine," she paused, and I heard the voice again. *His* voice--and wanted to reach through the phone and throttle him. "I'm not sure what your grandmother told you, but God knows she can be over-the-top."

"Which is why I love her."

Silence. Brenda Cook trying to figure out how to talk to her daughter. Something she should have gotten the hang of years ago.

"Mom," I said, softer this time. "Are you seeing someone?"

"Justine."

"Are you?"

A slight pause. "Yes."

"Okay," I said, my heart in a free fall. "Who is he?"

I sensed her relief at once. "His name is Paul. We met about a month ago."

Something in my heart warmed to her joy. She was in love and deserved to enjoy the glow of her long-awaited beau's adoration. Just like I'd been doing.

Could I really begrudge her that happiness?

I didn't. I begrudged her for not telling me, for sneaking around and trying to pass things off to Iris when she should have told me herself.

And I realized that I was disappointed. That I might always be.

"Why didn't you tell me?"

Another silence. I looked out the window as I drove south along 23. Dusk was just brushing the sky as the lights of Lantern Creek appeared across the bay.

"Mom?" I asked again, trying to convince myself that everything would be okay.

"I was afraid, Justine," she said. "You loved your father so much."

"And you didn't?"

"I did," she said, "And he's been gone a long time."

I gripped the steering wheel again, my knuckles white, wishing for a bit of my super strength to resurface so I could beat the hell out of something.

"Do you want me to meet him?" I swallowed, waiting. "Or something?"

"Yes," she whispered. "I do."

I took a deep breath. "Are you coming here?"

"Yes," she said, then reconsidered. "If you'll have us."

Us, a pronoun I had never associated with my mother, hovered in the air.

"When?"

She mentioned some dates in the next two weeks and I felt my heart sink because Iris was right, no time was a good time to meet the man who might replace Robert Cook.

Still, we settled on a date and when I hung up, I felt like I'd just eaten one of Mallard's extra rare hamburgers after running a mile in wet socks.

I was hoping Dylan would say just the right thing to lift my mood when I pulled into our driveway five minutes later, but his truck was gone.

I checked my phone.

No messages.

I walked into the bungalow and flipped on the kitchen light.

No wallet thrown on the kitchen counter, no black fleece jacket hanging from the coat rack.

He hadn't come home from class yet.

I glanced at the clock we had hung together above the kitchen sink.

10:30 p.m.

He should have been home over an hour ago.

I dug my cell phone out of my purse and hit his number.

Four rings and his voicemail kicked in.

The rare hamburger feeling came back in the pit of my stomach, this time compounded by the very real memory of the time he had been lost in the woods last summer. I hadn't known where he was then--had spent the better part of the night searching the Ocqueoc Falls watershed with only Pam's dog to guide me.

I took a deep breath, wondering if we were as normal as we pretended to be or if it was our destiny to freak out at the slightest peculiarity. Still, it was unusual for him not to check in. We'd made a pact, after all, and Dylan always kept his promises.

I tried to steady my spinning mind, thinking of the moment I'd found him in the woods with blood running from a gash in his arm. I remembered hauling him to his feet and rushing through the darkness while his attacker pursued us. I remembered running Henry Younts over with the truck only to watch him rise moments later as we sped off into the night.

Yep...no way in hell were we a normal couple.

I picked up my phone and hit his number again.

He picked up on the third ring.

"Hey, hon."

"Hey," I said quickly, hating my fear even as relief replaced it. "Where are you? I called and you didn't pick up."

"Sorry," he said, and I heard commotion in the background. Unfamiliar voices blending in disjointed symphony. "Some people in class wanted to go over our study guide. It's noisy, so I didn't hear my phone. I'll be home soon."

I listened to the spaces between his words. Jabbering voices, some female, above the clink of mugs and spoons.

He was at a coffeehouse. Having fun. Forgetting about my crazy mom and her boyfriend and our shared dreams of suicide.

"I should've called," he said. "I thought you were closing the bar tonight."

"I was," I said, running a finger over the grout in our kitchen counter. Wanting something like what he had at that moment. "But Mallard sent me home early."

"Slow night?" he asked.

"Yep," I said, wondering if he and his classmates were talking about better things than the happenings at a dive bar in the middle of nowhere. Hating myself again.

"We're almost done."

"Okay," I said, suddenly hopeful. "I'll wait up for you."

"You don't have to, baby," he said, and something in my heart sank despite the endearment. "I know you're tired."

"I don't mind," I said. "I just wanted to talk."

"We can in the morning," he said, the voices rising in the background again. "I love you."

The words he had resisted for so long came easily now. And I should have been content.

But I wasn't.

I put my pajamas on, scribbled a few lines in my journal and then lay in bed and waited, watching as my bedside clock inched past 11:00 p.m.

Then 11:30 p.m.

I got up, went to the bathroom, and got myself a glass of water. Peering out the window, I scanned the street for his headlights.

Nothing.

Ten minutes later I was beginning to feel embarrassed and went back to bed.

It was now past midnight.

I knew Dylan didn't have to work the next day and still his absence rubbed at the most sensitive part of my insecurity. Was this what "going back to school" was going to be like? Late night chats with hip college girls at a trendy Alpena coffeehouse, followed by nonchalant promises to "talk in the morning" when I needed him here, in the flesh, sympathizing with my plight?

How dare he study with ordinary people who had never heard of Henry Younts, let alone been chased through the woods by the murderous preacher? How dare he act like an average Joe getting his teaching certificate when I had a set of scars running across my wrists that said otherwise?

I was nearing a new level of anxiety when I finally heard his truck. To my surprise, I felt tears on my cheeks and quickly wiped at them.

Moments later I heard the kitchen door close softly. A few creaky floorboards carried him to the bathroom where I heard the sink turn on. Then he was in the doorway, stripping down to his boxer shorts and sliding under the covers beside me.

He touched my shoulder and I started.

"J?"

I rolled towards him.

"Were you awake?"

I tried to hide my face in the darkness, but he reached over and turned on the bedside lamp.

"What's wrong?"

I shook my head.

"I'm sorry, baby. I should've called. I didn't think it would take that long."

I shook my head again, embarrassed. "I'm the one who should be sorry."

"Why?" he asked, turning my chin so he could see my face.

"You went out with some friends after class. No biggie. I shouldn't think about seeing you bleeding in a forest with a carved-up arm. I should let you go and have a good time. I should--"

"Shh," he said, his lips finding mine in a soft kiss. "I get it. Remember? You don't have to explain yourself."

"Yes, I do. Again, and again, and again."

"It's okay," he said, his hand cupping my shoulder. "We'll get it figured out. Nothing's going to happen."

I took a deep breath, hoping he was right.

"Once I'm done with school, we'll be able to buy this place. We'll get old and fat together out on that front porch."

"Will we, Dylan?" I interrupted, not knowing why. Knowing it would scare him.

"What do you mean?" He pulled away. "Why would you say that?"

"The dream," I said.

"Doesn't mean anything."

"How can you know for sure?"

He sat back against the pillows, frustrated, and I hated myself for pushing things this far.

"We checked around. No one jumped off a cliff on Mackinac Island."

"Yet."

"Yet!" he said sharply, and I felt myself start. "We can drive ourselves crazy, or we can move on. Living in the past isn't good for our future."

I felt like he'd dumped a bucket of ice water down my shirt.

"Mom wants to bring her boyfriend here. I was upset about it and then when I got home you were gone, and you didn't answer your phone--"

"Justine," he said. "I told you I couldn't hear it."

"I know," I said softly. "It's okay. And you're right. I need to stop living in the past."

He slid closer, swept my bottom lip with his thumb, his blue eyes fixed on me in a way that tickled my stomach. "Let's make a deal not to worry unless we need to."

He may as well have asked me to break off a piece of the moon.

"Deal?" he asked again, incredibly adorable as he sunk beneath the covers, his hand sliding to my thigh in a way that spoke to what he wanted.

And I wanted it, too.

"Deal."

CHAPTER FOUR

The light hurt Amanda's eyes and still she opened them slightly, stunned by the brightness of her surroundings. At first, she thought she might be in the land she used to dream about as a child--a place where her parents lived together in a small house cupped by a hill, a creek running behind shaded by the branches of a willow tree that seemed to kiss its mirror image. She dreamed about it over and over, wondering how she could love a place that never existed.

Maybe she was there now, and if so, she would be content to lie in the grass and listen to the whispering stream forever.

But how she would miss her mother, and the friends she had made at her job in town.

And Troy.

The last one sent a shiver down the length of her broken body.

"Amanda?" someone spoke close to her ear. "How are you feeling?"

She tried to answer and felt nothing.

At her sudden movement there was sudden activity. People began to talk faster and feet to clatter on the floor.

Amanda tried to remember what had happened. She had a vague memory of letting go of the railing at Robinson's Folly and feeling her body fall through space with only the inevitable to stop it. She remembered her shoulders hitting the outcropped rock just above a cedar tree, her back exploding as though her skin had caught fire.

She tried to speak and realized there was a tube in her throat.

"Don't talk," the voice said, and Amanda realized it was a nurse. "We'll get your family here as quickly as we can."

Amanda shut her eyes, took a deep breath through her nose. The thought of her family did not comfort her as they consisted of her mother on one side and a smattering of rich, arrogant assholes on the other.

Oh, and there was Ethan, the man she was supposed to marry because he was an "appropriate choice" and if she wanted her inheritance she was going to have to play along.

Her wedding was less than two months away. The invitations had been sent, her dress ordered and altered, the bridesmaids selected from a pre-approved list that did not include any of her "downtown" friends.

Ethan would look handsome in his tuxedo, his brown hair falling across his forehead. His smooth face appealing in its youthfulness-- as though she were marrying a sophomore in high school instead of a man of twenty-six. He would say just the right things; raise his champagne glass at just the right moment.

Amanda pressed her lips together. She imagined her grandparents bursting through the door in a few moments, grateful that she was alive, angry that she had shamed the family, always lamenting the loss of their son before he could produce a legitimate heir.

Amanda imagined her mother coming in next. She saw her standing to the side, her long hair falling in a way that hid her face from curious eyes because something had happened after Daniel Calhoun's death that changed her, made her unfit to be the mother her daughter needed and so, the grandparents had stepped in, replacing Sara Bennett as though she were merely a child.

Amanda opened her eyes, looked around at the nurses who were moving freely about the room, and imagined how they would scatter once Ethan arrived, full of an arrogance that masked something Amanda hadn't figured out yet.

She thought of their private moments together, wondering why he hadn't pushed for more intimacy and realized for all his bravado, he was still just a boy waiting for her to decide what was best.

She thought about how different he was from Troy, a man whose authority seemed as natural as the sun rising outside her window.

Amanda imagined him coming in from the woods, the smell of an honest day's work on his skin and knew there was nothing so real to her in all the world.

Yes...if she could just find the strength to get out of bed and climb into Troy's pickup, they could escape to that little town in the Upper Peninsula he had told her about.

The room was silent for the moment as sunshine warmed her skin. Before the questions and accusations and disbelief. Would Ethan berate her? Did Troy know? And if he did, would he blame himself?

She tried to move her fingers, the morphine drip just easing the pain when a man's face flashed before her eyes.

She tensed on the narrow bed and bit her tongue, tasting blood.

He was old, his white hair thinning into wisps that seemed to fly away from the top of his head. He was lying in a hospital bed, people standing at loose ends until a little girl stepped forward and kissed his cheek.

Amanda watched the flesh she had touched turn color, tendrils leaching across the man's face like a dead branch.

She recoiled at the sight, her wrecked body seizing up as he sank down into his bed, his skin loosening as though he had stepped out of a Halloween costume.

Amanda's stomach retched as she watched the old man disintegrate into the hospital bed, the shell that had once been his body vaporizing in a cloud of sooty dust.

She swallowed, tried to still her racing heart as the image began to lift, the sunshine that had warmed her skin moments before returning in a comforting wave.

She turned her head, saw the I.V. bag and the slow drip sending drugs into her veins and wondered if they had done something to her.

"Amanda," a female voice whispered, and she turned again, stared at her mother for a brief moment before the others entered. She imagined Troy was there, too--his gaze catching hers as it had when he first saw her feeding the horses.

She mouthed her mother's name, unable to speak and the older woman took her hand and held it tightly.

"It's okay," her mother soothed, and Amanda thought how absurd the words seemed coming from a woman who had always been the child. "It's going to be okay."

Then Ethan entered, his voice husky as he stepped into the space she had reserved in her heart for someone else. "What were you thinking?"

She looked to her mother, then her grandparents, who had followed Ethan into the room. "We told the police you were looking for your dog," her grandfather said, his lips a thin line of displeasure.

"You have a dog, don't you?" her grandmother asked, fiddling with the latch on her expensive purse as she sank into a chair.

Amanda blinked, unsure what to think because his name was Charlie, and he had been dead over a year now.

"That's what happened, isn't it?" Ethan asked.

Amanda couldn't answer, and even if she'd been able to, she learned long ago not to fight them. And in that way, they were like the freighters that cleaved the narrow water of the Straits, forfeiting everything in their path.

At once a buzzer went off in the hallway, alerting the hospital staff to an emergency.

"My goodness," her grandmother said, turning in her chair. "What is the matter?"

"Looks like someone's taken a turn for the worse," her grandfather answered, smoothing down his gray hair and Amanda wondered if they remembered the night they rushed to this same hospital only to be told their son had died on the way.

Then, like some strange birds of prey, they moved to the hallway, her grandmother touching a nurse gently on the elbow and asking a few questions, the nurse answering despite her other duties because she knew who they were.

For an instant she was alone with her mother, who sank down into a chair and looked at her with the haunted eyes she had known since childhood.

If only she could find some way to get to her inheritance. Her mother could get a real house with a car that ran in bad weather and a washing machine that worked. She could stop stocking shelves at Dollar General to pay for what was missing.

What had always been missing.

"I know why you did it," her mother whispered, her eyes suddenly clear. "It's the same reason I wouldn't give you their last name."

Amanda looked into her mother's dark eyes, the eyes they shared, wondering what she meant.

"It's the same reason I never gave you their last name."

A bustling of fabric told them the grandmother had entered the room and Sara stood and then drifted into a corner as though she had no right to any other place.

"Such a shame."

Amanda raised her eyes to Ethan, who had come to stand beside her bed.

"The old man in the next room just died," he said, his hand finding hers. "It's a good thing his family was already here."

Her grandmother nodded, opening her purse, and pulling out a tissue. "The nurse told me his granddaughter had just kissed him on the cheek."

Amanda felt her chest tighten. The man she had seen step out of his skin like a child in a Halloween costume--the young girl bending over as black fingers flexed across his cheek.

He was real.

And he had died.

"Ethan," she tried to say, seeking the comfort he had never been able to give her.

"You didn't mean to jump, did you, Mandy?"

She didn't like it when he called her that.

"It was an accident, wasn't it?"

She looked at him with fear in her eyes. If she told him the truth then the money would be gone, and so would the little house and the new washing machine and the car that started on snowy mornings. Her mother would never leave Dollar General and Amanda would have to listen to the tourists' talk about their aching feet down at the fudge shop, wondering when her time would come.

If it would ever come.

She nodded, and Ethan's boyish face lit up in a way that made him seem happy. Reaching out, he pushed her hair from her face.

"I thought so."

"We were worried, Amanda," her grandfather spoke from behind, his voice ripe with displeasure.

Yes...she thought...I was worried, too.

Worried she would die.

Worried she would live.

Amanda felt her chest tighten as she thought about the man and his young granddaughter.

Maybe the two had played together in an old barnyard, the grandfather watching as she swung from a rope he had tied to a high beam after reading *Charlotte's Web*. And afterwards, when the sun hung hot and heavy, she imagined them wandering to a creek to swim in a hole filled with rocks and cold water.

Amanda had longed for that kind of life, but her grandparents had been distant and stern, caring only for their money and what her illegitimate birth had cost them.

But there were times when she would sneak off to sit beneath an oak tree hidden in a meadow above the shoreline. She imagined her grandparents without money- poor even, but with a joy often found in people who live simple lives. She saw a cabin where children ran barefoot in the yard, a place where her mother was welcome, the door swinging wide on its hinges.

And later, when Troy filled her dreams under the same tree, she imagined her grandfather's smile when he asked for her hand in marriage, knowing what a good provider he would be.

She saw them making plans to build a home together in the northern woods. He would train horses, and she would grow a garden, selling what they would spare on Saturday at the market in town. They would get to know their neighbors over fence posts and recipes, their lives sliding into something that was meant to be.

She saw a young boy with auburn hair and green eyes sleeping peacefully on Troy's chest while his sister grew inside of her belly.

She saw the days and weeks and years passing in a sort of contentment that could only be found with a man like Troy and felt fresh despair smother her.

Amanda shut her eyes, felt tears well behind her lids and envied the old man in the next room.

Because death could never truly be cheated.

She was living proof of that.

CHAPTER
FIVE

"**G**ood to see ya, Squirt!" Holly Marchand greeted me at the door with her typical exuberance.

"Hey," I said, bracing my Tupperware container of macaroni salad against my hip.

"Holly," Dylan leaned in from behind, touched her cheek to his in a brief show of affection before sidestepping us.

We'd come over for our weekly game of Euchre, which was really an excuse for the guys to grill and the girls to gossip. The events of the past week made this evening more important to me than usual. I hadn't had a chance to tell Holly about Mom's impending visit or my strange dream--and she was sure to have spirited opinions on both.

"So, whatchya been up to?" she asked once we were settled in the kitchen making bean dip for the nachos. "Sorry we had to miss last week."

"It's okay," I lied.

"Bill and Marty get antsy if we don't come over, and we've been trying to get out of it since March."

"Sure," I said, wondering why she called her parents by their first names, knowing she wouldn't be Holly if she followed social norms.

"Then all we do is sit around and listen to them complain about their lactose intolerance and plantar fasciitis. I tell you, Squirt, it better not be genetic!"

"It's not, babe!" I heard Dave call through the open window that overlooked the deck.

"Right answer, hot stuff," she shot back.

I heard Dave laugh as Holly put a hand over her mouth and giggled and wished Dylan and I could be so easy with our banter, but ever since he'd come home late from class the week before his mood had seemed tense, as though disregarding his own advice not to worry.

I'd asked him if everything was alright, and he assured me it was. Summer classes were just harder than he had expected. And more expensive. And no way could we ask his mom for a loan after he'd gone against her explicit orders and shacked up with me.

And so, I'd picked up extra shifts at Huffs to make up the difference, which meant we weren't spending much time together, which meant my prophetic anxiety about us drifting apart was becoming self-fulfilling.

"What's up?" Holly noticed my mood. "You're not your cute, bubbly cheerleader self."

I laughed. I would hardly describe myself as a bubbly cheerleader...but I looked like one, which meant my personality should match.

"Is it his mom?" she asked.

I shrugged, trying to downplay her question because no matter how hard I tried, the subject of Melinda Locke never failed to depress me. "I ran into her at Walmart two weeks ago, but she ducked down the frozen foods aisle to avoid me."

Holly smiled, flipped her long, chestnut hair over her shoulder. "Maybe she needed some pot pies."

I laughed. "She wouldn't lower herself."

"Good point," she nodded. "Do you still visit his dad?"

"Every Wednesday," I said, my voice reflecting the sadness I felt at never knowing Michael Locke when he was well.

"And she--"

"Doesn't."

"But his sister's still good with you, right?"

I shrugged, peeled the lid off the macaroni salad, and started opening drawers in search of a serving spoon. "She's a nice person, so she wants to help me work through my *problems*."

"As in she wants to be your shrink?"

"Yeah," I said, my mood sinking further than I believed possible on Euchre night. "Dylan wants to tell her the truth. He thinks she'd take it the best out of everyone."

"So, let him," she said matter-of-factly while opening the fridge, pulling out ingredients that seemed to have no conceivable culinary connection. "What's the big deal?"

"It would screw things up and I think," I paused, unwilling to admit my misguided psyche was now in the driver's seat, "I think his family would rather see him with a head case than someone who can bench press a freighter."

"Aw, Squirt," she shut the fridge, came to the table and dumped her findings in the center. "You only saved the entire world like some cute little She Hulk. You deserve some friggin' *credit*."

I shrugged. "Dylan knows...that's enough."

"And it's probably eating him alive."

I looked down, uncomfortable with how close she might be to the truth. "Maybe someday we'll spill the beans and I'll end up moving all of Melinda's heavy furniture."

Holly laughed, my humor deflecting further inquiries.

"Mom's bringing her boyfriend up next week."

Holly turned from where she was spooning sour cream into a bowl with a rubber spatula. "The guy she met in her pottery class?"

I nodded, glad she remembered something I had told her over a week ago--a new personal record.

"Ooh! You think they went at it like Patrick Swayze and Demi Moore?"

I wrinkled my nose. "That's really gross."

"He might be a hunk!"

"Just what I need. A smokin' hot stepdad."

"To go with your smokin' hot meathead."

I frowned.

Holly gave me a searching look, then threw the sour cream container away and came over to me. Glancing out the window, we saw our men grilling up a storm and therefore had no intention of eavesdropping.

"This smells like Dylan trouble," she said, "And I don't mean 'I wish I could tell Mommy about my superhero girlfriend' kind."

I laughed. "Dylan trouble has a smell?"

She tapped her chin with her finger. "Sandalwood with burnt toast undertones."

I nodded. "Impressive."

"I lived with you for three months. I smelled an awful lot."

I couldn't argue with that.

"It's just..." I began, unsure what to share. "School is different than I thought. He was out late with some classmates the other night--"

"Ladies?"

I looked at her like she had eaten a banana without peeling it. "He's going into education."

She nodded. "*Lots* of ladies."

"Yeah, and--"

"He's not exactly a turn-off."

I frowned again, my mood darkening. "I realize this, Holl. I just didn't know I'd feel so--"

"Alone?" she gave my shoulder a squeeze. "You're not alone. You've got me and Iris and Mallard and Adam."

"I want *him*," I said. "And he's so wrapped up in this."

"He's supposed to be wrapped up in this."

"That's not what I mean," I stopped, went to my Tupperware bowl and stuck my serving spoon in. "I just need--"

"A commitment."

I looked down, hating the way my eyes stung.

"You're still dewy young lovebirds. Give it time."

I chewed on my lip, thinking about what she had said.

We were living together. Sleeping together. Sharing our innermost thoughts, feelings, and desires. But beyond that, where was it going? It had been almost a year since he had declared his love for me as I lay dying in his arms. Maybe he'd felt undue pressure at the time and now- with so many scholarly girls who shared his interests popping up...

I put a hand to my forehead, surprised where my thoughts had taken me.

"But something else is going on. Something...weird."

She raised an eyebrow, referring to the almost prerequisite sense of the supernatural she'd acquired since last summer. If something was off with my chakras or a butterfly had flapped its wings in Bangladesh, she was now firmly convinced of her ability to sense it.

"Well," I stole another glance outside, saw Dylan leaning against the railing, his disarming smile in place as he laughed with Dave.

"I knew it!" she snapped her fingers. "Getting good at this, ain't I?"

"I dreamed about Dad."

I heard her rubber spatula stop mid-whisk and knew I'd gotten her attention.

"For real?"

I nodded.

"Ah, crud," she said, genuine fear in her voice and I wondered how deeply last summer had affected her as well.

"There was a girl on Mackinac Island. She was standing on a cliff and Dad pointed her out. Said she was going to break her wings. Then she just...jumped."

Holly's hand went to her mouth.

"You wanna know the really weird part? Dylan dreamed the exact same thing--"

"Holy friggin' crud, Squirt--"

"So, I started asking around and no one jumped from a cliff on Mackinac Island aside from some girl going after her dog and this girl didn't go after a dog. I mean, she jumped on purpose. Totally different thing, right?"

"Squirt--"

"I mean, it doesn't mean anything, right? Dylan says we should just let it go because we checked around, and we shouldn't worry unless we need to, but I really can't just forget about it. It's my *dad*, you know."

"Justine," she left the bean dip again, came to me.

"What?" I asked, alarmed now because Holly never used my actual name.

"I'm not really supposed to know this but, you know how I kinda know a lot of people."

Which meant she'd slept with a lot of men.

I nodded.

"Well, this guy named Joe that I had the hots for from Cheboygan has a sister who works over on Mackinac. Some fudge shop. Anyway...this girl and I still talk and the other day she saw the ambulance go by and hears about a girl being taken down the side of Robinson's Folly on a backboard."

I nodded again. "She went after her dog."

Holly shook her head. "Ends up she works with this girl who jumped and no way did she have a dog because she talked about her old one dying and how she wasn't ready for a new one."

I felt my fingers cover my mouth.

"I guess her family is super rich and--"

I felt my head fill with static. "Would cover up a suicide attempt."

"Your dream,-

I slumped against the counter. "Was real."

"Dylan's was, too," Holly paused, her eyes searching mine. "Is he--"

"Getting weird?" I said, my tone clipped. "Maybe some of Butler's magic wore off on him. Maybe *I* wore off on him."

"You *are* pretty tight."

I tried to smile, crossed my arms against my stomach, and walked over to the window. Dylan was laughing, taking a swig of beer, flipping the burgers over. Happy. Himself. Then he turned, saw me in the window and a shadow passed over his face.

And I hated myself for putting it there.

For always putting it there.

So, I smiled. Blew him a kiss.

He smiled back. Caught the kiss.

I moved away from the window, grabbed my macaroni salad and plopped it in the middle of the table.

"I'm not gonna tell him, Holl."

"Squirt--"

"He's so happy right now. This will screw everything up. He doesn't want a weird girl."

"He wants you."

I put a hand to my forehead. "He wants peace."

She frowned. "If you keep secrets that's the last thing you'll find."

I felt the truth of her words hit my heart.

"I'll tell him. Just not tonight."

She frowned again. "Promise?"

I held out my pinky, and she paused before linking it with hers.

"You're in deep now."

"I know," I said. "Now tell me the name of the girl who jumped."

CHAPTER
SIX

"Amanda Bennett," I repeated silently to myself as we played Euchre at Holly and Dave's kitchen table, a soft rain pattering outside that played back beat to my jumbled mind. I said the name again in my head, allured by what had happened to make jumping from Robinson's Folly a viable option to this girl.

I wondered what she looked like, how she walked or talked or dressed.

Wondered if she was injured.

If she was even alive.

"Spades are trump, J," Dylan reminded me as I laid my king over his queen.

"Oh," I said, laughing it off. "Sorry."

Dave shook his head. "Trumping your partner? I'd make her walk home."

Holly giggled, a nervous edge to her voice and I glanced at her, seated just to my left. She stopped, took a quick swig of beer.

She wanted me to tell him.

Now.

"She's not wearing her flip-flops," Dylan teased, his easy smile in place, my daydream lost in the happiness of the moment as we played cards with our friends like we had planned to when we decided to stay in Lantern Creek instead of a place where no one knew us.

I smiled, breathed deeply, the air smelling of rain and damp earth and some lost flower that had opened itself to uncertain light.

Dylan was happy.

I was semi- content.

Maybe I could pretend Holly had never told me about Amanda Bennett's attempted suicide from the exact spot I'd dreamed about.

"How're summer classes?" Dave asked, pulling me back to the moment.

"Not bad," Dylan shrugged, reached over and took a pretzel from the bowl we'd placed on the table when the bean dip ran out. "I'm going alone on this one."

Holly looked at Dave, did her nervous giggle again as I laid my cards on the table, ready to let Dylan take the trick for us.

"Keeping up?"

Dylan nodded, laid down the left and right bower, ace, and king of diamonds as Holly and Dave tossed their cards down in frustration. "More studying than I thought. Summer classes are accelerated so it's intense."

"But then it'll be over," Holly winked at me. Popped a pretzel in her mouth. "And you'll be home more."

"Not sure if I will," he said, and my heart skittered in my chest. "A group of us are going to study together for final exams."

"That so?" Holly asked, one eyebrow arched. "Who's in your group?"

Dylan cleared his throat, started dealing a new hand. "A couple of guys who already have degrees and want to be certified."

I looked to Holly, satisfied with his answer.

"And a girl starting out like me. She works as a vet assistant down in Alpena."

"Vet assistant," Dave echoed. "Like the lady with four chins who gives my mom's beagle her rabies shot?"

Dylan shrugged. "I think so. She got the job in high school."

"Yeah?" Dave asked, and I wanted to hit him over the head with the empty bowl of bean dip.

"Not much money there, and she heard there were some teachers retiring from Alpena," he paused, glanced at me again. "That's where she went to high school."

"Yeah?" Dave continued. "I used to date a girl from there. How old is she?"

I heard Holly make a low noise in her throat, but the boys didn't notice.

"Nineteen," Dylan laughed, and I was surprised at how upbeat he sounded.

"Green on the vine," Dave snickered, his eyes cutting to Dylan who looked down, shook his head as if to say he had no comment.

"She told me a story the other night about a married couple who brought in a Great Dane that ate a pair of the wife's panties. But when the vet got the underwear out they realized they weren't hers."

Dave laughed and Dylan stopped. Looked around. His eyes settling on me, and I glanced down at my hand.

Holly cleared her throat, knocked on the table. "Pass."

"Pass," I said. Thinking of the veterinarian's assistant. Hating her.

"Pass," Dave said.

"Hearts," Dylan answered, his voice low.

"How appropriate," Holly said while popping another pretzel in her mouth.

"Where does she work?" I asked quickly, shooting my friend a dirty look. "Iris wants a good place to take Joey."

Dylan's eyes met mine and I could see that he was sorry, that he wished he had never mentioned her or the story about underwear-eating Great Dane. "Water Way Clinic, I think. I don't know for sure."

"Hmmm," I said, grabbing a pretzel and twirling it between my fingers. "I'll have to go check it out."

"I'll come with you," Holly offered. "Moral support."

"Iris can check it out," Dylan said, his smile hesitant. "You need to relax for five seconds."

"Hey," Dave interjected, his laid-back persona erasing the tension Dylan's story had created. "Did I tell you guys about the huge morel my cousin found outside of LeRoy last month? He almost missed it but his girlfriend had to pee, and they were in the middle of nowhere."

Just the slightest reference to mushroom hunting was enough to distract Dylan, and so we passed the rest of the night in a semi-comfortable camaraderie, the vet assistant forgotten until we were driving home later.

Dylan noticed my mood, reached over, and took my hand. "I'm sorry about what I said back there. About Meg--"

"Meg?" I asked, her name as cute as the buttons I imagined were missing from her scrubs.

"The girl in my study group. I want you to know--"

"It's okay."

He shook his head. "No, it's not. I'd be pissed if you were talking about some other guy."

I looked up at him, smitten with his jealousy.

"In fact, I'd probably want to punch him in the face."

I smiled, reached up to touch his cheek. "I love you."

"I love you, baby," he said, pulling me closer, his lips finding mine in a soft kiss that could have been our first. "I know these last few weeks have been tough on you, but I'm doing it for us."

"I know you are," I assured him. "And it's the same reason I'm working doubles in the shittiest bar in Presque Isle."

He laughed, his fingers pushing a strand of hair behind my ear. "I'd be worried if you hadn't already smoked the Presque Isle Mafia,"

My laughter joined his, mingling in the air as he took my hand and led me into the house, flicking on lights we had a hundred times before, our routine established as he took my coat and hung it on the rack beside the door.

Then he was opening the refrigerator door, looking for a snack before settling on a glass of milk.

He carried it to the living room, sat down as we curled up on the couch watching T.V. and in my mind I was already tucked beside him in bed, the moon shining through our window as I turned my body into him.

As if we were married.

But we weren't.

I frowned as we scrolled through channels.

Why did it matter so much now, just months after we had settled into our cute little bungalow? Why couldn't I be happy with the status quo? The living together? The forever introducing me as "his girlfriend" as though we were freshmen on our way to the semi-formal?

Would he propose after I filled up all the pages in my journal?

Before?

Ever?

Maybe I could start my book off with the bit about the Almost Ex-Cop and his Cuddly Study Partner because the subject of Meg had stirred up a firestorm of discontent.

I frowned again, took the remote, and looked for something that involved flipping spouses while swapping tiny houses before stumbling across an old movie.

"Let's watch this," Dylan said, surprising me.

I turned, one eyebrow up. "Really?"

"Sure," he smiled, slid an arm behind my shoulders. "Bogart always gets the girl."

I looked back at the screen. "Not this time."

He took a slow sip of milk, his blue eyes following the action from across the top of his glass. "What happens?"

I tilted my head to the side, the gray light casting a nostalgic haze and just for the moment I was Ingrid Bergman on the tarmac.

"He sends her away."

Dylan glanced at me. "Why?"

I thought about it, wondering the same thing. "Because he wants her to be happy."

"But don't they love each other?"

I nodded. "Yes."

He shook his head. "I don't get it."

"Neither does she," I said, snuggling against his arm as he tightened it around me. "So, he has to do the thinking for both of them."

"I couldn't do it," he said while propping his feet on our coffee table, ready to settle in as the piano player named Sam began "As Time Goes By." "I'd come after you."

"You would?" I teased, knowing what his answer would be, wanting to hear it anyway.

"Every damn time."

I moved closer, guilty that I'd thought of Meg as anything other than a classmate when an image of Amanda Bennett came to mind.

I looked at him, intently watching a movie I had loved since childhood and felt my heart bend beneath the weight of my love. I wanted to tell him what I knew, wanted the knowledge to draw us together but knew it would do just the opposite.

And so, I shut my mind to the thought and watched as Rick and Ilsa fell in love again, my heart heavy against the flicker of Old Hollywood.

AMANDA LAY IN THE BED, the tubes that numbed her pain entangling her arms like a silicone octopus. She looked out the window and saw a tiny patch of blue sky and couldn't distinguish it from any other piece of sky anywhere else in the world.

But she knew she was in St. Ignace, in the hospital, unable to speak or move her legs and aching for a man she had yet to see. She wondered if a tree grew somewhere in the distance and if she would ever be able to catch a glimpse of something that would mark her place in the world.

Ethan had visited earlier, had sat beside her and held her hand while he talked about their wedding. He told her he still had every intention of marrying her and that it didn't matter if she couldn't walk or talk.

She reached down, tried to touch the spot where her IV needle pierced the soft skin inside her elbow, and wanted to pull it out and run away. If she could just get to her mom and head north everything would be okay. They could live on a couple of acres if they could both find jobs. If her mother could *keep* a job. And Troy would be there to help.

Wouldn't he?

They left things badly between them. He was hurt. Confused. Frustrated. And he had every right. Amanda knew it was one of the reasons she had walked calmly to the top of Robinson's Folly and jumped.

Because life without him made no sense to her.

And life with Ethan made even less.

She wondered if Troy knew. If he cared. If he had found another woman to tell his wild and rustic stories to.

He was handsome, with thick black hair, green eyes, and the strong arms of a lumberjack who wrangled horses in his spare time. Amanda had heard talk on the island about the new hire who had come to work with her grandparents' riding horses. He was known to be good with the ones the others couldn't handle...but Amanda hadn't believed it. Most likely he was another opportunist looking to leach money from a wealthy man.

And even though she was eager for a glimpse of him, she had walked down the big hill by the Grand Hotel every day to her job in the town, saving the money she made scooping ice cream for tourists, waiting for the moment she and her mom made their getaway.

But the time never came, and the money she saved went to pay doctors because her mom was getting worse, talking about Amanda's dad and how she had known he was dead long before the police told her.

And then she met Ethan, and three weeks later he had proposed, and she had accepted even though something inside told her to wait.

But Amanda was tired of waiting, of hoping for things to change and before she knew it, the life she had imagined under the oak tree vanished like all the dreams of her childhood.

Until she had gone to see the horses and made the mistake of feeding one a sugar cube through the paddock fence.

She closed her eyes, smiled at the memory of Troy calling to her from across the yard, asking her what the hell she was doing.

She stood still, not used to being reprimanded by the people who worked for her grandparents.

So, she kept quiet- because she didn't know anything about that horse and if she should be feeding him sugar cubes, she only knew it was her money that paid for everything she could see and this man was talking to her like it didn't matter.

Troy was furious, his eyes wild when he told her the horse was diabetic and the sugar could make him sick and did she know how much money that animal was worth?

She looked down, studied her tennis shoes, letting him go on because she was somehow intrigued--as though he knew something she didn't, as though he were in charge when clearly, he wasn't. And something inside the girl who only knew men that drew power from money took notice.

She apologized, not telling him who she was for fear of ruining the moment and making him remorseful, not himself, because the innate honor in this man would prompt him to apologize.

And she didn't want to see that.

They talked about the other horses and soon his mood changed. He relaxed, leaned against the fence, his green eyes crinkling at the corners when he talked about how he had been making real progress with the one she'd been feeding. Amanda looked at his hands, saw that they were calloused and rough from heavy labor, and felt something slide into place for the first time in her life.

She thought about a future with this sort of man--his arms slung over the paddock fence and fought the urge to reach up and touch his hair, to push it out of his face and knew she needed to go before someone saw her.

She turned, thanking him for letting her know about the horse, and he called to her, telling her he was going down to The Pink Pony later that night and did she want to meet up for a drink.

She said yes, she would like that very much.

Amanda thought back to that first date, the song "Brandy" playing low in the background as Troy sang along for a couple of measures, changing the words to match her nickname. Making her smile.

They talked about their jobs, and he had admitted to watching her through the large window while he sat on the porch of the Mustang Lounge. And Amanda realized that she had noticed him, too, wondering why he made her remember those afternoons beneath the oak tree.

She watched him that night on the deck of The Pink Pony, the angles of his face softened by the fading light, all rules forgotten in a rash moment that could have ended in disaster if Ethan saw her.

But he was on the mainland for business, and they passed the night getting to know each other--and afterwards--wanting to learn more. A first date led to a second, and then a third and a fourth and before long Amanda had a full-blown clandestine affair on her hands.

Which made her wonder why Troy hadn't come to the hospital.

Maybe he was angry. Or frightened.

No. Troy Phillips had respect for wild horses and the way a tree might fall in the woods, but never the mundane intrigues of people like her grandparents and Ethan.

She looked out the window and felt someone enter the room.

Turning back to the door, she felt her breath suspend, certain she had conjured him up from some sort of whimsy.

He looked so good in his white shirt and canvas pants, his hair cropped short for the summer and Amanda tried to reach up, to take him into her arms but the pain clamped down hard.

He came to her, pulled a chair to the side of the bed.

"I have to make this fast."

She nodded, tears welling up. She was tired of fast. Of hiding.

"Why did you do it?" he asked, taking her hand, rubbing the top with his thumb.

She opened her mouth but no sound came out.

She was mute. And the doctors didn't know why.

"Mandy," he asked again. "Can you talk?"

She looked at him, her eyes large.

"Can you write on something?"

She glanced down, ruined arms the only answer he needed, tears fresh in her eyes, clogging her throat and making her choke.

"I'm sorry," he said, his own eyes watery. "Please tell me it wasn't because of our fight."

Yes...their fight. She told him about Ethan, and he had exploded. No surprise there. He wanted to know when she was going to break it off, tell him to go to hell. Tell them *all* to go to hell. But she couldn't answer, and he stormed off to the logging site.

Later that day she went to the landing and into the woods where he was cutting trees. A dangerous thing, he said when he saw her, so angry he threw his chainsaw. Why didn't she leave him alone if she was going back to Ethan? And Amanda cried, covered her face with her hands and told him it wasn't that simple--she had doctor bills and no way to pay for it unless she married Ethan.

Troy came to her, took her shoulders there in the woods with the other cutters watching and told her he would take care of her.

Why couldn't she believe that?

She looked down, a wild hope building so fast the wind stole it.

Then she told him no one ever helped her unless there was something in it for them, and why would he be any different?

Troy looked at her, the shock showing plainly on his face before turning to leave, the idea of climbing to a place so high she would not survive the fall forming in her clouded mind.

"When you get out of here, you're coming with me," Troy said, his eyes holding hers. "I'm not giving you back to him."

She felt words beat against the lips that had once allowed her to not only tell but show him how she felt.

Please... she thought, her heart racing. Please hear me...

I HEAR YOU.

Her dark eyes widened, her body tense on the bed.

She heard the voice as plainly as if someone had been standing beside her.

Troy noticed her distress.

"Mandy?"

HOW CAN YOU HEAR ME? she asked--feeling awkward in the attempt--a baby forming words through a mouthful of soft food.

"Mandy?" Troy was standing now, searching for a nurse.

She looked around him, caught sight of a boy standing outside her room. He was watching her, a woman Amanda assumed was his mother standing beside him.

Then she turned, her eyes locking on Amanda.

"Come on, Adam," she touched his shoulder.

The boy looked at his mother as she took his hand, leading him to another room and another hallway where he wouldn't be able to hear her and Amanda began to panic.

DON'T LEAVE ME!

He stopped, turned to look at her again.

HELP ME!

A long pause.

I'LL TRY.

CHAPTER
SEVEN

"So, you'll be up here the day after tomorrow? Great..." I said, trying to sound enthusiastic as Mom gave me the lowdown on her Presque Isle County itinerary.

A week had passed since our Euchre game, a week of Dylan cramming for tests between sessions with his sketchy study group while I agonized over whether to tell him the suicidal girl from our dream actually existed.

I'd come close one night over a home cooked spaghetti supper. I was feeling particularly domestic, basking in the belief that nothing could come between myself and the object of my affection, a man who was trying to study Algebra between bites of garlic bread.

He squinted while looking at a linear equation, and I was reminded of the glasses I'd imagined him in, thinking I might buy a pair that screamed "Hunky Nerd" when I blurted out my quasi-confession.

"I think there might be something to that dream we had."

He looked up. "What?"

"Holly knows some people on Mackinac Island."

He laughed. "I'll bet she does."

I frowned. "I'm serious, Dylan."

He put his garlic bread down on his plate, pushed the Algebra book away.

"I thought we agreed to let it go."

I took a breath, my words measured. "Aren't you curious? I mean...we had the *same* dream."

I expected him to react in anger, but he didn't, he just reached across the table and took my hand.

"Please," he said the word softly.

"What?" I asked, feigning innocence.

"I can't do it."

"Dylan?" I had asked, genuinely concerned now.

"I can't get pulled back in."

"Into what?" I asked, searching his face for something of the man who had been studying linear equations moments before.

"I'm in school. We're starting over."

"I know," I said, worry boiling in the pit of my stomach.

He shook his head, continued to rub my hand before turning it over, his index finger seeking the scar that lanced my left wrist. "I look at these every day and I can't," he paused, swallowed. "I'm sorry. I know you want to find out what the dream means."

"Dylan--"

"I just want to protect what we have and," he paused, drew a shaky breath.

"Tell me what happened at the Falls," I said, my words measured, my heart on fire.

He shook his head. "It won't change anything."

"Yes, it will," I said, my voice breaking.

"No," he insisted. "If I talk about it, it's like it's happening all over again."

"Dylan," I whispered, circling the table, taking him around the shoulders. To my surprise, he buried his head against my chest.

"Life is so good right now. I'm doing what I should've done before Mom shipped me off to law school and you're going to write your book. Don't you see how that could all go away? Your visions could start coming back. The blood. And *other* things."

"You mean Henry Younts?"

I felt his muscles tighten. "Nothing would surprise me."

"That won't happen. I won't let it."

"You can't control it, so please...*please* leave it alone or you might see me up on that cliff."

I felt the breath leave my lungs, stunned by his words.

"Okay, baby," I said, tightening my arms around him. "I won't talk about it again."

He looked up, his blue eyes hopeful, and the expression made me ashamed that I had ever considered telling him about Amanda Bennett. He needed this assurance from me, needed to know I would do everything in my power to prevent a repeat of the summer before.

"Justine, are you there?" Mom asked, her voice a sober reminder of what I would be facing when she rolled into Presque Isle County two days from now.

"Yeah," I twirled a long piece of hair around my finger. It was hot outside and the humidity always made it wavy. Dylan told me I reminded him of the heroine in a book his English Lit teacher had forced the class to read--one who did nothing but wander the moors and pine for her lover.

But he was off with his study group tonight and wouldn't see me in my full glory unless I waited up.

Which sounded very appealing.

"Justine!" Mom was mad now. I wasn't paying attention to her grand scheme to introduce me to Pottery Class Paul.

"I'm here, Mom. I'm--"

"Daydreaming?" her voice had a hard edge.

"We have a lot going on up here."

"This is important to me. Paul is important."

"Mom--" I interrupted. I didn't need an argument before she came. I didn't need an argument at all. "This isn't easy. I'm not used to thinking of you with anyone besides *Dad*."

"Well, I had to get used to thinking of him with Pam," she sighed. "So, there's that."

I didn't say anything, the anger that consumed her during my childhood still burning with an intensity that surprised me.

I stood up and looked out at our backyard, thoughts of our Euchre game and how Dylan's face had changed when he talked about Meg swarming like summer mosquitoes. I pictured him kissing her, holding her, or worse yet--making love to her and felt the food I'd eaten for breakfast rise in my stomach.

Yes, jealousy could kindle one hell of a fire.

"I'm sorry you had to go through that," I said at last. Meaning it- and something seemed to soften inside of me as I waited for her response.

I heard her clear her throat. "Mary is going to meet us at your house."

"That sounds great," I lied, assuming Mary was the daughter and not some stranger Mom had invited into our ridiculously small bungalow. "We'll have the spare room made up for you."

"She may stay the night if that's all right. She doesn't see her father very much."

"Sure," I lied again.

"Thank you," Mom said, and I imagined Mary on the couch, Mom and Paul snuggled up in the guest room while Dylan and I slept a few feet away.

We would be one happy, partially blended family.

Dad excluded.

I turned from the window and walked back towards our kitchen table, still rattled, knowing I would have to put on a happy face and act the part even if I didn't want anything to do with Mom and Paul and Mary and--

I NEED YOU, SIS.

I stopped so quickly I smacked my leg on the kitchen table.

"I'm nervous about this and I'm sorry if..."

"Adam?" I said before I could stop myself.

"Adam?" Mom repeated. "Is he there?"

"No!" I blurted. "I'm by myself."

THERE'S A GIRL WHO NEEDS OUR HELP.

ADAM--

I'M THE ONLY ONE WHO CAN HEAR HER.

"Justine?"

"Yes," I answered. Feeling dizzy.

CAN YOU HELP HER?

I CAN'T. IF DYLAN FOUND OUT--

HE'D WANT YOU TO.

HE'S CHANGED. HE'S SCARED.

"I'll see you on Friday."

"Okay."

SHE'S IN THE HOSPITAL.

"Please remember that this is hard for me, too."

SHE TRIED TO KILL HERSELF.

I put my head in my hand. Felt consciousness slipping away.

WHAT'S HER NAME?

"And Paul has nothing to do with what happened between your father and me. Give him a chance."

I opened my mouth to respond and found that I couldn't. Blackness enveloped me the same way it had the summer before at Salmon Fest.

"Justine?" my mom repeated. "Are you there?"

I swallowed. Lowered myself to the floor before I fell and split my head open.

TELL ME HER NAME!

He paused.

AMANDA BENNETT.

I'M NOT sure how long I lay on the kitchen floor, my left cheek plastered against the linoleum, when I heard our land line ringing.

I blinked hard, reached for the receiver.

I hadn't wanted a land line, had said it was too expensive, but Dylan insisted it would make the bungalow feel more like a home.

He also liked an alternative way to contact me as I always seemed to be losing my cell phone or forgetting to charge it or any number of minor infractions that irritated my law-enforcement beau.

I sat up, scooted over to where the phone sat on its cradle, and answered with a throaty, "Hello?"

"Justine?" Dylan's voice jolted me. "Are you okay?"

I squinted into the sun that was pouring through our kitchen window, then looked around. My cell phone lay where I had fallen. Mom must have hung up. Called back. Hung up again. And called Dylan.

"I'm not sure," I tried the dingbat approach. "I got really dizzy."

"Did you pass out?"

"Umm," I mumbled, rubbing my cheek. "I think so."

"Okay. Just sit tight. I'll be home in five minutes."

"No," I tried to backpedal. "We can't afford for you to lose the shift."

"Are you kidding me?" he said, his voice rising.

"We took a hit when you went to part-time."

A pause. "You think that's something I care about right now?"

"I'm feeling better," I persisted, scooting over to the table, laying my forehead against one of the chairs. "So, if you come home, you'll just have to help me do laundry."

Another pause. "Then I'll help you do laundry."

I mustered up a giggle, hoping it would deflect him. "I might even make you fold your own clothes."

He chuckled. A good sign. "We don't want that."

I waited, my heart hammering in my chest.

"Your mom called."

I stood up, braced myself against the back of the kitchen chair for support. "I wish she would just *chill out*."

"J--"

"I'm super stressed and I didn't eat any breakfast and then I just...I don't remember."

He was silent. Thinking.

"Is it like what happened on the bleachers when you met Mom? Or the break wall with Stoddard?"

"Dylan--"

"Maybe it's starting again."

"Maybe I'm pregnant." I blurted out.

It was a cheap diversion. But it worked.

I heard him clear his throat, imagined him doing the mental math. "Um," he finally said. "How--"

"It was a joke," I said, irritated.

"Oh," he was awkward now, embarrassed with his response. "Not that I wouldn't be happy. Just...later on."

"For sure," I echoed, realizing he was right and now would be a terrible time to add our supernatural, albeit cherubic offspring to the mix. And a wedding would need to come first, preceded by a modest engagement ring we'd purchased from my tip money at Huffs.

"Now Paul's daughter might stay the night and it's just getting to be--"

"Too much?"

I put a hand to my head. "I don't know how to pull this off."

"You don't have to pull it off," he said. "You just have to *be*."

I smiled.

"You always say the right thing."

"Can I have that in writing?" he laughed, the mood lighter and still I felt the poignancy in the silence that followed.

"Promise me, J."

"What?" I asked, knowing what he wanted.

"Promise me it's not starting again."

I swallowed. Pausing would make him wonder. Make him worry.

"I promise."

I could almost feel his relief. "Sure you don't want me to come home?"

I giggled, heat splaying across my skin. "I want you to come home, but not to do laundry."

"Down, Tiger," I could hear the amusement in his voice. "Want me to call your mom back?"

"I would love you forever."

"Done," another pause. "See you tonight."

"Yep," I said, wondering if I sounded too chipper for a person who had just passed out, feeling guilty the next minute because there was absolutely no way to make him understand why I would help a girl I'd never met, a girl who could make me break a promise to the man I loved.

The next minute I was grabbing the keys to the Jeep and taking off for Three Fires Lodge, a quaint assembly of cabins I'd been cleaning every Saturday morning for the past year.

Pam Mallory--my boss and Adam's mother--was not expecting me, but that didn't matter. She had an easygoing manner that was lacking in my own mother--something I always imagined must have appealed to Dad. I found her in the main lodge going over paperwork, her curly hair pulled back in its customary ponytail.

She looked up when she heard the front door open and smiled brightly.

"Justine."

"Hey," I said crossing the distance between us. "I thought I'd drop in for a visit."

She frowned, pushed her paperwork aside, and leaned forward.

"Did Adam talk to you?"

I started, unnerved by her question.

"He's been acting strange since we visited my friend in the hospital. Maybe you can get to the bottom of it."

"Sure thing," I tried to smile. "But there's one catch."

She raised an eyebrow. "What is it?"

"Don't tell Dylan I was here."

"What?" she said, and I sensed her surprise. We'd been everyone's golden couple for the past eleven months and I hated to relinquish the title. "Why?"

I looked down, embarrassed. "He doesn't want me to do this anymore."

"Do what?"

I shrugged my shoulders. "This *stuff* that Adam and I do."

Pam gave me a searching look.

"What stuff?" she asked. "Dropping by to check on your brother?"

I shook my head. "You know what I mean."

"But it's who you are. Who you *both* are."

I shook my head, tried to downplay her words. "Doesn't matter. Do we have a deal?"

"Justine--"

"Do we have a deal?" I repeated, sticking out my hand, hoping she would take it.

She didn't like it, I could tell. She didn't want to deceive Dylan, didn't want *me* deceiving Dylan, and she probably knew--as I did--that everything would unravel once I pulled on the loose thread that was Amanda Bennett.

"Okay," she said, her voice firm as she took my hand. "Adam's inside the house."

I touched her shoulder in passing, climbed down the back steps and towards the cottage hidden behind a copse of birch trees, Ocqueoc Lake sparkling beneath the hot haze of an afternoon sun.

I knocked twice, then entered and found my brother on the couch, a video game he loved playing across the screen. He turned when I came in, stood up and came to me quickly.

Adam was only eleven years old, but we stood almost eye to eye. He was growing, changing, his curly hair shorter than it had been last summer, the soft lines of childhood replaced with muscle.

Immediately his fingers went to his ears, and he began to make a low sound in his throat.

I'M GLAD YOU'RE HERE.

I pulled him into a hug.

"What's going on?"

DAD CAME TO YOU, DIDN'T HE?

I nodded. "How did you know?"

HE CAME TO ME, TOO.

I felt guilty at once. The first thing I should have done after my dream was talk to Adam. But I'd shut him out--the only person he could communicate with.

Until Amanda...

"What did he say?"

TO FIND HER.

"Why?"

I THINK SHE'S LIKE US.

"How?"

SHE TOLD ME THE OLD MAN IN THE NEXT ROOM WAS GOING TO DIE.

I pulled away, looked into his eyes. "She's in a *hospital.*"

SHE SAW A LITTLE GIRL KISSING HIS CHEEK. SHE SAW IT ALL BEFORE IT HAPPENED.

I tensed. A person who could predict death wasn't someone I wanted Adam mixed up with.

"Does she talk to you a lot?" I asked, a strange twist in my gut.

ALL THE TIME.

I sat down on the couch, the video game paused on some ultra-challenging level, the mountain troll avatars bobbing in repetitive motion against a fantastical backdrop.

"What can I do?"

SHE NEEDS YOUR VOICE.

"My voice?"

HER BOYFRIEND NEEDS TO KNOW WHAT'S GOING ON.

I frowned. This was beginning to sound less like a rescue mission and more like an episode of *The Young and the Restless*. But Dad had told me to find her--told *Dylan* to find her even though he was currently burying his head in the proverbial sand.

And now Adam had been pulled in, too.

"So, we're supposed to sneak into the hospital and tell the boyfriend that she communicates with you in her mind?"

THERE'S A CATCH.

I made a face. I hated "catches."

SHE'S ENGAGED.

"Oh, geez," I rubbed at my temple. "Let me guess...the fiancé and the boyfriend are not one and the same?"

HER FAMILY WOULD CUT HER OFF. SHE NEEDS THE MONEY TO PAY FOR HER MOM'S DOCTORS.

"This is starting to sound like a really bad idea."

I CAN'T DO IT ALONE.

I frowned, my resolve weakening. "Dylan doesn't want me to do this stuff anymore."

WHAT STUFF?

"Us," I gestured to him. "This weird stuff we do."

He pulled away, looked in my eyes, the low noise in his throat again and I scrambled to explain.

"He's just scared. He saw some bad stuff after I passed out at the Falls."

TELL HIM TO JOIN THE CLUB.

I bit my lip, wondering if he was suffering in the same way Dylan was.

"Your mom knows something's up. What should I tell her?"

TELL HER I WANTED YOU TO PLAY VIDEO GAMES WITH ME.

"Adam--"

SHE'LL JUST TRY TO STOP US.

"Maybe we should let her."

DAD TOLD US TO FIND HER.

Yes...there was that. We needed to listen to the father who was always one step ahead of us when it came to flushing out danger.

And he had given his life for us, so the least we could do was sneak into a hospital and telepathically communicate an injured patient's desires to her secret boyfriend.

"Okay," I said, shaking my shoulders as though loosening up before a fight. "How do we do this?"

TROY COMES TO THE HOSPITAL WHEN ETHAN'S AWAY ON BUSINESS.

Troy? Ethan? People I'd never met. People who could jeopardize my relationship with Dylan. And for what? A stupid dream? Why didn't I just chalk it up to my overactive imagination and tell Adam to go back to his mountain troll avatars like any other eleven-year-old on summer vacation?

I knew the answer but didn't want to say it.

Think it.

Be it.

"Okay," I said, touching my head to his. "Just tell me when."

CHAPTER EIGHT

Sunlight was streaming through the window of Amanda's hospital room. She was sitting up now, propped against a mountain of pillows and looking outside at a concrete parking lot. Ethan's black Cadillac was parked close to the entrance, but he had yet to reach her room.

She was starting to feel better now, less lonely because Adam had been keeping her company in her mind, reassuring her that his sister could help. Amanda didn't understand but Adam told her they spoke without words--that they had something to do with what happened down in Lantern Creek the summer before.

Amanda remembered her co-workers talking about it. A man was shot while poaching on state lands. His son was implicated but had since disappeared. But that wasn't the whole truth... The sister was involved, had made up a story about being put on suicide watch because she didn't want the real story to get out.

She was special, too--could access strength the boy didn't have. But her boyfriend was a cop and would try to stop her if he found out.

Not that Amanda could tell anyone. That was the whole damn point...

She opened her mouth and tried to push air through her windpipe as she had millions of times before. A simple action that had produced her voice for the last twenty years.

She looked down at her hands, tried to shift her weight on the hospital bed. Her shoulders were healing and so was her back and yesterday she had been able to use the bathroom like a semi-normal person. The doctors were calling it a "miraculous recovery" considering the extent of her injuries and the height from which she had fallen.

And still one answer eluded them.

Why couldn't she talk?

Despite this question, they were going to send her home in a week. With help, of course, at which point the grandparents had offered to pay for a nurse. It was the least they could do, after all, and Ethan had agreed, insisting that she be moved downstate where he did most of his business. He had planned to relocate after the wedding but there was no reason to wait.

Amanda wanted to scream her mother's name, Troy's name, any name to make him realize she was not one of the pieces on his expensive chess board.

But she couldn't. And her heart had broken as she pictured Troy coming into her room and finding it empty. He wouldn't know where she was, couldn't know because she wasn't able to tell him.

Unless...

Amanda stopped eating that day. Started sleeping more. Pushed her morphine button with fingers that were growing stronger.

Ethan noticed the change when he came to visit two days later. He pulled the doctor aside and touched him lightly on the elbow, his charming smile in place. Why was she losing weight and sleeping all the time? Could they take her off the morphine? Transfer her to a larger hospital?

Amanda listened while she pretended to be sleeping and reached out to Adam.

CAN YOUR SISTER HELP US?

He didn't answer and she started to panic. Maybe he was getting tired of her and decided to abandon her? She waited while Ethan and the doctor argued, listened while he threatened to pull her family's financial backing and the doctor coughed, tried to placate him but Amanda knew better.

Ethan would get his way.

Like always.

The next moment Adam's voice was there, telling her his sister was coming, and she almost wept with relief.

She wiggled her fingers, remembering the conversation as though it were a lifeboat in a November gale. She was improving now and maybe, just maybe, she could write Troy a note if she could grip a pencil.

"Mandy," Ethan's voice jolted her, made her start as he leaned over her bed. His boyish face so different from Troy's.

"Are you in pain?"

She nodded.

"You haven't eaten much in the last few days."

She could only stare at him, hoping that he would believe it was dangerous to transfer her downstate. For a moment she fantasized about pulling the old Romeo and Juliet trick with Adam serving as Friar Lawrence, tipping Troy off to her whereabouts after an elaborate Mackinac Island funeral.

"I love you, Mandy." Ethan said, and she wanted to close her eyes, pretend she was somewhere else. "I've loved you since the first time I saw you at that god-awful cocktail party your grandparents threw at the Jockey Club."

She swallowed, remembering the twinkling lights and humid air, Ethan standing apart from the others, smitten in his jacket and tie.

"You were so different from the other girls. Like you didn't belong to this world."

She looked at him, wondering if what he said was true when he leaned closer, pressed his lips to her forehead.

She turned her head, pretended to be in pain as Ethan took her hand in his.

"Do you think you can write something down?"

She stared at him, unsure how to respond.

"And if you could, what would you say, Mandy?" he asked, his hold tightening until her fingers tingled beneath the tension. "Because I have a feeling you've been lying to me."

She shook her head, her eyes large as she fought to pull away.

"Am I hurting you?"

She took a deep breath, nodded.

"Good."

She wasn't sure she heard him right, tried to pull away again, but he squeezed tighter.

"I watched you move your fingers before I came in. You haven't eaten in days, Mandy. Come to think of it--you haven't eaten since I mentioned transferring you downstate."

She looked at him, wanting to spit in his face.

"Well, I'm taking you to another hospital whether you want to or not. That doctor is going to give you medicine when I tell him to, and if you don't eat, he's going to put a feeding tube right here," he reached down, traced her belly button through the thin hospital gown with his index finger. "You won't be writing any notes, Mandy. Your games are over."

She gasped before she could help it, felt her hand bend backwards as he twisted it and bit the inside of her mouth.

"Do you understand what I've said to you?"

She nodded, sweat breaking out across her forehead.

"That's a good girl."

Amanda slumped down in the bed, her breath staggered as he released her and took a step backwards.

"And if I find out there's another man," he whispered, his smile a tight stretching of skin that meant nothing. "I'll kill him."

∼

It was nine o'clock on the night before Mom's arrival, and I was stuck bar tending with Mallard Brauski. I had a million things to do but Dylan was off with his shady study group, and I didn't want to obsess over it.

Easier said than done.

I berated myself for letting it bother me, telling myself he was only there because he wanted to make a better future for us and not to ogle the young vet assistant.

I glanced around the bar, peeked outside at the parking lot.

"Hey, Mallard--"

He poked his shaggy head out from the alcove behind the bar.

"Don't you even *think* about leavin'."

"No one's here and--"

"I'm here," Shaw bellowed, taking a swig of Blatz. Placing it on the bar, he swiped at his wet mustache. "Glad your grandma knows how to treat a fella better than you do."

I scowled, then turned my back to him. I'd spread my to-do list in front of the bar mirror, and it was getting longer by the minute--a side effect of my most recent bout with Brenda Cook-Induced OCD.

I chewed on my bottom lip, the picture of concerted concentration, and scanned the list: bake two pans of lasagna, finish the laundry, wash the sheets in the spare room, dig up blankets for Mary, clean the carpet, and whatever else looked like it might have an unknown substance on it.

"Flats!"

"Huh?" I turned around, found Shaw tapping an empty bottle on the trough.

"Can't take care of one fuckin' customer and you wanna split. Must be somethin' on her mind, Shaw."

"Must be," he echoed. "Iris told me you have a big shindig comin' up tomorrow night."

I nodded, reached over, and adjusted the to-do list.

"You should give her a break, Mal."

Mallard chuckled as he appeared from behind the alcove with a misshapen hamburger. Dropping the plate in front of Shaw, he said, "She can handle herself."

"Little runt like her?" Shaw laughed. "You sure about that?"

"Pretty sure," Mallard grinned, and I smiled, turning back to my list.

Sweep the front porch. Find a recipe for some spectacular dessert. Bake aforementioned spectacular dessert. Did I have "clean the bathroom" on the list?

I looked up into the mirror, saw the back of Mallard's head and Shaw's white beard and behind it the smattering of card tables that gave Huffs its effervescent charm. I saw the jukebox blinking red and blue and green to the beat of some Hank Williams song about a lonesome cowboy. I saw the haze that lingers in places where people have smoked cigarettes over long periods of time, the soot on the tabletops, the dark corners that seemed to lengthen.

I went back to my list, wondering if the local grocery store would have all the ingredients for the lasagna and if I should use ricotta cheese or cottage cheese, or both, and would Paul smile at me when we were introduced, take my hand, and become the father figure I'd never wanted.

Would Mom crack under the pressure, or would Dylan's charm and my organizational skills be enough to trigger an involuntary relaxation response?

One evening.

One sleepover.

I could do it.

I could be a hostess to Paul and his daughter and whoever else happened to walk through the door because at this point, it wouldn't have surprised me if Dad himself decided to join us.

Mallard laughed and I looked up into the bar mirror again. Shaw was biting into his hamburger, saying how terrible it was while rings of smoke told me they had just lit up. The haze hung in languid waves, gathered in the shadows behind the tables, Hank Williams wailing away when--

Something moved in the corner. Something large and fast and dark.

I turned quickly, knocked a bottle of Old Grand-Dad whiskey off the shelf where it shattered at my feet.

"What the fuck!" Mallard turned on me. "Flats?"

"I--I'm sorry," I stammered. "I saw something in the corner."

Shaw laughed; took another bite of the burger he'd been complaining about. "You got rats in here, Mal?"

There was a long silence.

"Might be," Mallard finally agreed, his eyes holding mine. "What was it?"

I paused, "Something big. Like...a person, maybe."

"A *person*?" Shaw shouted, turning on his squeaky stool to glance behind. "Someone sneak in while I wasn't lookin'?"

"Nah," Mallard waved it off, but I could tell he was rattled. "Get a broom and dustpan and clean that shit up."

"Okay," I agreed. "Where'd you put them?"

He looked at me for a beat and then led me around the corner and into the storeroom.

Once alone, he took my elbow and backed me into the wall, a strange fear in his eyes I'd never seen before. "What the fuck was it?"

"I don't know."

"Like hell you don't."

"Well," I said, wiggling free of his grasp. "I've been having weird dreams."

He tilted his head to the side. "How weird?"

I shrugged. "Well, if I had to classify them, I'd say they were pretty darn--"

"Fuck me," he interrupted, running his hand through his hair. "Was it that big bastard what was shot in the woods last summer? Was that what you saw?"

"I don't think so," I mumbled. "It might have been a shadow. This place doesn't exactly have the best lighting."

"Shit, Flats," he said again, pivoting on his heel. "*Shit.*"

"It wasn't anything."

"You sure about that?"

I put a hand to my forehead, tried to keep my composure. "I don't want to be a freak again. I don't want to beat up roughnecks and start bleeding for no reason."

"That went away, right?" Mallard poked me with his index finger. "You're a wimp again, right?"

I shrugged my shoulders. "I think so... I mean... I've never really had to use my strength but sometimes Dylan tickles me in bed and I try to fight back, and then he pins me down and--"

"I sure as hell didn't need that picture in my head."

"Sorry--"

He looked at me long and hard, reached up to scratch at the nape of his neck. "Guess there's only one way to find out."

We emerged from the storeroom moments later, Mallard carrying the broom and dustpan.

"You gonna clean up her mess, Mal?" Shaw bellowed.

"Nah," Mallard waved him off. "I'm gonna arm wrestle her for the honors."

"Shit," Shaw took a last bite of burger and pushed it away. "Look at her chicken arms."

"Hey," I feigned offense. "I used to be pretty good back in the day."

"Well, git on with it, then," Shaw laughed. "This might be the only show I get all night."

Mallard circled to the other side of the bar. Leaning over, he locked his elbow in position while I gripped his hand, my eyes telling him to give it all he had, or Shaw would never let him forget it.

And I would never forgive him.

Then Shaw pounded the bar with his fist and I felt Mallard's fingers tighten around my own. He was scared that he would lose.

Scared that I would win. Scared that once a door was opened something terrible would walk through it.

Our arms didn't move at first, and a part of me wanted to call it good right then and there and live with the assumption that I was, indeed, a wimp again. Then, little by little, Mallard began to advance--pushing my arm backward towards the bar. I felt my wrists tingle, the hard wood boring into my elbow, making it numb.

My arm sank lower, relief circling my body like a second skin when I remembered what had triggered my strength before.

I should have let him drown...

Jamie Stoddard was there, leaning up against the Jeep and then the next moment he was face down against it. I felt his pulse between my fingertips, but it was only a memory. Jamie was gone and I knew I was going to have to dig deeper if I wanted a true answer.

I tightened my muscles, a picture of Dylan and Meg laughing over a triple mocha latte materializing before me. He was smiling, interested in her stupid panty-eating dog story when his hand reached up to touch her cheek. Moments later, I watched him guide her lips to his in a gentle kiss.

"Damn!" Shaw yelled as if from a great distance. "She's kickin' your ass!"

I tried to shake the image off, remembered that Dylan was with her at that very moment and watched Mallard's arm bend backwards.

"Git him!" Shaw cheered, his Blatz spilling as he raised it over his head. "He ain't ever gonna live this down."

Mallard's eyes met mine over our clenched fists and at once I saw his terror, his desperation. The rage was there, exploding behind my eyelids as the picture of Dylan and Meg took on a life of its own.

But beneath was something far more powerful.

The lie I hadn't been able to shake since that day at the community pool.

A good man would never stick around if my own father hadn't.

I squeezed my eyes closed.

I was supposed to be done with this.

Over it.

But I wasn't.

"Git him!" Shaw cried again.

But I couldn't.

In one motion, Mallard pinned my arm so quickly I winced in pain.

"Got ya," he croaked, his nerves shot as he reached a shaking hand towards his half-empty pack of cigarettes.

"Guess you did," I said, shaking my hand out. "I'll clean up."

Shaw chuckled. "Ya got spunk, Chicken Little. I'll give ya that."

"Fuck," Mallard said, out of breath as he lit up. "She's the one holdin' the broom, ain't she?"

Shaw grunted, draining his beer and paying his tab. Moments later he lumbered out the door and Mallard and I were alone.

"Git outta here, Flats," he whispered, one hand at the back of his neck.

"You won," I said, wanting to believe it. "Fair and square."

He shook his head, "It wasn't no fair and square and you fuckin' know it. Somethin' threw you, otherwise--"

"Don't say it."

"I'm gonna say it because you gotta stop livin' with your head up your ass thinkin' you're something you're not."

"It doesn't matter," I laughed while dumping the dustpan of glass into the garbage can. "I'm still a wimp. You just proved it."

"Flats," he said again. "Go home."

"My shift's not over."

He put a hand on my shoulder. Squeezed.

"Yeah, it is."

"Mallard--" I whispered, my voice breaking. "I don't want it to come back."

"Don't matter what you want."

"What if," I said, thinking of the shadow. "He comes back?"

He paused, took a long drag, and then blew the smoke out slowly.

"I guess you'll have to kick his ass again."

I stopped, leaned the broom and dustpan against the bar, and looked up at him.

"But what if--"

"You'll handle it."

I felt my nose tingle.

"I will?"

He smiled, ruffled the top of my head.

"Bet my life on it."

CHAPTER NINE

The day of Mom's arrival had finally come.

I'd gotten up early and started baking the fabulous dessert. Dylan was working the morning shift at the station and then coming home to help with last minute details.

Although he'd been plenty helpful the night before.

I'd come home from Huffs, unsettled about the shadow and how close I'd come to beating Mallard in the arm-wrestling contest, and was surprised to see his truck in the driveway.

"Hey--" I said when I entered the house to find him seated at our table with a mixed drink in his hand. I had to admit it was a romantic scenario, minus the relaxed yet mindful heroine.

He was wearing a white collared shirt, the first two buttons undone, and I found my eyes drawn to the small triangle of skin, wanting to place my lips there.

"You're home?"

He smiled and I felt like a child who had just caught a balloon before it floated away.

"I wanted to be here."

I sank down into a chair, thinking about the shadow, knowing it would ruin everything.

"I've missed you," I said.

He placed the drink in front of me, brushed the top of my hand with his fingers.

"I've missed you more."

I smiled again, took a small sip, and let the bourbon numb my frenzied mind. Mom was coming. Paul was coming. Adam was on standby, waiting for some guy named Troy to show up so we could rescue a girl named Amanda.

And I was waiting on Adam.

But not tonight.

We talked about Mom, and as I spoke, I watched Dylan watch me and knew he understood what was breaking my heart.

"Robert Cook will always be your father."

I looked down at my hands, suddenly embarrassed. "Why doesn't it feel that way?"

He reached across the table, took my hand. "Because you want to please your mother."

I sighed, wondering if he was right.

"Paul might be a good guy."

I laughed. "I'm sure he is."

"Then leave it at that," he said. "It doesn't have to mean anything more."

I sat, looking at the low lights playing in lazy circles around the edge of my glass and began to cry.

Dylan stood up and came to me. "It's okay."

I shook my head, my hands over my face. "No, nothing about this is okay. I don't want him here and I don't want her here and I sure as hell don't want *Mary* here--"

He knelt in front of me. "All we have to do is get through it."

I looked at the face I'd come to love with such abandon and leaned forward, my mouth seeking his.

His arms were around me in an instant as we stood, still kissing, and moved toward the bedroom. I didn't protest even as the ever-expanding to-do list floated through my mind. What I needed most was him making love to me- and afterwards, holding me while I fell asleep.

He laid me down on the bed and undressed me in a way he hadn't in a very long time. He was tender, as though we were lovers seeing each other for the first time, and I felt myself blush under his gaze as he shrugged out of his own clothes.

"You're beautiful, J," he said as he dropped beside me, his fingers running the length of my hip and across to my thigh. "I know I don't tell you that enough."

"You make me feel it," I answered, closing my eyes as I rolled beneath him, pulling his hips down to meet my own. I felt his breath stagger and smiled, thinking of the pleasure I could give him after weeks of tension and uncertainty.

Our lovemaking was slow and dreamlike--aided by the bourbon and our tired minds--I felt his skin like a heated sheath above me, sliding and folding until the intensity broke free and I cried out his name, my nails digging into the firm skin of his shoulders.

He followed moments later, collapsing on top of me, kissing my cheeks and lips in a way that made me feel like a piece of glass that must not be broken.

I burrowed into his neck, smelling the scent of his damp skin, feeling such bliss I thought I might dissolve into the night.

That memory was certainly better than the present moment as I stood in the kitchen, wishing the fabulous dinner would cook itself. The time had come, and I had to put on a good show for Mom who had yet to see my new home.

My first home.

My only home.

Dylan arrived at noon, and I kissed him at the door, memories of the night before lingering in our touch. It must have been on his mind, too because he chuckled and said, "We're gonna be late if you don't stop."

"In that case, you'd better start chopping," I teased while grabbing a knife and cutting board.

"Not exactly a turn-on, J," he grinned while coming towards me again, tickling me in the way I'd described to Mallard and for a split-second I wanted to fight him, see how far I could get but the moment passed.

Nothing would ruin the day faster than kicking my boyfriend's ass. And still, he must have sensed something in my hesitation, my stillness--because he pulled back.

"What's wrong?"

I looked at him, my gaze lingering on the flecks of silver that sometimes appeared in his eyes.

"Sometimes I wish I was still strong."

"I don't," he paused, unsure if I was joking. "And you are."

There it was. The answer I wasn't expecting. And I loved him for it.

An hour passed. Then two. The lasagna was in the oven. Mom and Paul were set to arrive any time and Mary would follow later.

I tried not to think about my mom sleeping with another man as I spread a blue tablecloth across the leaf Dylan had brought in from the shed. The room was beginning to fill up with delicious smells, not the least of which was Dylan's shampoo from the small space beneath the bathroom door.

I heard the shower running, felt it gather in a strange, slow momentum, a hum that just matched the sound I'd always associated with white noise, building and building until...

I saw something drop on the floor in front of me, a small splatter of liquid I knew was blood--the same that had come the first time I'd met Dylan and had everything to do with Amanda Bennett and the totems I'd destroyed the summer before.

I made my way to the counter, remembering what had stopped my visions before and saw the knife I'd been cutting vegetables with laying the sink.

I heard the shower turn off, heard the curtain being drawn across the metal rod and knew Dylan would be out in a matter of minutes.

I reached for the knife, pushed the tip into the pad of my thumb. Blood spouted from the wound, and I bent over, dropping the knife where it clattered against the side of the sink.

I waited as the pain slowly wiped the vision from my eyes, felt my knees tighten up and gripped the counter while turning on the water. Shoving my hand under, I felt someone standing behind me and prayed he hadn't seen anything.

"What'd you do?" Dylan asked.

"Nothing," I said quickly. "Just grabbed the wrong end of the knife."

He peered into the sink, then looked at me and knocked on my forehead. "Get it together, Cook."

I laughed, my knees still shaky. "No promises, Locke."

He paused, looked at my thumb again. "I'll take that cut over the last one I bandaged up any day."

I looked at him quickly, his words breaking new ground between us. "You bandaged me up?"

He glanced away, uncomfortable with what he'd revealed. "Adam and I tore up the bottom of his shirt. You were bleeding so bad we thought--" He cleared his throat. "You might not make it to the ambulance."

I looked down at the knife in the sink. "I guess I have no idea what you guys went through."

I felt him squeeze my shoulder. "That was the plan."

"Dylan--"

"I'm good with it. No reason to bring it up when everything turned out good."

"I don't know," I said, thinking his approach might be labeled 'avoidance behavior' by any therapist worth their salt. "It might make you feel better to talk about it."

"Doubt it," he said, his brevity a thing I'd come to expect where the subject was concerned. "And it's no good for you, either."

I frowned. "You sure about that?"

"Yep." He smiled again, trying to distract me, and doing a damn good job. "And your mom just pulled in."

I tensed, turned to look out the kitchen window. Sure enough, a strange car had just pulled in behind the Jeep. I felt my mouth go dry as I watched the man behind the wheel lean close and touch the side of her face.

The next moment they looked back at the house and I moved away.

I took a breath. Then two. Then ten.

A light knock at the door.

Mom's knock.

I moved towards it and put my hand on the knob, feeling like a million pounds of crazy was about to invade the piece of heaven I'd created with Dylan.

I stood still, unable to turn it and Dylan moved behind me, touched my elbow with is fingertips.

"J?"

On the other side of the door was a woman whose approval I craved, a woman who now wanted mine.

"Justine?"

I tightened my grip even as I felt the door jar beneath a second knock.

Dylan moved closer, and I felt him lean into me, his breath just touching my ear. "Open the door, baby." ."

I did, blinking as Mom stepped across the threshold, blocking the light.

Her pixie cut had grown out and now hung just below her shoulders. She'd gotten blond highlights as well, ones that made her look younger. She took another step forward, wondering why I was mute when Dylan leaned over and extended his hand.

"Thanks for coming up."

I backed away and looked at the man who was standing behind her.

He was tall, with salt and pepper hair and a five o'clock shadow I suspected was intentional. His jeans were new, his white button down and sports jacket an appealing juxtaposition.

"Mom," I breathed as she entered the kitchen. Stepping aside, I hoped she would be pleased with what she saw.

She had something under her arm, some sort of salad she had picked up along the way that had strawberries arranged in a semi-circle on top.

"Justine," she leaned in, gave me a quick peck on the cheek. "This is Paul."

"Paul," I said, unable to form another word behind it.

He extended his hand. "Nice to finally meet you, Justine. Your mom has told me all about you."

Like how I kill creepy Lutheran preachers in my spare time...

"And I've heard about you, too," I lied.

Paul nodded as if he believed me, and then entered the kitchen. We stood awkwardly in the small space for a moment before Dylan offered to give them both a tour.

Mom jumped at the chance by handing me the salad.

"Yes, please. Justine has never owned a home before."

Paul nodded, it seemed to be all he was able to do, before putting a hand on the suede coat I hadn't offered to take for her.

"Well, this certainly looks like a great starter home," he said.

I bit my lip before I said something nasty while Dylan pretended not to notice.

The tour took all of ten minutes, with Mom nodding over my choice of shabby chic bathroom décor and how I had chosen to arrange my towels. We paused for a moment at our bedroom. I had made the bed nicely, pulling hard on the comforter to make it look like a five-star bed and breakfast, but no one could escape the reality of what usually happened there besides the usual eight hours of shut-eye.

Dylan's cough moved us along to the second bedroom.

"This is where you'll sleep," I said, giving the space a panoramic sweep of my arm for emphasis.

Paul stuck his hands in his pockets. "Are you sure there's room for us?"

"Yep," Dylan leaned in before I could add my fifteen cents. "Can you come out back, Paul? I need some advice on a new belt for my mower."

He looked to my mother, and I saw her nod almost imperceptibly. It was okay. He could go with "The Boyfriend" and do manly things in the backyard like talk about lawnmower belts although I wondered if Paul had ever mowed his own grass.

As soon as the screen door slammed, I felt myself tense up again.

Mom smiled, sat down at the kitchen table I had set to accommodate an extra three, and touched my tablecloth gently with her fingertips.

"So?" she asked, and I looked at her closely, unable to believe she could really be blushing.

"He's good-looking," I said quickly, feeling dumb because she was obviously searching for something more.

"And?"

"He seems nice."

"*And*?"

I leaned against the counter, crossed my arms over the yellow blouse I had chosen for its summery allure.

"I've only known the guy for ten minutes. What do you want me to say?"

She smiled again, put her chin in her hands like a smitten schoolgirl.

"Mom--"

"I know you think I'm moving too fast."

I shook my head, "I don't think that--"

"It's been eleven years."

I shifted my position against the counter, leaned over to look at the lasagna bubbling in the oven because nothing had prepared me for the fact that my mother might truly be in love.

"I haven't felt this way since..." she trailed off, thinking the same thing I was.

"That country chapel tucked so far into the woods no one was able to find it?"

She blushed again, looked down at the tablecloth, and smoothed an imaginary wrinkle.

Mom was happy. Fun. Free.

And I had no idea how to deal with her.

"I never thought I'd feel this way again."

I took a step towards her, wanting to offer something but ended up suspended in space, unable to move in either direction.

"Please be happy for me."

"I am."

"No," she reached up, took my hand, and squeezed it. "I mean *really* happy."

"Mom," I said, my voice weak. "All I've ever wanted was for you to be happy."

She nodded again. "I know. I know you have. And now I can. With Paul."

"Mom," I began, feeling something slide out of place. "You were fine before you met him."

She laughed, smoothed the tablecloth again. "You of all people should know that's *not* true."

I didn't want to psychoanalyze her but this goofy behavior was starting to make me long for the Brenda Cook who always had her shit together.

Or at least pretended to.

The oven buzzer went off and I turned away, grabbed a couple of mitts, and pulled out my masterpiece. Mom stood, took the plastic lid off her salad, and began to toss in silence. I glanced at the backyard and saw Dylan standing by the shed we used as a garage in cases of extreme necessity. He and Paul were talking, laughing, and I felt grateful to have a mate who tethered me to earth with his good nature and common sense.

He looked up, saw me at the window and smiled, and I felt my heart do a somersault, unable to believe in some primal recess of my brain that he was mine.

YOU NEED TO GET TO THE HOSPITAL.

I started, unable to process his sudden intrusion as Mom dumped her salad in a bowl. The next moment Dylan's voice was at the back door as he and Paul came in.

I'M IN THE MIDDLE OF SOMETHING RIGHT NOW.

"Dinner smells great, hon," Dylan said while planting a quick peck on my cheek.

"Thanks," I smiled, trying to block my brother out. Knowing it was useless.

GET OUT OF IT.

I took the lasagna and placed it in the center of the table with the garlic bread. Mom's salad and my platter of cut veggies came next. The brownies would be a tasty culmination to be relished later.

I CAN'T.

"When is Mary coming?" Mom asked as she sat down, spreading her napkin carefully across her lap.

"Any time," Paul answered, his hand going to what I assumed was Mom's knee under the table. "She usually gets out of work at four."

Mom nodded, said something like "Umm" as she took a bite of lasagna.

"Where does she work?" I asked, trying to make conversation while dishing up the salad and Paul smiled, appreciating my feigned interest.

"Water Way... it's a—"

"Vet's office," Dylan said, shifting beside me.

"Yes," Paul nodded, a piece of lettuce skewered on his fork while a sick feeling began to press on my stomach.

"I think I hear her now," Mom offered, and I listened as a car pulled into our driveway, a door slamming moments later.

"Is Mary--" I began.

"Meg," Paul corrected, glancing at my mother. "Her name is Mary-Margaret, but we haven't called her that since she was ten."

Mom laughed. Dylan and I didn't.

He looked at me, trying to tell me everything would be all right when the knock came. Light. Courteous. Pert.

Like the little tramp herself.

Dylan stood quickly, walked towards the door, and I wanted to chase him down, grab his arm, and tell him no way in hell was he letting her into our home for brownies and a pajama party.

But I didn't because all I could do was sit like a blob while my boyfriend went to greet the girl he'd been spending the majority of his evenings with.

The door opened slowly, and I watched as the color drained from the face of a young woman who looked every bit the nineteen-year-old she was. Her hair was long and brown and shiny and straight. Her eyes were dark, too--a striking contrast to Dylan.

"How--" he began.

"Dylan?" she asked, not understanding.

"Meg?" her father stood up.

"Paul?" Mom chimed in, leaving me with nothing to say and pretty close to completely miserable.

I stole another glance as she entered the kitchen. Yep-- perfect right down to the mole on her right cheekbone that looked like something Marilyn Monroe had planted. She was holding some sort of dessert--a pie she had probably baked in her own kitchen with her cute little hands, a dusting of flour across her nose.

Yes, Mary--aka Meg--was as delightful as I'd expected.

And her sudden appearance had disturbed Dylan, which bothered me.

I stared but tried not to as she sat the pie down and stood before the sink where I'd stabbed myself with a knife only an hour before.

My gaze shifting to Dylan, I could sense his discomfort in the hunch of his shoulders, the tense ball of his fist on the door frame, the way he glanced at me as though he'd ate the last double fudge brownie.

And now the girl that had gotten him all worked up would be sleeping mere steps from our bedroom door. And if Paul and Mom got married...

I'd never get rid of her.

I looked down at my plate as my nose began to tingle.

TROY WILL BE THERE TOMORROW. YOU NEED TO COME.

I swiped at my cheek and stood quickly. Advancing towards Meg with all the confidence I could muster, I extended my hand.

I'll BE THERE.

CHAPTER
TEN

I lay in bed, gazing up as our ceiling fan sliced the darkness, wondering if Dylan was awake and how we were going to deal with the hot, young thing sleeping right outside our bedroom door.

The dinner had been strained--Mom and Paul confused.

Meg seemed disconcerted but went on to explain that she and Dylan were taking classes together and wasn't it an incredible coincidence that he was dating her father's girlfriend's daughter.

A coincidence... Her dark eyes held his for a beat, then darted off in another direction as she commented on the rooster clock above the sink, the dishes that were a concoction of His, Hers, and Dollar General--anything to distract us from what was in her heart because I knew it had settled on Dylan.

Not that I blamed her.

Women looked at him all the time.

He just never looked back.

I shifted towards him and put a tentative hand on his chest, felt him stir.

"Dylan?" I whispered. I didn't want Meg to hear. Didn't want her to think we weren't sleeping in a cocoon spun from the threads of our own romantic bliss.

"Hmmm," he mumbled.

I thought about what to say.

After dinner, we showed Meg around the house, pausing again at our bedroom door, which she barely approached in her haste to move on.

Yes...she had it and tried to cover it up by talking incessantly about the classes they were taking together and wouldn't it be awesome if they both got placed in the same school after they passed their MTTC exams. She would teach English Language Arts, and he would teach American History across the hall. She'd heard that two teachers were retiring from Alpena High School.

"I want to stay in Lantern Creek," Dylan offered, and my heart rose at his rebuff.

"Sure," Meg replied, her cheeks red. "Closer to home."

Thankfully, Mom had been willing to pick up the slack conversation-wise. I finally got the long-awaited story of how she met Paul and their first date at a restaurant my father would never have set foot inside.

Because he had taste.

The thought surprised me, and I bit my tongue before I said something crappy. There was really no reason to hate Paul besides the fact that he had fathered a daughter Dylan seemed smitten with. Besides that obvious faux pas, he seemed attentive to my mother, was mannerly in some of his actions, and had a keen fashion sense that was sure to set Lantern Creek on its ear.

Yes...he was an ideal "first boyfriend," and I had to admit Mom had taken a long time getting around to it, which made it hard to begrudge her happiness.

"Dylan?" I asked again and he stirred.

"What?"

"What happened with Meg's parents?"

"What?"

"Meg's parents," I repeated. "What happened?"

He rolled towards me and touched my face, one finger lingering beneath my chin. "Baby... it's almost two o'clock."

"Does she have any brothers and sisters?"

"Justine."

"I mean, I thought you might know something about her besides the weird stories she tells about the cheating clients at her clinic."

"We only talk about our classes when we study. I'm not going to cross that line, not when she's--" he trailed off.

"In love with you," I finished, the words I'd wanted to say since I first saw her face blanch in my doorway tumbling free.

He chuckled under his breath. "She's not in love with me."

"Oh, yes she is."

"She's young."

"And beautiful."

He paused. "We're just friends."

"I think I know when a girl has the hots for you," I said while propping myself up on one elbow, the wavy hair he loved so much spilling over my shoulders in a way I hoped he found alluring. "I've had plenty of practice."

"Shhhh," he silenced me. "She'll hear you."

"So what?" I said. "It's not like she's trying to hide it."

"Justine," he said, pulling me down into his arms and I wondered if she could indeed hear us on the other side of the door.

"Don't you think she's pretty?" I asked, wanting to see his face in the darkness.

He laughed. "I'm not answering that question."

I lay silently, waiting, until he became uncomfortable.

"Yeah, she's pretty."

"And smart," I offered. "Sounds like a straight A student."

"Maybe," he sighed. "I don't know."

"Quite the combo."

"Justine," he said again, more gently this time. "Stop doing this to yourself."

"Doing what?"

"This *thing* you do when you think I might leave you. I'm not leaving you. I'm *never* leaving you."

I felt my cheeks burn with embarrassment and snuggled further into his arms.

"You were upset when you saw her in the doorway."

"I shouldn't have been talking about her the other night."

"You were talking about her because you were *thinking* about her."

"Justine," he said, shifting on the bed. "I've been with that group a lot and it's only natural--"

"But she--"

"Isn't you," he interrupted, and the next moment I felt his lips seek mine in the darkness.

Possessiveness overtook me in a rush, and I placed my hand on his stomach, following the fine hair that ran from his belly button beneath the band of his boxer shorts. I lingered there as I often did; waiting as he became aroused but instead of rolling me beneath him, he took my hand and placed it back on his chest.

I felt his heartbeat skip rope beneath my fingers and wanted to tell him his gesture hurt me--but I didn't. There had been enough talk for one night and in the morning Meg would be gone and I would be on my way to the hospital in St. Ignace to help a girl I'd never met and if Dylan found out...

But he wouldn't find out because he was working all day and I had an alibi and it was only this one time to get Adam off my back.

"I love you," he whispered as he nestled me into the crook of his arm, and I stared at his profile in the darkness until his breath became steady and his hand slackened in mine.

Turning, I traced his jaw line with my fingertips.

"I hope that's enough."

CHAPTER
ELEVEN

I was almost there.

Only the Mackinac Bridge stood between me and the place I'd been dancing a slow tango with for the past two weeks. I turned and looked at Adam, his brown hair blowing in the breeze because he preferred his window down on this hot, summer day.

He seemed lighthearted, carefree, and I could only imagine it was because he now had a partner in crime.

"Almost there," I said, not sure why I spoke the words aside from the small part that wanted us to be normal.

WHAT DID YOU TELL DYLAN?

I shrugged, the lead in my belly turning sour and sinking toward my toes. I'd told the group currently at my bungalow to make themselves at home because I was taking Adam to lunch, not bothering to consider if my actions were rude, hoping they would all be gone by noon.

"That I was hanging out with my favorite baby brother."

I'M YOUR ONLY BABY BROTHER.

"Never say never."

He looked at me, put a finger to his ear.

DID YOU SAY WHERE WE WERE GOING?

I shook my head. "I didn't tell him, but he didn't ask questions."

HE DIDN'T?

"He's working today. Then it's off to cram with his study group which means he's way too busy to come looking for me."

It was Adam's turn to laugh.

HE'S NEVER TOO BUSY FOR THAT.

I smiled, slowed down as we began our drive over the five-mile expanse of the Mackinac Bridge.

"He's been distracted lately."

WITH WHAT?

That was the million-dollar question, wasn't it?

He'd gotten up for work just after sunrise, pausing at the door to make sure Meg was presentable before walking into the living room. I sat up, trying to be quiet and caught a glimpse of her through the open doorway.

She seemed to be sitting in a puddle made from the folds of our favorite blue blanket, her sweatshirt hanging from one shoulder in a way that made her look like a petulant schoolgirl.

Which was pretty much the truth.

She was just about as perky as someone could be first thing in the morning as she stretched, seemingly surprised to see Dylan emerge from his bedroom at exactly the time he said he needed to leave for work the night before.

"Hey," Dylan whispered, trying not to wake me.

"Hey," she answered, her voice throaty.

"How'd you sleep?"

"Not so good," she replied, drawing her long hair over one shoulder and I wondered if he would take the bait.

"Help yourself to anything you need."

"I wish," she whispered, and it made him stand up straighter.

One glance over his shoulder and I slunk down into the pillow, pretending to be asleep. "I know this is awkward."

"That's the understatement of the century."

"It is for me, too."

"It doesn't have to be."

"What's that supposed to mean?"

"Dylan--"

"We talked about this."

"I know. I just didn't expect to be spending the night outside your bedroom door."

He paused, the silence filling my mind with scenarios his words should have discouraged.

"I had no idea her mom was dating my dad."

"I'm going to be late."

"Dylan--"

"See you in class."

And he had gone, walking through the living room and shutting the kitchen door with an extra *umph* that made me wonder what sort of message he was sending the scorned nymphet. And why he had talked to her at all or labeled their time together "awkward," hinting that they had already "talked about this."

And now I was stuck explaining my love life to my little brother.

"There's a girl in his class," I paused, wondering what he would think and if I should even be talking about this when we had bigger fish to fry. "He likes her, I can tell. Her dad is dating Mom if you can believe my rotten luck."

THAT IS ROTTEN LUCK.

I reached over and turned on the radio, hoping it would ease my tension. Moments later the Beach Boys burst on the scene, telling me not to worry and I wished I could take their advice.

DID I MENTION I HATE BRIDGES?

I glanced at the outside lane and the pitiful guardrail that separated us from Lake Huron, hundreds of feet below.

"Did I mention I hate driving across them? You owe me *big* time."

I DON'T WANNA DO THIS ANY MORE THAN YOU DO.

"You could've told her to take a hike."

NO, I COULDN'T.

It was true, and I loved him because of it.

We were halfway across and I adjusted my grip on the wheel. Dylan had driven across once before when I'd had a hankering to visit the Upper Peninsula last fall. After a trip to Tahquamenon Falls and a lightning-fast picture with a honey-crazed cub at Oswald's Bear Ranch, I'd fallen asleep in his lap while he drove us home.

I chewed on the inside of my lip, wishing he was here instead of patrolling the back roads of Presque Isle County, thinking about a girl who was likely in the "awkward" position of using his shower right now.

I wrinkled my nose, wondering if she would swipe our soap as a memento when I saw someone walking beside the guardrails up ahead.

"What's that guy doing?" I asked, squinting into the sun.

Adam glanced at me.

WHAT GUY?

I pointed. "The one up there."

WHAT ARE YOU TALKING ABOUT?

I motioned again, irritated, until we drew closer, and I saw the side of the stranger's face.

He was tall, with shoulder-length blond hair that seemed to ignite in the sun, his easy-going gait suggesting he spent time following the wind and weather.

I felt my palms perspire as the Beach Boys died in my ears.

"Dad," I said weakly, startling Adam.

WHAT?

My mind was suddenly drawn to the first time I'd seen Esther Ebersole at the lighthouse the summer before. Holly had been standing beside me, oblivious to the fact that a woman was wandering the shoreline with a fresh bullet wound in her chest.

WHAT DO YOU SEE?

I slowed down, wanting to open the door and usher our dead father into the back seat, knowing deeper that something was wrong because Dad would never come to us in this way.

We were beside him now, and he stopped walking, turned slowly, and for an instant, I saw the face of the father I loved.

"Muffet," he mouthed, his hand coming up as though he were about to touch the side of the Jeep.

Adam jerked in his seat beside me, his hands splayed across the dash.

HE SAID NOT TO STOP!

I started, pushed down on the accelerator when the face of my father began to melt like the shimmer above hot asphalt. Hazel eyes became black, his warm smile sliding into something that should have died years before.

"Shit!" I cursed, my grip lost.

WHAT DO YOU SEE?

"Red Rover! He's right there..."

I felt my hands float across the top of the steering wheel as Adam reached over, his face white.

GET OVER!

We were passing him now and his head swiveled slowly, following our forward motion when I saw something in his hand. Something cinched with rawhide and dripping with a dark substance I knew was blood.

"He has the medicine bag," I gasped, barely able to touch the gas as my foot began to shake uncontrollably.

I imagined our Jeep lifting off the road like a kite catching the breeze, somersaulting as the lake reached up to catch us in her palms.

I tightened my grip, determined to gain control over what was pulling us toward the edge when my right leg exploded in pain.

My mind cleared and I heard the Jeep passing over the grating on the roadway. Glancing down, I saw a small trickle of blood on the outside of my thigh.

I looked at Adam, who was holding a paper clip he had unbent, the glove box open in front of him and realized he'd just stabbed me with the only thing he could find.

I gripped my leg, glanced behind as we swung back into our lane. Henry Younts was gone.

"Damn," I whispered, my whole body shaking as sweat broke out across my chest and forehead. "We were going over."

I'M SORRY, SIS.

"You saved us."

WAS IT HENRY YOUNTS?

I nodded, my breathing still shallow, my leg pulsating. "He had the medicine bag."

I HEARD DAD'S VOICE. HE TOLD ME NOT TO STOP.

He looked at me then, his large eyes frightened and for a moment, I was reminded of how young he was, how much he had suffered and my heart hurt for his lost childhood as much as my own.

Minutes later we paid our toll and pulled over on a grassy area just past the exit ramp. Laying my forehead against the steering wheel, I gulped air and waited while the breeze cooled my clammy flesh.

WE NEED TO GET TO THE HOSPITAL. MAYBE AMANDA CAN TELL US WHAT'S GOING ON.

I looked up at him. "You think she can help?"

SHE'S LIKE US.

I shook my head, laid it back against the seat and closed my eyes. "There's no one like us."

Moments later we were back on the road, both silent as we pulled into the parking lot of the St. Ignace hospital.

All was quiet as we entered through the automatic doors and made our way across the lobby. A sleepy woman who was eating a Snickers bar was sitting at the front desk. She glanced our way, then sat up straighter as we walked by.

"Can I help you?" she asked, and I shook my head, grabbed my brother's elbow and pulled him to my side.

"We know where we're going," I lied, flashing what I hoped was a convincing smile and it seemed to work because she continued to peel the wrapper before stuffing the rest of the candy bar in her mouth.

"Need a Band-Aid?" she asked, one chocolaty finger pointing towards my leg and I glanced down, nodded, and took one out of a bowl she had sitting on her desk.

She smiled, seemingly satisfied with her good deed and when I looked back a moment later, she was licking her fingers.

"Where are we going?" I asked my brother as he steered me down another hallway.

THIS WAY.

WE ROUNDED A CORNER. A nurse's station was on the right, several people bustling around or hanging out, not looking. It was as if we were invisible, which made me wonder if they'd notice if I'd been walking around naked instead of my usual white tank top, cut off shorts and flip-flops.

I looked down at my toes, painted a summery shade of pink and smiled. Dylan had dared me to walk back to Lantern Creek in these flip-flops, his humor making a bad situation more bearable.

I wished he was here to crack a joke now.

"I'm transferring Miss Bennett to a different hospital," I heard a voice rise just inside the room to our left.

Adam grabbed my elbow and pulled me aside as a man hurried from the room to the nurse's station. He was well-dressed, his tone suggesting that he was used to giving orders and having people follow them.

THAT'S ETHAN. HE'S NOT SUPPOSED TO BE HERE.

"Well, he is," I hissed, wondering if this was the boyfriend- realizing seconds later he was the fiancé and an old-fashioned rumble was going down if Troy showed up anytime soon.

"What does Troy look like?" I whispered, scanning the hallway.

An old lady with a walker was making her way towards us, followed by a nurse rolling an I.V.

HE LOOKS LIKE THAT GUY FROM SUPERMAN IN A LUMBERJACKY KINDA WAY.

I glanced at my brother.

IT'S TRUE.

I shook my head, then peeked down the hallway and saw Ethan leaning over the counter, trying to sweet talk a nurse who seemed irritated. I heard the phrase "Power of Attorney" float above their heads and wondered if our plan was going off the rails before it began.

I looked at the nurse again. Things didn't seem to be going well. Ethan couldn't take Amanda until the "right person" got there. They weren't legally married, after all.

"Her mother's not well," he said, his tone sharp, and she looked up quickly. Ethan spread his hands on the counter as though he was delivering an ultimatum to an insubordinate employee. "Any judge would declare her incompetent."

The nurse lowered her voice, glanced around to see if anyone was listening. "You would be transferring her against medical advice. The POA would have to sign paperwork."

I backed up against the wall, wondering why I had ever agreed to come here when Ethan finally lost his patience with the nurse. He was leaning back now, his hands kneading the counter top. He couldn't make the "Power of Attorney" cloud disappear despite the names he'd been dropping like breadcrumbs in a fairy tale forest.

Turning quickly, he stormed back into Amanda's room.

"Can I help you," the nurse finally noticed us. She stood up, rounded the counter with a questioning look when another person entered the hallway.

He was about six feet tall, with black hair and a powerful stride, his clothes spotted with some sort of grease I could only assume came from working with a chainsaw. He approached, the smell of sawdust filling my nose as clear, green eyes focused on me, a look of confusion twisting his face into something I recognized in myself.

And I had to admit, my brother had been spot on about the whole "Superman" thing.

"Miss?" the nurse said. "Who are you here to see?"

"Him," I said, pointing to Troy- who had just realized something was wrong.

"And who are you here to see?" she asked him, and he smiled, shrugged his shoulders.

"Her."

The nurse paused, looked at Troy a beat longer than she should have, then sat back down at her desk.

"Who are you?" he asked, his voice lowering, his eyes darting toward Amanda's room.

"Ethan's here," I whispered, wondering how he would react.

He stood up straighter. "What?"

"Amanda's in trouble."

"What do you mean?" he asked, pulling us aside and into an alcove. "How do you know her?"

Adam squeezed my hand.

TELL HIM.

I looked up at Troy, undone by how intently he was watching me.

"I'm Justine. This is my brother, Adam."

His eyes darted between us before settling on me.

"What I'm about to say won't make any sense, but my brother"-- I paused, swallowed past the fear that made speech difficult--"talks to Amanda."

Troy stepped back, dropped his hands to his side, and looked out into the hallway again. Glancing back at us, I saw a hard glint in his eye. "Amanda can't talk."

"She can," I said, holding his gaze. "My brother can hear her."

He crossed his arms over his chest. "How can he hear her?"

I took a breath. "In his mind."

Troy was silent, and for an awful moment, I thought he was

going to laugh, or turn us into the woman eating the Snickers bar, or run down the hallway and burst into Amanda's room and get into a fistfight with Ethan.

But he didn't. And so, I looked up again and saw that his eyes had widened. As though he wanted to believe it was possible.

"Ethan wants to transfer her to another hospital."

"*What?*"

"We have to hurry."

Troy held up a hand. "You're telling me your brother heard this...in his mind?"

"That's exactly what I'm saying."

"Okay." He leaned back, the smell of sawdust stronger now. "If that's true, tell me where we went on our first date."

I looked to Adam and felt like something was beginning that we could never undo.

"The Pink Pony."

Troy's face slackened as his hand absentmindedly rubbed the dark stubble on his chin.

"What song were we listening to?"

I paused, my brother's voice clear and strong.

"Brandy, but you changed the words to--"

"Mandy," he finished, leaning against the wall. "No one knows that--"

"I'm sorry, Troy. I know this sounds crazy but my brother--"

"Doesn't talk."

"But he hears things. And I hear him."

"And he's telling you that Mandy's in trouble?" he asked, reaching for a chair. Sitting down slowly.

I looked at Troy, wanting to comfort him but knowing there was no comfort for the world he was about to enter. And if we lingered too long in this purgatory, we would lose time when what we really needed to do was get Amanda out of the hospital and...

I bit my lip.

I hadn't thought about where we would go, but that wasn't my problem. I had a life back in Lantern Creek that came complete with a quirky group of friends and a super-hot boyfriend and I'd only agreed to tell Troy what was happening, so he could swoop in and save her like...

Well...Superman.

Ethan's voice rose from somewhere down the hallway and in an instant, Troy was on his feet.

"Cocky little shit."

I touched his arm. "Let him leave on his own. We can't cause a scene or my plan won't work."

He looked down at me.

"Your plan?"

I nodded, my eyes cutting to Adam.

CABIN TEN NEEDS A NEW ROOF. MOM CLOSED IT DOWN FOR THE SEASON.

I swallowed, stole a glance down the hallway again.

"Let's go."

CHAPTER
TWELVE

Ethan had just left the room and Amanda found it hard to breathe. He had threatened the hospital staff with everything in his power and still they would not release her. Not without her mother's consent. So, Ethan had gone to persuade Ms. Sara Bennett to come down to the hospital so that she could sign the necessary paperwork. He was making phone calls already, getting his lawyer lined up--and the grandparents, if necessary. They were family, after all--and Sara could hardly be seen as competent in comparison.

ADAM, WHERE ARE YOU?

He didn't answer, and she felt the familiar blanket of fear smother her. Maybe he hadn't been able to get away, or his sister had decided to bail, or Troy had packed up and left town with a girl who could stand on her own two feet.

Amanda tried to straighten her right leg and felt it shriek in protest. If she could only get out of bed, then maybe she could stumble down the hallway and into the parking lot.

But where could she go so that Ethan wouldn't find her?

Troy lived above her grandparents' stables on Mackinac Island. It was impossible to hide her there and with no one to care for her when he went to log jobs during the week...

She straightened her other leg as a bolt of pain ripped through her body.

She heard footsteps moving down the hall and shut her eyes, terrified that Ethan had returned to take her by force.

"Mandy."

Troy's voice was like a breeze on sunburned skin. She saw him come towards her bed, followed by Adam and a girl she had never seen before.

She was petite, with wavy blond hair that hung almost to the middle of her back and large, expressive eyes that widened when she entered the room.

In fact, Amanda was pretty sure she had skipped right out of a Disney movie, which made her wonder how she could help when she seemed better suited to nursing orphaned kittens or twirling through a field of daisies.

"Mandy," Troy repeated as he came to her side. "Did you send them here?"

She nodded, felt his hand come up to touch her cheek.

"I can't believe it."

The sister came forward, leaned over so she could look at her more closely and Amanda saw that her eyes weren't brown or blue or green, but something that danced the line between all three.

"My name is Justine, and we're going to help you."

Amanda nodded, feeling like she could trust her even though they had just met.

"When is Ethan coming back?"

Amanda glanced at Adam, who turned to his sister.

SOON.

"We don't have much time," she said. "We need to get you out of here."

"And we need a place to take her," Troy said, and Amanda hated that she had become a burden. That her choice to climb to the top of Robinson's Folly had led them here.

"We have a place," Justine answered, touching Troy's arm as they moved into a corner to talk.

Adam came to her bedside. His eyes were worried, anxious. Uncertain.

WHERE AM I GOING?

MY MOM OWNS A FISHING LODGE. YOU'LL BE SAFE THERE.

WHO WILL STAY WITH ME?

WE WILL.

YOUR MOM?

WILL HELP US.

He smiled at her and she felt her heart lift. They were going to get her out, take her to a place where Troy could care for her. She would grow stronger and when she finally got her voice back...

Justine was coming back now, Troy following, and he leaned over her again, put his hand to her face.

"You trust them?" he asked softly, his green eyes searching hers as they had in the past, and she nodded.

"Then I trust them, too."

She smiled as he brushed her lips with his own. Memories of their nights together in his loft above the stables lingered in her mind, making her wonder if she would ever feel the touch of his hands again and not recoil in pain.

"Excuse me," a voice from behind broke the moment. "It's time for her medicine."

Justine took her brother's arm and backed up, allowing the nurse to enter.

Troy, on the other hand, eyed her I.V. bag suspiciously.

"What are you giving her?"

The nurse was the one Ethan had been threatening earlier, and she seemed to flush under Troy's gaze.

"Just some morphine. She paused, looked down, and fiddled

with some buttons on the base of the I.V. "She wasn't listed as having any med allergies. Because you'll need-"

"No," Troy smiled, and the nurse relaxed--the color creeping down her neck. "Just curious."

"Are you?" she ventured, her eyes rising from the base up to the I.V. bag, "A relative?"

Troy shook his head. "Just a friend."

The nurse nodded, "She's doing well considering the circumstances."

Troy shoved his hands in his pockets, rocked back on his heels. "That's a relief."

"Yes," she replied, although it seemed like she wanted today more when Justine spoke up.

"Can we take her down the hall in a wheelchair? Get her out of the room for a bit?"

The nurse looked at them, unconvinced that Amanda should be moved. Troy smiled. "Your shift ends soon, doesn't it?"

The nurse nodded, the color high in her cheeks again, wondering why he would ask, and Amanda held her breath, wondering the same thing.

"We'll be sure to tell your boss what a good job you did dealing with that jerk"--he paused, glanced at her name tag--"Amy."

"He was something else," she grinned, her guard down. "Actually threatened to have me fired."

Troy shook his head, his displeasure evident and Amy looked away, pushed a piece of hair behind her ear.

"How's your pain?" she asked, and Amanda looked at her, realizing how Troy's charm had completely discombobulated the nurse.

"We'll bring her back in ten minutes." Troy smiled again, his gaze darting from the nurse to Justine.

"That's good because her fiancé will be back--"

"Sure. Will you help me find a wheelchair?" Troy smiled and Amy turned in the doorway, a slight smile brushing her lips.

"I saw one in the hallway," she offered, moving away while Troy followed.

Hushed voices carried into the room as the three waited, wondering what was being said.

When Troy returned moments later, he was alone.

"Hurry," Justine whispered to her brother, who moved to secure the chair.

Amanda winced as Troy's arm slid behind her back, pushing her shoulders forward.

"I'm sorry," he apologized. "I don't want to hurt you."

Moments later they were wheeling her out the door and past Amy, who had returned to her desk, her eyes lifting for just a moment as they passed by.

"Thanks again," Troy said, his tone holding something that Amanda couldn't distinguish.

But she didn't care if her boyfriend was flirting with the day nurse.

He was getting her out- taking what was his.

And God help them if Ethan ever found out.

CHAPTER THIRTEEN

I couldn't believe I was smuggling a suicidal clairvoyant out of the St. Ignace hospital in broad daylight.

I watched as Troy wheeled Amanda down the hallway and into the parking lot to his truck. Once there he lifted her into the passenger seat as though she weighed no more than a toddler.

I looked over my shoulder.

No alarms were sounding, no staff rushing to see why we were shoving a critically injured patient into a rusty blue pickup. A shift change coupled with lunch seemed to be all that was needed to successfully whisk Amanda Bennett away from St. Ignace Hospital.

"Follow me," I said over my shoulder as I forced myself to walk towards the Jeep--*Dylan's* Jeep--which had now been used in some sort of criminal activity.

I tried to steady my shaking hands as I climbed inside. Then I was pulling out of the parking lot, wishing the distance between myself and Three Fires would vanish. And still I had an hour to scan every passing car for Ethan, every long shadow cast across the Mackinac Bridge for Henry Younts, my nerves shot to hell when my cell phone rang.

"Hey," I answered with a breezy nonchalance I hoped would fool Mom.

"Are you on your way back from lunch?"

I wondered why she cared what I was doing since she and Paul had planned to head over to Traverse City.

"Yep," I lied.

"Our plans have changed. Paul thinks he should talk to Meg since--" She trailed off. I gritted my teeth, wanting to forget the debacle of the night before.

"They have some classes together. That's it."

She sighed. And I hoped Paul wasn't sitting beside her, pitying me again.

"It's obvious that they have feelings for each other. Paul wants to talk to her. You need to let him."

I glanced in the rear view mirror. Troy was tailgating me, his hands clenched on the steering wheel, which meant I needed to ditch the drama and get moving.

"They're in class tonight."

"Paul's asking her to skip."

I laughed, "And miss a chance to stare at Dylan for two hours without blinking? I don't think so."

"She agreed, Justine. She's upset--"

I squinted at the road, then the rear view mirror, half expecting to see a dozen cop cars tailing me, my boyfriend included. "It's not like she didn't know he had a girlfriend."

Mom paused, "She's young."

"That's obvious--"

"She had no idea you were my daughter."

"Well now she *does*!" I spat, my voice peaking, and Adam glanced at me. "And you can tell Paul to tell her to keep her meaty paws *off* my man!"

"Justine--" Mom began, trying to placate me. "He's taking her to dinner. I need somewhere to go while they talk."

"Go to her house."

Mom paused. "She has a roommate."

"You can paint your nails."

She was silent.

"Not sure when I'll be home."

"You told Dylan you'd be back this afternoon."

I looked at Adam. "We wanna hang out. Do brother-sister stuff."

I heard her sniff. "Am I just supposed to catch a seven o'clock movie?"

"I don't know," I was exasperated now. Troy was almost at my bumper, Amanda slumped beside him. "And I don't know why Paul wanting to have a heart-to-heart with his floozy of a daughter is suddenly my problem."

"She's not a problem. She's nineteen years old and Dylan was well aware of--"

I pushed on the pedal, rage exploding behind her insinuation, and sent the Jeep whizzing down 23. "Don't you say it," I said. "Don't even think it."

"Justine--"

"I gotta go."

I hung up, swung off of the road and onto the gravel driveway that led towards the Lodge, my heart in my throat, wondering if Pam would let us hide Amanda in Cabin Ten and what we would do if she refused.

HOW'D THAT GO?

I turned to him, trying to figure out if he was joking when my cell phone rang again.

"*What?*" I snapped, annoyed before I realized the caller was Dylan.

"Hey, hon," he said, his tone light, and I envied his oblivion. "Your mom wants to have dinner with us tonight."

I gritted my teeth, irritated that she had manipulated him to get what she wanted.

"Paul wants to talk with Meg. She's skipping class."

"So you are, too?"

"I'm caught up," he paused, unsure how to take my question. "We could spend some time together."

"Sounds great," I said, loving that he wanted a quiet evening at home even as I plotted how to get Amanda inside Cabin Ten without Pam seeing us.

"It's a good thing," he said. "Meg really needs this time with her dad."

I wondered how he knew what Meg needed, exactly, if all they ever talked about was school, and how he'd become privy to her daddy issues, which were running a close second to my own.

"Well, we all want Meg to get what she needs."

He paused. "I didn't mean it that way."

I sighed, exhausted, and glanced in the rear view mirror again.

"I just want to *stop* talking about her."

He was silent. Hurt. And I needed to get off the phone.

"I'm sorry--" I began.

"Don't apologize."

"I'm just really sick of this."

"I am, too."

I saw the sign for Three Fires up ahead and continued up the driveway.

"I gotta go," I said, my tone clipped.

He paused again. "Are you okay?"

I swallowed, wanting to tell him the truth as I passed the main lodge. "I just want to spend some time with my brother without getting hassled every three seconds."

He was silent again. Caught off guard. We never argued.

"Dylan--"

"It's okay. I won't bother you again."

"That's not what I meant."

"See you tonight."

I glanced at Adam, disturbed, and hung up before parking the Jeep in front of Cabin Ten.

The next moment Troy was at my window.

"Is this it?"
I jumped out, shoved my hands in my back pockets and nodded.
"How's she doing?"
He shook his head. "She's hanging in there."
I turned towards Cabin Ten.
"Let's get her inside."

CHAPTER
FOURTEEN

"You don't have to do this, you know?" Troy said as we pushed Amanda towards the cabin. "Yes, I do," I insisted.

"No," he said again. "You don't."

"Troy--"

"I'm thankful," he continued, turning once to see if anyone was following us. "I don't know what I would've done if you hadn't shown up."

I felt heat rise to my cheeks.

"I take that back," he grinned. "I probably would've beat Ethan's ass."

I smiled, thinking how unfair that match would be, then glanced at the girl in the wheelchair, trying to imagine what she had been like before her jump from Robinson's Folly. Watching her for a moment, I saw it in the smattering of freckles the summer sun had given her. She loved the outdoors, had spent afternoons wandering the cedar-lined trails of Mackinac Island with Troy and I could imagine the two of them making a home for themselves in some lovely part of the northern woods.

But until that day came, we would take care of her until she could tell us why Dad had pointed her out in a dream or Henry Younts had decided to stretch his legs on the Mackinac Bridge. Once that was settled, I might finally understand why my comeback summer had suddenly morphed into a hot mess.

"What the hell is going on?"

I jumped, spun in a circle, and came face-to-face with a livid Pam Mallory.

"Pam," I began.

"Save it," she put a hand up, looked at Troy and Amanda like they had just beamed down from an interstellar burger joint on Mars.

"Ma'am--" Troy began, clearly flustered, "I should sic Rocky on you for sneaking out here."

I paused, unsure if she was joking. "Sic Rocky--"

"You know what I mean."

"Pam," I gestured to the wheelchair. "This is Amanda Bennett. And Troy..."

I glanced at the man in question.

"Phillips," he muttered.

Pam looked from Troy to Amanda, then glanced at Rocky who had plopped down at her feet. If I hadn't seen him hot on Dylan's trail the summer before, I would never have believed the black lab could move faster than a mosey.

"I've heard of you," Pam said, and I tensed. "I knew something was up when Adam and I were at the hospital, so I asked around." She paused. "And speaking of that, where is that kid of mine?"

I glanced behind, saw Adam standing in the doorway of Cabin Ten, and motioned him over.

He moved to his mother's side, and she put an arm around him, drawing him closer. "What happened to her?" she asked, more to Adam than us, and Troy stepped forward, ready to explain.

"She had an accident," he offered, uncomfortable with revealing more. "A fall."

"A fall?" Pam repeated, and I saw Amanda shrink in her seat, unable to meet anyone's eyes.

"She can't talk but Adam can hear her." I moved closer, put a hand on her arm. "Dad told us to find her."

She paused, shaken by my mention of Robert Cook.

"He did? Why?"

"We don't know," I explained, "But her fiancé wants to take her downstate. She needs to stay here and--"

"Fiancé," Pam interrupted, her eyes cutting to Troy. "Who're you?"

He took a breath, straightened his shoulders.

"The man who loves her."

Pam raised an eyebrow. "Usually they're one and the same."

"Not this time."

Rocky stood now, pushed his head under her hand. I watched her scratch his neck, knew she was considering our crazy proposal.

"I'm not one to judge," she said after a few moments and I let my breath out, a rush of relief spreading across my chest. "But I don't like this idea."

"We can take care of her," I countered.

She held up a hand. "You have enough on your plate to feed an army. And you," she turned to Troy. "I assume you have a job or two or ten."

He chuckled. "Yes, ma'am."

"So, just to be clear, I'll be doing most of the work."

We stood silently, unable to argue and I felt her eyes settle on me.

"Adam rope you into this?"

I glanced at my brother.

"Dylan won't like it, you know."

I saw Troy move out of the corner of my eye. "Who's Dylan?"

"Her guy," Pam answered for me. "And he's sharp. He'll figure it out."

I looked at the ground. "Not if I can help it."

"We're sorry," Troy offered, the charm he'd displayed at the hospital replaced with sheepishness. "We didn't want anyone to see us."

"You drove by the front window, so you did a crappy job of it."

Adam shuffled from foot to foot and his mother grabbed his hand and squeezed it tightly.

"Is this what you want?" she asked.

I felt his answer in my heart and let the moment pass because this moment belonged to them.

"Do you want to help her?"

I watched as Adam looked to Amanda, watched one hand go to his ear as he began to make the low noise I recognized.

Pam looked at me, her gaze lingering before moving back to her son.

"That settles it, then," she said.

I glanced at the others, my eyes widening.

"Pam--"

"Robert told you to find her," she said, pausing at the door of Cabin Ten. "That's good enough for me."

AMANDA WAS RESTING AT LAST. They had placed her in a bed with clean sheets and the woman named Pam came with painkillers she stashed away from an old wisdom tooth surgery.

It wasn't morphine--didn't kill the hurt like the I.V. line had, but it would work.

Now the others were in a strange huddle in the kitchen, talking about who would take care of her and Amanda felt like a child, straining to hear their words, hoping Troy would take the lion's share but knowing that was impossible.

Amanda imagined her grandparents getting suspicious when their prized horses started acting up. They would wonder where the handler was, would question him when they caught him taking his apartment steps two at a time. And if his answers didn't make sense, they would follow him to this beautiful place and search the cabins one by one until they found her.

Amanda looked out the window, her fear spreading like frost on a windowpane.

"Mandy," she heard Troy's voice and turned to see him bending over her, his eyes full of something he didn't want to tell her. "Pam and Adam are going to be here during the day."

She felt herself stiffen. The eleven-year-old was going to take care of her while his mom ran a fishing lodge during tourist season.

Troy sensed her distress, placed a hand on her shoulder and squeezed. "It's only until you're better. Until you can talk or write or something..."

She swallowed, caught his eye, and knew he wanted her reassurance. So, she smiled.

"Justine and I'll come when we can," he paused, his head dropping and Amanda knew he didn't want to leave her. "We can't screw this up, Mandy."

Then Pam was there, asking her if she wanted something to eat, pausing awkwardly when she realized Amanda couldn't answer.

"I'll put some soup on," she turned to the others. "And someone needs to find her mother."

Amanda looked to Troy, who said, "Her mother's not well."

"Not well?" Pam echoed.

"Mandy's dad died in a motorcycle accident before she was born," he explained, his eyes shifting to her again. "She was never the same after."

"I'm sorry," Pam said, her voice soft. "I know how it feels to lose someone you love."

Amanda felt her heart open to this woman, and then Justine was there, telling them she had to leave.

"I'll be back tomorrow," she said, glancing at Pam. Then Troy.

He nodded, his face holding an uncertainty she had never seen before. One by one the others left, leaving her alone with Troy who seemed uneasy as he paced the room, trying to make her more comfortable by drawing curtains in some rooms and opening windows in others.

After eating the soup Pam had warmed on the stove, he cleared the dishes and came to sit beside her again, and she wanted to talk, to tell him she loved him, but the moment passed in a silence so sharp it was painful.

Time together was not making her feel better. Only worse.

Restless, he searched the room for a pencil and some paper. Finding both shoved in a drawer with a deck of old playing cards, he placed them in front of her.

She looked at these simple tools, knowing what he wanted her to do and reached a finger out. Looping it around the pencil, she tried to squeeze as a trembling pain stopped her cold.

"I'm sorry," Troy said, sliding the pad of paper away. "I thought it could help."

She looked away.

"Do you want to lie down?" he asked, perhaps seeking respite from her company, and she nodded. Moments later she was settled in bed with Troy leaning over her, a scenario she would have desired under different circumstances.

"I'll be in the next room," he said, his gentleness edged with tension and Amanda nodded again before closing her eyes.

She lay still for several minutes before focusing on the sound of a blue jay outside her window, its bitter call a contrast to the veil of slumber Pam's medicine had created.

She drifted off, pictures of the people who had rescued her melding until she could not tell them apart. And then another face-- one she did not recognize--separated itself from the rest.

A pretty brunette with a mole on her cheek.

She was standing beside a man with a face Amanda felt she should know, and he reached down, took the girl's hand.

Suddenly the girl took a step forward, looking straight at Amanda even as her feet began to sink into something soft. Water was pooling over her knees, lapping at her waist. The man said her name--pulled at her hand as his grip began to loosen. The water was coming faster, and soon the girl was struggling as the waves lapped at her neck.

Amanda felt her body spasm. It was happening again...just as it had in the hospital. She saw the girl's skin loosen, her head collapsing into the shell of her skull only to dissolve into a sooty dust that blew away in a dry wind.

Amanda stiffened, tried to sit up as another person came into view, a large man with black eyes and a smile that seemed to be broken.

She drew a breath and heard her voice for the first time since she had jumped from Robinson's Folly.

"Who are you?"

He took a step closer, breathed in the dust that had once been the girl with the mole on her cheek.

"The Bad Man."

Amanda screamed, the sound both welcome and terrifying as she fought the sleep she had welcomed before.

"Mandy!" Troy was there, shaking her as gently. "Wake up."

She felt the dream choking her and fought to draw a full breath.

"Mandy!" Troy's voice again, this time close to her ear, and she knew he was trying to hold her still on the bed.

She felt her shoulders come up, felt herself moving away from the awful picture of the girl and the water and the man whose smile made her feel like she was freezing.

She opened her eyes, the blue jay's call in her ears.

She blinked hard, looked up at Troy, and he reached down, pushed her hair back from her forehead.

"You were having a nightmare."

She felt her eyes fill with tears.

He pressed his lips together, his voice breaking. "I can't stand to see you go through this."

She wanted to tell him to save his breath because it served her right to go through this after climbing over the fence and letting go of everything that mattered to her, including him. But all she could do was lay there while Troy looked down, his eyes flecked with worry, wondering when death would come for the girl with the mole on her cheek.

And if she could do anything to save her.

CHAPTER
FIFTEEN

I breezed into my kitchen later that evening with an easygoing air I did not feel. Throwing my purse on the counter, I wondered how long it would be before Mom arrived, hoping she wouldn't mind leftovers because I was in no mood to cook.

I met Dylan as he came in from the living room with a troubled look.

"J--" he began, and I went to him, laid my head against his chest while wrapping my arms around him.

"I'm sorry," I said, not knowing why but wanting to make things right because crazy kidnapping escapade aside--he was still the most important person in the world to me.

"Don't," he said, his arms tightening around my back. "I'm the one who should apologize."

I pulled back and felt love snuff my fear like wet fingers to a flame.

"This thing with Meg has gotten out of hand."

I felt myself stiffen, unsure where the conversation would lead us.

"You said you were tired of talking about her."

I blew out my breath. "
"I am, too."
"Dylan--"
"I'm gonna drop my class."
I pulled back. "No--"
"I can take it next semester."
I looked at him, wanting to kiss him and slap some sense into him at the same time.
"We can't afford it."
"We'll figure it out."
"But you're working so hard. You'll get behind."
He put his forehead against mine, took a strand of my hair, and twisted it around his finger in a way that spoke to the intimacy that came so naturally to us.
"I can't keep spending time with a girl who has feelings for me."
I looked up. "She told you that?"
He nodded.
"And?" I asked, wanting to smack that beautiful mole right off her cheek.
"I told her I was in love with you."
I raised an eyebrow. "And how did she take that?"
He shrugged. "I didn't see her again until we had dinner. That's why--"
"She was upset," I interrupted, relief sweeping my body for the first time in weeks.
"I see how this hurts you and I can't do it anymore. Not after we've worked so hard to put the past behind us."
I looked down, a picture of Troy and Amanda stashed away in Cabin Ten calling me out for the hypocrite I was.
"I know it's been hard not looking for that girl. I want you to know I appreciate it, and I love you for it."
I couldn't have felt worse if he'd punched me in the gut.
"Thanks," I managed.
"But it's worth it," he insisted, his eyes seeking mine if only to

assure himself that I wasn't hiding anything. "The further we get from last summer the less likely it is to come back."

"Do you really believe that?" I asked, knowing I had to bring a shred of my true self to this conversation. "Because the gifts Butler gave my family are a part of who I am. Who *we* are--"

"You mean you and Adam?" he asked, his tone defensive.

"No," I insisted. "*You* were the one who saved my life in the woods. *You're* the one who shared my dream. It's a part of *us*. Butler wanted it that way."

"Well, I want it different," he said, his tone clipped. "And I can't live like that. Especially where you're concerned."

I tried to smile even as a part of me turned to stone.

"You don't know how it feels to not be able to protect you."

"I can take care of myself, remember? It's part of the 'super-human strength' economy package."

"No, you can't," he interrupted, taking another step back and I felt the same argument coming on and realized I was never going to be able to tell him about Troy or Amanda or the man I'd seen on the Mackinac Bridge. "You couldn't stop the bleeding out at the Falls. I *barely* stopped it and if we keep messing around with this stuff, I'm going to lose you for good."

I looked into his eyes, took his hand in mine. "Tell me what happened."

He sighed. "I'm not getting into that right now."

"Well, when *are* you going to get into it? I want to know--"

"No," he said, one hand up. "You don't."

"Dylan," I said, my voice a whisper. "I want to be there for you, but I don't know how to do that if you don't tell me what happened."

He softened, came towards me again. "You *are* here for me, living and laughing and driving me nuts when you lock your keys in the Jeep and I have to leave work to get the spare set and I love absolutely everything about it," he paused, his eyes holding mine. "Which is why I'm dropping the class."

"Dylan--"

"We'll figure it out. We always do."

"Okay," I said, my heart warming with his words. "Just promise I don't have to work triples with Mallard Brauski to make up for it."

He laughed, the dark mood forgotten as Mom pulled in the driveway--a bizarre repeat of the day before minus Paul and his adorable daughter.

Fifteen minutes later we were seated around the table eating leftovers.

"Have you been watching the news?" Mom asked and I almost dropped the plate Dylan was dishing my lasagna onto.

"Nope," he answered without looking up.

"Really?" she persisted. "You should turn it on."

"Really," he asked, taking her plate. "Why?"

"We hate the news," I said quickly. "Can't stand it, actually."

Dylan laughed. "I wouldn't go quite that far."

"A patient was kidnapped from the St. Ignace hospital today," Mom said, her eyes flitting between us.

"Hmmm," Dylan mumbled, not incredibly interested.

"Her family owns half of Mackinac Island, so they're searching everywhere." Turning to me, she asked, "You were up that way today. Did you hear anything?"

I gripped my fork, began to saw at my lasagna like a logger with a bucksaw.

Dylan glanced at me. "You went to St. Ignace today?"

I shrugged, tried to downplay the remark. "Just to Mackinaw City. Adam wanted to try someplace new."

"Mackinaw," he repeated. "That's pretty far."

I shrugged again, gave a goofy smile. "Gotta keep the Boss Man happy."

Dylan seemed suspicious at first, but was quickly distracted by Mom, who wouldn't stop talking about the one subject I wanted to avoid.

"They think they were driving a blue pickup."

I was starting to panic, and so blurted out something I felt sure would distract her.

"Dylan's dropping his class."

She glanced at him sharply, and I tried to ignore the look he shot me, the one that said he had wanted to tell her himself.

"Will you get behind?" she asked, her fork making a clinking noise that seemed to speak of her disappointment.

"Yeah," he answered. "But I'll catch up."

"Meg will be upset."

"I'm not sure why," Dylan said quickly, and I sensed his irritation.

"She's not going to disappear, you know."

I felt my muscles tighten and reached for Dylan's hand under the table. He took hold and squeezed, his grip assuring me that he would handle my mother.

"We know that."

"I know it might be awkward at first but you're just going to have to learn how to deal with her."

"And we will," Dylan said, his words measured, "But I don't need to sit beside her in class every night to do that."

"Hmm," Mom said, ruffled by his reasoning and I took another bite, hoping she would drop the subject I'd had the idiocy to bring up.

AMANDA SAW ANOTHER ONE.

I started. Took a bite of lasagna to cover it up.

ANOTHER WHAT?

ANOTHER DEATH.

I stood up, began clearing the table in an effort to exclude myself from the conversation.

"Hey, hon--" Dylan began, "I'm not done with that."

"Sorry," I said, putting his plate back while sweeping the table for errant silverware. The next moment I was at the sink, turning on the faucet as hot steam began to surround me.

MAYBE THIS IS WHY DAD WANTED US TO FIND HER.

I thought about it, knowing he was right.

WHO DID AMANDA SEE?

A BRUNETTE WITH A MOLE ON HER CHEEK.

I felt the dish I was holding clatter against the counter top. The conversation paused behind me, but I didn't dare turn and look.

THERE WAS SOMEONE WITH HER.

I gripped the counter top as scalding terror threatened to send me to my knees.

DYLAN?

I DON'T KNOW.

I closed my eyes, tried to breathe in slowly but found my lungs would not allow it.

HE SAID A NAME.

I closed my eyes.

WAS IT MEG?

A pause before, **YES.**

I bent my head, gripped the counter top to keep from collapsing.

SHE WAS DROWNING--

BUT DYLAN--

WAS TRYING TO SAVE HER.

Of course, he was.

DID HE... I couldn't form the next word.

IT WAS ONLY THE GIRL

I took another breath and felt my lungs expand, ashamed of the relief that crushed me.

THERE WAS SOMEONE ELSE.

WHO?

I felt my brother pause, felt tiny beats of dread bounce between our minds until they centered on the person we feared the most.

HENRY YOUNTS.

CHAPTER SIXTEEN

I was vaguely aware of the dish in my hand as it slid to the floor and shattered at my feet.

"J?" I heard Dylan's voice, and in an instant, he was beside me. One look at my face and he grabbed my arm. "Are you okay?"

I pressed my lips together, nausea twisting my stomach like a rag being wrung of water.

"Get her to a chair," Mom said and I felt them lead me the few steps to the kitchen table, where I sat down, dazed.

"Justine," Dylan repeated. "What's wrong?"

I wanted to tell him the truth--that for eleven horrific seconds I thought he might die--that his safety status was still tenuous in my opinion and that letting him out of my sight seemed about as appealing as walking barefoot across the Dollar General bathroom.

"Justine," Mom said, unnerved with my silence and I put my head in my hand, rubbed at my temples.

"My head hurts."

I could feel Mom and Dylan exchange glances over my head, a subtle shift in the air, an intake of breath that told me they wanted to know what the hell was going on. "Are you sick?" Dylan asked.

I looked into his eyes and felt my own fill with tears, realizing for the first time what he had suffered at the Falls.

"Hon," he said, tenderness softening his voice. "Please tell me what's wrong."

I thought of Meg, thought of her drowning while Dylan tried to save her and felt hopelessness overtake me.

"I need to lie down," I said quickly, and Dylan helped me to my feet, walked me to our bedroom while shooting Mom a look that said he would try to figure out what was going on.

Once there he shut the door softly, helped me into bed, and then sat beside me as I curled into a ball, my breath labored, my head pounding.

A long pause before, "Did you see something?"

I looked at him quickly, wondering how long he had known.

"I think," I began, reaching for his hand. "I think you might be in danger."

He leaned closer, touched my cheek.

"Why would you think that?"

"Just a feeling."

He pulled back. "What did you see?"

I closed my eyes, tucked my chin into my chest.

"Justine," he said, firm now. "Tell me the truth."

I knew I had to come up with an answer that would satisfy him but confessing to a quasi-kidnapping wasn't something I was ready to do.

"I keep dreaming about Henry Younts."

His hand tightened in mine.

"Dreams," he paused. "Or visions?"

I felt shame course through me, shame for the gifts Butler had given my grandmother and hated that I had to hide something so sacred from him.

"I don't know," I said, the tears coming again. "I saw something at Huffs the other night."

He didn't say anything at first.

"What was it?"

I looked up, wanting to believe that he would love me even if it meant walking back into the shit show we'd survived last summer.

"A shadow."

He chuckled. "That place is full of shadows."

I swallowed. "It moved... like a person."

He pulled back. "Did it look like... anyone?"

I shook my head, not wanting to tell him how real Henry Younts looked on the side of the Mackinac Bridge.

"Why do you think I'm in danger?"

"I saw you," I began, my fear for his safety outweighing everything else. "You were with Meg and Henry Younts was there and you were trying to save her."

He drew a long breath. "And you saw this in a dream?"

I nodded, feeling like a child.

"Or was it a vision?"

I reached over, took his hand again. "I don't know. I--"

"Yes, you do, J."

"It's all so confusing."

"No, it isn't. You're either having them or you aren't."

"Dylan--"

"Have you been looking for that girl?"

I felt my stomach kink up again and wished we'd eaten something besides leftovers.

"*Have you?*"

A small flame of anger licked at my skin, and I sat up suddenly.

"What if I have? Would that be so wrong? I don't want anything to happen to you-"

"And I don't want anything to happen to you."

"Then *listen* to me!"

He put a hand to the back of his head, "I'm trying."

"No, you're so afraid of what happened at the Falls you're making *everything* about last summer."

He stood up. Angry now. "How can I stop making everything

about last summer when you almost died in my arms? Am I supposed to just forget that it all started with visions and your dad and Adam talking to you in his mind? Do you really want to go there again?"

I drew a quick breath, frightened by his words and how close they might be to the truth.

"I'm only going to ask you one more time to stop looking for her," he said, his eyes holding mine with an intensity I hadn't seen before. "I told you I couldn't live that way and I damn well meant it."

I gripped my pillow tighter.

"So that whole bit about never leaving me is only valid if I obey your orders?"

He shook his head and began to pace the room.

"Dylan--"

"I don't understand why you would do this to me after I fought so hard to save you."

"I'm not *doing* anything to you!"

"Yes, you are," he said. "And it makes me wonder if your dad is more important than anything else."

I looked at him, unable to answer.

"Including us."

I shook my head, "No."

He paused, sat down on the side of the bed. "You know I still dream about it sometimes."

"What?" I sat up, desperate. "Dream about what?"

"About that night at the Falls. Only this time you don't make it, this time I put my hands around your wrists and your skin goes cold."

I felt fear break across my shoulders like a rogue wave, my hands gripping our comforter as though it could tether me to earth.

"And Adam starts crying, starts making this terrible sound that I didn't know he could make and after a minute I realize it's not him making the noise. It's *me*."

I sat, unable to speak.

"And then I wake up and there's that split-second when I think it might be real and you're really gone and I roll over and touch you, to see if you're breathing. If you're still alive."

I touched his arm, unprepared for his confession.

"And I can't tell you how it feels when I know you're okay. When I can hold you and feel you against me."

I stared at him for a moment, stunned into silence when a commotion in the kitchen drew our attention. Voices were rising and falling and somewhere in the mixture I thought I heard Paul.

And Meg.

"I'm sorry," Dylan said, his voice resigned and the only thing I hated more than our argument was their timing. "I shouldn't have said anything about it."

"No," I just managed. "You need to... I need to--"

"We should go out there," he cut me off, trying to put some distance between himself and what he'd said and I nodded, swung my legs off the bed, and stood there, unable to move.

"J?" he asked, one hand reaching for me. "Come on."

I nodded, then allowed him to lead me from our bedroom.

Moments later we were standing before Paul and Meg in the kitchen, Mom standing between us with a look that told me she was planning to run interference.

"Ready, Brenda?" Paul said quickly and I sensed that their talk had not gone well.

"Of course," she replied while grabbing her coat. "Thank you for dinner, Dylan. Justine--"

"You're welcome," Dylan said, extending his hand to Paul.

The older man looked at it for a beat before grabbing Mom's coat from the rack beside the door. Moments later he was moving her out the door, a gesture I may have appreciated under different circumstances.

We heard the car start, heard it pull out of the driveway, and I was left wondering why Paul would forget his most precious possession, and so turned to Meg, who stood shifting from one foot to the other.

Seconds passed in silence. I opened my mouth, wanting to tell her to get the hell out of my kitchen when I remembered what Amanda had seen.

"Dad and I talked," she said. "And he wants me to apologize."

"Meg," Dylan put a hand up. "Please, don't--"

"I read into something that wasn't there," she continued, her finger going to a strand of long hair and twisting it, her eyes never meeting mine. "Or maybe I'm just stupid."

"You're not stupid," Dylan said, and I hated how he jumped to her defense, how his body tightened as though he wanted to move towards her when he'd just talked about dropping the class they shared.

"Well, I feel that way," she confessed, her dark eyes locked on my boyfriend as though they were the only people in the room. "Here we are just getting to know each other, and I screw things up. Dylan told me he had a girlfriend. I just didn't know it was you."

"Well...it's *me*," I laughed, not knowing how to take her half-baked apology, still unnerved by the fact that she wouldn't look at me.

"Meg," Dylan said. "I'm going to drop our class."

Her eyes narrowed almost instantly as she crossed her arms against her chest.

"That's really dumb."

"No, it isn't."

"You'll have to take it next semester. You'll get behind."

"I'll figure it out."

She paused, unable to argue and for a moment I felt sorry for her, knowing I would fight tooth and nail to keep him.

"Why are you doing this?"

"Because I can't stay in a class with someone who has..." he paused, not wanting to continue. "Feelings for me."

The room seemed to drop ten degrees as her eyes finally found mine. She uncrossed her arms and I took a step back, unsure what particular hell this scorned schoolgirl was about to unleash.

"*Feelings?*" she repeated. "Is that the nice little label you've chosen to give it?"

"Meg--"

"You told me you wanted to spend time with me."

My boyfriend put a hand up as though warding off an attack. "I just needed some help with school."

"*You* suggested we study together."

I took a step back, let my arm drop to my side.

"And that night at the coffeehouse when you reached down to get the book I dropped?" she said, a slight smile on her lips. "Did you tell Justine about that?"

"Meg," Dylan repeated helplessly. "It was a mistake."

"What?" I asked, my throat frozen. "What was a mistake?"

Meg turned to me, her face smug and I wanted to tear that gorgeous mole right off her cheek. "He gave it back all right. But then he wouldn't let go of my hand. Held it under the table the *whole damn night.*"

"What?" I barely managed, my breath shallow. "What is she talking about?"

Instead of answering, he moved towards Meg and grabbed her elbow. "You need to go."

"Don't touch me!" she jerked away, images of them holding hands at the coffeehouse while I waited at home like a sucker playing through my mind like a Hallmark movie gone wrong.

Dylan had encouraged her, had led her to believe he wanted to spend time with her.

Which meant there was something wrong with us.

"Get out of here," Dylan ordered, angrier than I'd ever seen him. "*Now.*"

I sank into one of the kitchen chairs with no memory of moving my legs, feeling like I would willingly feed Paul's daughter to Henry Younts if it meant I could wipe her off the face of the earth forever.

"I'll go," she said, her voice raw with hurt. "But you'd better watch your back, Justine. He's not who you think he is."

I closed my eyes, put my head in my hands, unsure if Meg had followed through with her promise to leave or was lurking outside our kitchen window, hungry for a glimpse of the chaos she'd created.

"J," Dylan touched my shoulder and I looked up, shocked that I could still find him attractive at a time like this. "Just hear me out on this."

"I don't understand," I said, my voice next to nothing. "I was waiting at home for you. You told me not to worry."

"You don't need to worry, baby."

"But you held her hand."

"She reached for me. I didn't know what to do."

"Here's an idea," I said, my voice rising. "How about telling her to back the fuck off!"

He ran a hand through his hair, beautifully miserable. "It wasn't that easy."

"And why wasn't it easy?"

He threw his hands up. "She was helping me pass--"

I shook my head, and he stopped, willing to do whatever I needed.

"Just tell me what happened."

He took a breath and cleared his throat, more nervous than I'd ever seen him. "It's true I asked her to study with me. It was stupid, I know--but we had other people with us, and I didn't know any other way to keep up with summer classes."

"Dylan--"

"We'd just had that dream about the girl on Mackinac Island and you were talking about your dad again and for some reason I just wanted--"

"Something normal."

"Yeah," he said, his voice dropping. "I didn't want to worry about that stuff anymore...about *you* anymore."

"And Meg helped you forget."

"No," he said. "I'll never forget."

I pulled my hands away, anger sparkling around the edge of my vision.

"Then why won't you tell me what happened at the Falls!"

He shook his head. "If I talk about it, it's like it's happening all over again--"

"But it's *not*, Dylan. Even when you have those dreams, that's *all* they are!"

"I understand that--"

"Do you?" I laughed while standing up. "Because it seems like you have plenty of rules for me but none for yourself."

"Justine--"

"I need to go."

"No," he said, desperate now as he grasped me around the shoulders. "You're tired and you're upset, and I don't blame you. But I'm not letting you leave like this."

"You're not *letting* me?" I asked, my eyes narrowing.

"I'll go if you want me to, but you're in no condition to drive."

"No *condition*?"

"You're upset and when you get this way you can't think straight and--"

Anger ignited my body as I moved against his weight. The next instant I felt his hands give way as he slid against the wall, unable to move as Jamie had against the side of the Jeep the summer before.

"Justine--"

I stared at him for a moment, wanting to hurt him like he'd hurt me.

"Let me go."

He moved against me, and I felt the first cold fingers of fear, followed closely by shame as I backed away. He stood for a moment after I'd released him, his breathing staggered, his fear palpable.

"It's back, then?"

I looked down and nodded.

"How long have you known?"

I shrugged. "Long enough."

He took a step closer, searching my face. "She means nothing to me, I swear to God."

I grabbed the jean jacket that was hanging beside the front door.

"You know me, J, and you damn well know I'd never do anything to risk what we have."

I turned quickly, and he flinched, a small movement that hurt more than anything else that happened that night.

"I'm sorry," I put my hands up while backing away. "For everything."

"Justine," he said from the doorway. "Please don't leave."

I walked down our steps, turned once to look at him.

"You left first."

CHAPTER
SEVENTEEN

I climbed in the Jeep, ready to drive aimlessly around Presque Isle County until I figured out what to do about Meg and Dylan and Amanda and Troy and Mom and Paul and everything else that had turned a perfect summer into something I didn't recognize.

I knew Dylan would give me the rest of the night to cool down, but the reprieve wouldn't last forever.

Six minutes later I pulled up at Dave and Holly's. It was late, but they were known night owls, so I didn't feel bad about ruffling their feathers.

Holly answered the door in her bathrobe after I'd been knocking for what seemed like an eternity, her hair a disheveled mess that spoke to the privacy she may have wanted.

"Oh, hey ..." I stammered. "Sorry I didn't call--"

"You okay, Squirt?" she asked, stepping aside so I could enter. "You look like friggin' crud."

As if to prove her point, I swiped at my nose with my forearm and burst into tears.

Dave, who was hovering somewhere in the peripheral, cleared

his throat and announced now might be a good time to start that book he'd been dying to read.

Holly smiled, mouthed the words "Dave doesn't read," and motioned for me to sit down on the couch.

I did as she asked, fresh despair replacing the anger I'd felt in Dylan's presence.

"Want something to drink?"

I nodded, and she got up, made her way to the kitchen, and poured water into her favorite *Scooby-Doo* cup.

"What the heck's going on?" she asked once she was seated beside me. "I haven't heard much from you lately."

"I know," I nodded. "This thing with Amanda Bennett has turned into a nightmare."

She leaned forward, always ready for a juicy story. "What happened?"

"Have you been watching the news?"

She turned to look for Dave, then spun back to me. "We didn't have the T.V. on. You know..."

I bit my lip, hoping she wouldn't go into detail.

"Well... we snuck her out of the hospital and now she's staying in Cabin Ten with her boyfriend. I don't think the cops are onto us yet, but it won't be long."

"*Boyfriend?*" Holly echoed, not surprising me in the least.

I swiped at my nose again. "She's got a fiancé, too"

"Are you friggin' serious?"

I nodded, "The boyfriend is an honest-to-god lumberjack."

Her eyes widened, one hand going to her heart.

"Looks like Superman."

I heard her gulp, one hand reaching for the *Scooby-Doo* cup.

"And on days he's not using his chainsaw to cut down monster trees, he tames stallions on Mackinac Island. You know--just your average side job."

She shook her head, leaned back against the couch, and blew a stray piece of hair off her forehead. "Monogamy sucks!"

"Holly!"

"Just kidding! Tell me more."

"We're all taking turns keeping an eye on her--me, Pam, Adam, and Troy."

"Sign me up for a shift!"

I frowned, and she grabbed a bag of barbecue chips from the coffee table. "Does Dylan know?"

I twisted the fingers of one hand with the other. "I might have let the cat halfway out of the bag when he confessed to having a fling with his teenage study partner."

Her eyes widened as she leaned towards me. "The one who told him that jacked-up story about the Great Dane?"

I nodded. "Oh, but wait, it gets better. She also happens to be Paul's one and only adorable daughter."

"Your Mom's *boyfriend?*" she hit me on the shoulder. "Get outta town! That is some twisted shit. I hope he got down on his hands and knees and begged your forgiveness."

I swiped at my nose again.

"So how many times did they...you know..." she took out a chip, popped it in her mouth. "*Do it?*"

I looked down, embarrassed to admit the torrid affair I'd hinted at was nothing more than an episode of *Little House on the Prairie*.

"He didn't...I mean...*they* didn't...he just held her hand but--"

She nodded, still chewing. "Emotional affair."

I looked down. "He wants something normal."

She patted me on the knee. "Aww, Squirt, you're as normal as they come."

"What've you been smoking?"

She put her head against mine. "Dave and I were just talking about how you've been kind of *boring* lately."

"Boring?" I echoed, trying not to take offense.

"He got stuck behind you on Main Street about a month ago when I sent him out for the stuff to make my bean dip." She smiled. "You know my bean dip."

I nodded, irritated. "So, what?"

"He wondered if you were auditioning for a part in *The Slow and the Curious*."

I frowned, trying to remember what I'd been doing a month ago, feeling like that life had never existed.

"There were some good garage sales and Dylan wanted a new coffee table for the living room and I had to look *really* close at all the stuff in the yards."

"It's okay," she threw an arm around my shoulder. "Going 2.8 miles per hour in a bustling downtown district during tourist season does not define who you are."

I wrinkled my nose, took a chip from the bag and looked at it carefully. "Well, apparently I'm not *boring* enough for Dylan."

She leaned back. "So, what're you gonna do about the girl and her smokin' hot boyfriend? I mean, I have a few ideas but--" Her eyes got misty for a moment as she fished in the bag for another chip.

I shrugged. I had no idea what Troy and Amanda's plans were beyond getting her back on her feet again and off to that little town in the U.P. where they could ride their matching Palominos into the sunset.

"You're gonna have to tell Dylan, you know."

I looked at down at my hands. "I know."

"I warned you."

I shrugged again.

"Squirt--"

"I don't wanna go home."

She patted my knee again, fished for another chip and then discarded it when it was too small. "So, stay here."

"He'll wonder where I am."

"So, let him."

As if on cue, my cell phone rang. I looked at it vibrate on the table and knew how worried he would be if I didn't answer--and let my voicemail kick in.

"Good girl," Holly nodded. "This one needs to sting a little."

I felt my shoulders droop. "But I'm lying, too."

"Only because he's being the meathead we know and love. I'm telling you, a little space is just what the doctor ordered. He's got issues he needs to deal with. And I don't just mean with *you*."

"Karen?" I whispered, feeling like I was unearthing the dead.

Holly nodded, rolled up the bag of chips and clipped it. "He's been through the ringer, for sure. But I guess it makes up for the charmed life he had before everything hit the fan."

I put my head in my hands, not sure if she was making me feel better or worse.

"He'll snap out of it once he realizes you're not going to break into little pieces. Heck, you're the toughest Squirt I know."

I looked up. "I am?"

"Sure," she stood up, walked to the kitchen, and stuffed the chips back into a cupboard that looked ready to explode. "I don't know many people who can flat line twice and live to tell about it."

"What?" I asked, unsure I'd heard her right. "Flat line?"

"Yeah," Holly looked at me for a long moment. "In the ambulance. Didn't he tell you?"

I shook my head. "He doesn't like to talk about it...like...*at all.*"

She sat back down, patted my knee. "See what I mean about *issues*?"

"Yeah," I said, hating that she was right.

"Have you ever talked to Adam about what happened out there?" she asked, her eyes holding mine with all the seriousness I'd ever seen her muster.

"Not really," I shook my head. "He's only *eleven*. And..." I trailed off.

"You want Dylan to man up?"

I nodded, her words striking an angry chord in me. "How did you know about it?"

"I was the first one at the hospital and remember Joe from Cheboygan? The one I had the hots for right before I met Dave?"

I frowned. Holly had the "hots" for an innumerable number of guys and "Joe from Cheboygan" wasn't ringing any bells.

"Well, he used to be a mechanic, but then he switched and started working as an EMT, and he was on duty that night and..." she smiled, her eyes misty again.

"Dylan didn't tell you?" I asked.

She shook her head. "Dylan was a basket case."

I looked down at my phone, tears clouding my vision when I saw he'd left a voicemail. I tried to imagine the horror he'd experienced in the back of the ambulance while the medics tried to save my life, tried to understand the pride or fear or stubbornness that kept him from talking about it, and realized he had been struggling in a way I could never understand.

And for the first time I understood why holding Meg's hand under the table at a coffeehouse seemed appealing.

I picked up my phone, listened to his voicemail, and felt my heart bend.

"I know you're mad at me right now, but I just want to know where you are and that you're safe."

Moments later I was dialing his number, his voice a bittersweet reminder of all the things I had yet to learn about the man I loved.

"I'm okay," I assured him, thinking of all the times he'd rolled over and held me in the middle of the night. "I'm at Holly's."

He was quiet for a moment. "Thanks for letting me know."

I felt my throat swell, knowing I couldn't erase the awful things he'd experienced the summer before.

Or the summer before that.

"I'm sorry I didn't answer. I know--"

"It's okay. I'm okay."

"I'm going to stay here tonight."

"Sure."

"I'll see you tomorrow," I said, the assurance holding something so pure it was painful.

He paused, his voice low. "Promise?"

I took a breath, wondering if I could ever make things right again.

"Promise."

∼

I SLEPT CURLED up on Holly's couch that night in the clothes I'd smuggled Amanda out of the hospital in, thoughts of Henry Younts and Meg and why a girl Dad had told me to find was seeing all of this as she lay crippled in Cabin Ten swirling in the back of my mind like a snow globe.

There had to be a reason Red Rover was back in the game, and I knew it was because of the totems.

I thought back to the medicine bag, discarded with the snakeskin, jawbone, antler, shell, and feather. I assumed the fire had burned everything but had to admit I wasn't paying close attention after slitting my wrists.

I thought back on those awful moments, remembered the agonizing pain shooting up my arms as I followed the outline of the medicine wheel, Adam by my side. I was sure I'd gotten to four of them...but the one in the center--the one that prolonged the life of Henry Younts and his son.

I frowned, rolled to my other side, and stuffed Holly's Hello Kitty pillow under my neck in a way I hoped wouldn't cause lasting injury. Putting a hand to my wrist, I traced the scars that were a testimony to how my life had changed since leaving Webber. The next moment I was touching the line that lanced my left kneecap, my finger moving along the knotted tissue that had marked me as prey in Henry Younts' eyes and thought of Jamie Stoddard.

He walked out of the Alpena hospital and into oblivion last August, and I assumed he'd wandered off to die alone with only memories of Esther Ebersole to comfort him. But what really happened after the snakeskin no longer protected him?

I shifted to my other side, readjusted the pillow and pictured

Ocqueoc Falls, wondering why I'd never gone out there to make sure everything had burned like it was supposed to, knowing deeper it was for the same reason Dylan didn't want to talk about what happened in the back of the ambulance.

I swallowed hard, looked across the room, and was surprised to see a figure standing in a darkened corner.

But experience had taught me not to panic. The warm feeling that accompanied this person could only mean one thing.

"Muffet," he came out of the darkness, sat down on the side of the couch.

"Dad," I said, my voice full of the love I wanted to give.

"I'm sorry," he replied, his hand reaching out to rest on my knee, but I didn't feel his touch, only a heaviness where it should have been. "I never wanted you to go through this again."

"Again?" I repeated. "What do you mean?"

"Something went wrong at the reversal."

I sat up, "Dylan--"

"Took you before it was finished."

I thought back, remembered his whispered confession of love before darkness swallowed any memory of what had happened to the totems.

"What do we do?" I asked.

"What should have been done last summer."

"But," I began. "I don't know where to start."

"That's not true," he smiled in a way that made me feel like he might still be alive and waiting for me down on a bar stool at Huffs.

I put a finger to my lips, chewed on a nail. "I could go to the Falls."

"Then hurry."

"Why?" I asked, my voice rising, wondering if Holly and Dave could hear me having a conversation with my long-dead father in the middle of their living room.

"You're getting stronger."

A strange warmth spread across my skin, a feeling that told me

I'd never wanted my connection with Butler to end and that any dream of a normal life tucked away in our bungalow may have been Dylan's alone.

"But so is he."

"Amanda Bennett--"

"Is your only chance of stopping him."

"But why now?" I asked. "It's been a year."

"Exactly."

"Dad--"

"Everything has a season."

"A season?"

"Things grow strong in the summer sun."

I thought about what he had said, thought about the sun and the moon and the stars spilling into autumn, then winter and spring until they aligned with something that seemed to make perfect sense.

"Like Henry Younts?"

He paused. "You have the bird, now find the bridge."

The next moment my father was standing up, walking away and I watched him go without protest, my mind scrambling for purpose.

Knowing sleep was impossible, I stood up, scribbled a note for Holly and started looking for my tennis shoes.

Then I was heading for the Jeep, climbing inside and taking off into the night towards Ocqueoc Falls.

CHAPTER
EIGHTEEN

I couldn't say I was happy to be hiking to the scene of the most horrifying moment of my life, but I knew I had to act fast if I wanted to stop Henry Younts.

The trail head to the Falls was just as I remembered, and as I slid from the Jeep, I had to remind myself that Red Rover wasn't lurking on the other side of the river, keeping pace with me and Dylan as we sprinted for safety.

Still, the woods seemed strangely familiar, the night sounds a chilling reminder that nothing really changed despite my desire to believe otherwise.

I grabbed a flashlight but made a promise to myself to only use it once I'd gotten to the island. I didn't want to attract attention, and the best way to maneuver through the darkness was the same way the animals did.

A short time later I heard the rushing of the Falls and knew I had to stay on the western bank. The blackness seemed to part like a heavy curtain as my eyes began to adjust, and so I stopped, listened for any sound that might be out of place, and heard nothing.

I was at the edge of the marsh now, memories flooding my brain of Adam jumping the water, and Dylan--pushing my brother aside before we could finish what we'd started.

I paused, my toes on the edge of the bank when I heard someone in front of me, their movements just brushing my ears. Squinting into the darkness, I saw a person move out on the island and dropped to my knees.

How could someone be out here in the middle of the night? No one knew about this place besides a handful of people, half of whom were dead.

I waited, crouching in the darkness as the person bent down, searching for something.

Moments later they stood, walking towards the other side and I waited until I heard him jump the water before crossing on my own.

Once there, I crouched down again, waited a few moments before turning on my flashlight and searching for the medicine wheel I had drawn with my finger the summer before.

It was there--charred to blackness and with splashes of my blood dotting it like some grotesque version of the Rorschach test. I blinked once, unable to believe it remained intact exactly as I remembered it.

But then I thought of the shaman, remembered his love for Odessa and Cal and knew the same power protected this place as well.

I stood and walked in a slow circle, stopping once to listen for the return of the man I'd seen. I tried to remember where each totem had been placed and if there was any way to prove they had been destroyed aside from the scattering of ash that seemed to speak for itself.

Dropping to my knees again, I traced the lines, my fingers digging into dirt and ash and dried blood. Frantic, I followed the spokes to the center, to the place where I had pushed the snakeskin into the soft earth--and found nothing.

No ash, no splattering of blood that meant the fire Adam created had met certain death . Nothing but the memory of the man I'd seen crouching where I was now, stealing what rightfully belonged to Odessa Cook.

I stood, scanning the forest for any sign of movement and knew he had at least a ten-minute head start on me.

I thought of Dylan, saw him walking into the hospital with my blood staining the front of his shirt--Adam standing beside him in numbed terror.

I thought of Henry Younts--his black eyes staring at me from the small space between Iris' door frame and felt fury set fire to my veins.

I moved to the side of the island, stood looking into the black forest, and felt the wind move with me, felt it move around the person I sought as my eyes narrowed on a tiny speck of movement far ahead and between the trees.

I took off running, leapt the water and landed well clear on the other side. Once on the ground, I sprinted towards the man I'd seen, towards the person who stole my last chance for a peaceful life with Dylan.

I thought about this stranger, thought about twisting my fists into balls and driving them into his face until blood poured from his nose and mouth and ears.

The forest seemed to fold around me as I ran, my feet silent as I closed the gap between us, a dark coat floating behind like a scarf in the wind, leading the way.

Seconds later my foot found a branch, breaking it in two and the man started, turned, and took off at a dead run.

I gritted my teeth, unsure where he was leading us until the forest began to widen, the trees to separate. Moments later a car flashed by, followed by another. We were running parallel to a road but the person in front of me didn't waver or turn or slow down. Instead, he ran full speed into the narrow opening of pine and birch and began sprinting towards a vehicle parked on the shoulder at least fifty yards away.

I bent down, felt my legs pump like some heated mechanism I had no control over, and watched the distance between us dwindle to nothing.

The next moment he was inside the car, pulling the door shut as I slammed the full weight of my body against it.

The car rocked on its wheels, and he turned, darkness masking his features before I heard the doors lock against me.

The next second, I raised my elbow and punched it through his window like a piston, glass shattering in a rainstorm of confetti as the car lurched forward.

"Fuck," he cursed and I reached through the opening. Grabbing a handful of hair, I slammed his face against the steering wheel once, then twice.

The next second he was tearing at my arm, adrenaline kicking up and I felt his fist connect with my jaw in a way that made me stumble backwards, my chin a blossom of pain.

Then he was tearing off down the road, his tires squealing against silence and I watched for a moment before bending over, my elbow cut deeply, my jaw throbbing to the beat of my heart.

"Shit," I muttered, touching my face with my fingertips. Approaching headlights told me to get off the side of the road, and so I staggered into a cluster of pines and slid into a seated position.

I sat there for several minutes, bruised and bleeding and now that my supersonic rage had subsided, exhausted. But even these things seemed insignificant considering what had slipped through my fingers.

I sat until my breathing stilled, then staggered to my feet and began the slow trek back to the island. Once there, I washed my elbow in the river, felt cool water soothe burning flesh, and then stumbled on towards the Jeep.

Once inside, I tried to piece together what had just happened.

Dad told me to hurry.

Now I knew why.

I checked the time.

5:27 a.m.

Dylan would be leaving for work in an hour and the last place I wanted to lick my wounds was on Holly's couch. Instead, I made the half hour drive back to the bungalow, parked on a side street where I knew Dylan wouldn't see me, and fell asleep.

CHAPTER NINETEEN

I woke up to blinding sunlight and my neighbor's lawnmower four hours later. Disoriented, I pulled myself into a seated position and tried to remember what had happened. One glance in the rear view mirror told me I was going to have one hell of a bruise to explain, one glance at my elbow made me wonder if I should have swung by the E.R. on my way home.

Instead, I drove around the corner and parked in front of our shed.

Dylan's truck was gone. My plan to delay the inevitable a success.

Moments later I stumbled into the house. All was quiet, but he had left a note for me on the kitchen counter, one I took with shaking hands.

J--I love you. Always

I smiled, thinking of the man who had left for work just hours before, his injured girlfriend sleeping inside her Jeep after chasing a man through the woods and bashing his head against a steering wheel.

I thought about the man's face, smeared by darkness, and the car--a black sedan that looked like hundreds of others I might see daily and felt hopelessness overtake me. I stopped, touched my elbow, and considered my next move.

The snakeskin was gone, but that didn't mean I was giving up.

I remembered how it felt to hurt him and fought to stem my anger. I needed to be calm, to think logically, realizing moments later that's where Dylan came in.

But I couldn't go to him with a busted lip and bruised jaw, so I did the next best thing.

I called him.

He picked up on the first ring.

"Justine--"

"I'm home," I said, my heart unraveling at the sound of his voice. "I got your note."

He paused, trying to think of what to say. "I meant it."

I smiled. No one could ever accuse Dylan Locke of being insincere.

Another pause, and I sensed his awkwardness--as though he was gathering the courage to ask me on a date. "Do you work tonight?"

I touched my elbow, winced in pain. "Mallard said he might call me in if they get busy." Which really meant I was taking the afternoon shift at Cabin Ten and needed an alibi until Pam came by later.

Still, I couldn't leave him hanging, not when every bone in my body ached for things to be right between us.

"I'll see you after," I said, wanting to please him, hoping he would be sleeping when I got home.

"Okay," he said, and I could tell he wanted to say more, but was weighing his words carefully. "I want you to know I'm taking what you said seriously. About Meg and the--" He paused. Cleared his throat. "Vision."

"Dylan--"

"I know you can't control it. I just want--"

"I know what you want," I interrupted. "I want it, too."

"You do?"

"I always have."

"Good," he said, relieved, and I couldn't help but imagine how fast things would go south if he could see my face right now. "I'll wait up for you."

I smiled into the phone, thinking how his words would have thrilled me yesterday, wanting to kick myself for going crazy on the guy in the woods before hanging up.

Walking towards the bathroom, I caught a glimpse of myself in our hallway mirror and cringed. I needed to take a shower, change into clean clothes, and scrounge around for some breakfast.

Then I needed to get my brother and talk to Amanda Bennett.

My first three tasks completed, I fished around under our bathroom sink and found a tiny first aid kit shoved behind my lifetime supply of Q-Tips. I smiled to myself, knowing Dylan must have picked it up somewhere because no way in hell did I think about stuff like that.

Ten minutes later, my inaugural attempt at dressing a flesh wound was complete. I looked down, pleased with the results before examining my face in the mirror. The cut that split my bottom lip was an angry red, the bruise on my jaw swollen and purple, and if Troy asked me about it...

My thoughts snagged on him like dry skin on a sweater, my mind alive with the thought that he could help me.

Ten minutes later I was on my way to Three Fires with the fledgling hope that Troy Phillips would untangle the mess I'd gotten myself into.

I just had to tell him everything first.

Amanda sat at the table in Cabin Ten, her bones aching from spending a restless night in a strange bed, watching Troy prepare a small meal for her.

The night had been a struggle, the fear palpable as she resisted sleep for fear of seeing the man with the black eyes.

Adam knew who he was, told her he had something to do with what happened to his sister the summer before.

But he hadn't said anything else and Amanda suspected he didn't want to frighten her.

Too late for that.

She woke up early the next morning and Troy was there, helping her in ways that made her love him more, turning on the news so they could get a better understanding of their situation.

The Sheriff of Mackinac County was holding a news conference, talking about the task force he had assembled to locate the missing woman. He encouraged anyone with information to come forward, saying the search would likely extend into neighboring counties in the next two days.

Ethan was on next, talking about his "sizable assets" and how he would "spare no expense" in tracking down the lunatics who had kidnapped his fiancée.

He went on to say that he believed the motive for the abduction was money, and he fully expected to receive a ransom note.

"You think that son of a bitch would pay enough to get us that cabin," Troy asked, his smile telling her he had his own opinion and Amanda wanted to laugh like she always did when they talked about their life together.

Once he had saved enough money to buy the land he wanted from the time he was a boy.

But she couldn't laugh, couldn't write or do anything but sit and stare at the man she loved, wishing she could go back and make a different choice.

He placed a bowl of soup in front of her, and she ate in slow, painful sips. The medicine Pam brought that morning were half the dose of the day before, and Amanda knew what she was hoping.

What they all were hoping.

A light knock at the door startled them. They hadn't been expecting anyone and Troy stood, put a hand to her shoulder as if to assure her that he would take care of whoever was out there.

He opened the door slowly, cautiously, and Amanda was shocked to see Justine on the threshold, a bruise swelling on her jaw line, a cut splitting her bottom lip and Troy stepped back, ushered her inside quickly.

Amanda watched her enter the cabin as though a light had been turned on and wished for a bit of that magic. She'd had it once--on the night Ethan had noticed her at the cocktail party and the afternoon Troy called her back to the paddock fence. She remembered the soft glow of the lights later that evening on the waterfront, the band playing a slow song as he led her from their table--excitement tempered with the barest breath of fear.

"Justine," Troy said. "What happened?"

She stepped inside and stood awkwardly, as though waiting for permission to exist.

"I," she began, and Troy gestured to a chair, pulled it out and Amanda felt something inside of her turn over. "I need to tell you something."

Troy sat down beside her, his hands moving towards some sort of bandage she had wrapped around her elbow.

"I went after someone in the woods last night."

"You *what?*" Troy said, an angry edge to his voice and Amanda wondered how deeply Justine's sudden appearance had affected him after a night in the company of her silence.

"Yes," Justine began, her fingers going to the table, tracing the lines as she told a story that seemed impossible for Amanda to comprehend, a story about people who had lived hundreds of years before she was born. The man with the black eyes was there, trying to save his son but losing his soul instead. She spoke of totems and magic and cameo broaches and barn dances out past Millersburg as though the people were characters in a story she had loved since childhood--a lineage she traced through her father to the love of an Ojibwa Shaman--a woman named Odessa Cook.

She spoke of Amanda's visions as though they could help them kill the Bad Man and Amanda watched Troy, saw his face change into something she had never seen before and knew he believed every word.

"You're full of surprises, you know that?" he joked, his laughter stilted, as though he was trying to figure out how to make sense of what she'd said.

"That's what they tell me," she replied, and Troy reached out, touched her chin and Amanda had to force her eyes downward.

"Are you hurting? I could get you some of Mandy's meds."

Justine's eyes moved to Amanda.

"No," she said quickly. "She needs them more than I do."

"That elbow looks pretty bad."

She shook her head again, smiled. "I just wanted to ask her some questions."

Amanda wondered how she could help, realizing moments later that Adam must have told her about the girl with the mole on her cheek.

"The person you saw in your dream," she held up her phone, showed her a picture of a distinguished looking man with his arm around a young woman. "Is this her?"

Amanda looked closer, felt the breath suspend in her throat, and nodded.

"And the person she was with," she scrolled to another picture, held it up.

Amanda looked again, recognized the man and knew he was special to her. Knew that she loved him.

She nodded again.

She watched Justine put a hand to her face, watched her wince as her fingers brushed her swollen jaw before she whispered, "Was he okay? I mean...did he--" She stopped, struggling with how to form the next word.

Amanda paused, absorbing the power she held over this woman if only for the moment.

"Please--" she whispered again. "Did you see him die?"

She shook her head--saw Justine draw her first full breath since entering the cabin.

"The girl," she stopped again, looked to Troy. "Do you know where she was?"

Amanda tried to remember, tried to think about where the girl might have been.

"It's okay if you need some time," Justine assured her. "I just thought--"

"She's tired--" Troy interrupted.

Justine nodded. "Sure."

"If something comes up she'll tell Adam."

Justine nodded again, obviously upset.

"Maybe when she's had some rest. She didn't sleep last night."

"Yeah."

Troy's face softened. "I know you're frustrated."

She looked down at her hands.

"Which is why I hate to leave."

Amanda felt her heart speed up.

"I'll call you tonight," he said while standing up and moving around the room--gathering his things. Anxious to go. "And I'll find her mom."

"Her mom?" Justine echoed, standing up as well, following him to the couch where he'd laid his coat.

"She needs to know Mandy's okay."

"Sure," Justine said, her hands a worried knot at her waist.

"I'll find out what's going on when I get back to the stables," he told her, leaning over to touch her lips to his own. "No one's going to find you."

She wanted to believe him, wanted to believe that Justine would take good care of her this afternoon but all she wanted was her voice and arms and feet to carry her into something that made sense.

Troy walked towards the door, Justine close behind. Amanda saw the two of them step beyond the threshold, their voices low until he glanced at her, his eyes resigned--and shut the door between them.

CHAPTER
TWENTY

I stood just outside the door of Cabin Ten, Troy in front of me, his green eyes registering about every emotion I'd ever felt in my twenty-three years on earth.

I knew he was worried about Amanda, knew he wanted to help, and now I'd just dumped most of my personal baggage into his lap like the desperate woman I was.

"I'm sorry to put this on you," I said, moving with him as he walked to his blue pickup truck. Once there, he opened the passenger door and threw his bag inside.

"You're not putting anything on me. We're in this together."

I smiled, liking the sound of what he'd said, wishing he would linger while the sun made its slow arc over Ocqueoc Lake.

"Thanks," I said.

He shut the door to his truck, leaned against the side.

"Does your boyfriend know what's going on?"

I looked away. "I haven't told him yet."

Troy let out a low whistle. "He's gonna know something's up when he sees your face. And if he's anything like me, he's gonna kick someone's ass."

I shrugged, knowing he was right. "It could've been worse."

He paused, his eyes holding mine. "I'm glad it wasn't."

I smiled, unprepared for the warmth his words stirred in me.

Troy seemed to feel it, too, because he cleared his throat, shifted his weight as if to say he was ready to leave when just moments ago he'd been willing to stay.

And so, I changed the subject.

"What did you tell that nurse at the hospital? She described a short, bald man wheeling Amanda down the hallway."

He smiled. "I told her the truth."

I raised an eyebrow. "The truth?"

He laughed, crossed his arms against his chest. "She knew Ethan was a prick. All I told her was that Amanda's mom would straighten everything out. She knew it was the right thing to do."

I smiled, put my back against the truck, and looked up into the sky.

"And your charm had nothing to do with it?"

He grinned. "You tell me."

I felt my cheeks flush, knowing he'd backed me into a corner I didn't want to be in.

"You didn't have to help me, either," he said.

"Troy--"

"You won't take the fall for this."

"Oh," I said, a wave of heat radiating from my cheeks. "What do you mean?"

"If they find us, I'll tell them it was my idea-- that I made you do it."

"No," I said at once, unsure why I would argue.

"You and Adam can walk away."

"Why would you do that?" I asked. "It was my idea to bring her here."

He paused, looking at me again in a way that made me feel vulnerable.

"There are good people in the world, Justine. And you're one of them."

Then he was circling to the front of the truck, ready to go and I knew he had a schedule to keep, that people were counting on him.

"Is there any way you can keep an eye on that girl Amanda saw? Just until we find the guy who took the snakeskin?"

"I can try," I said. "But I have no idea where to find him."

"Never say never," Troy smiled again, climbed into his truck, and I put my hand on his windowsill, wanting to hold him in place. "We'll find it. I promise."

I looked down before he could see how his words affected me.

"See you soon."

I stepped back, hoping that was true, feeling guilty because Dylan was supposed to make me feel this way, not some lumberjack in love with the girl stuck in Cabin Ten.

I stood watching while he drove down the gravel road, swinging wide when he passed my brother walking in the opposite direction.

I raised my hand, waited until he came closer, his brown eyes going wide as they took in my face.

WHAT HAPPENED?

I put an arm around his shoulder, touched his head to mine and breathed in the sweet smell of his hair.

"Let's go inside."

I SPENT the better part of the day with Amanda and Adam cooped up inside Cabin Ten, checking my face periodically in the mirror, praying the ice pack I was using would help the swelling go down, so I wouldn't have to tell Dylan about bashing a man's head against a steering wheel.

So far, I wasn't having much luck.

I told Adam about Dad, told him what had happened on the island, but he was as confused as I was.

And scared.

Amanda sat at the kitchen table, her spirits lighter in my brother's company, and I could only imagine what they were talking about, feeling a strange twist in my middle that was interrupted when Pam came with more medicine.

She stopped dead in her tracks when she saw me, her eyes shifting from my face to my elbow.

"What happened?"

That was the question of the day, and so I answered with a condensed version of the night before.

"You saw a man *steal* the snakeskin?" she asked, her face incredulous.

I nodded.

"What did he look like?"

"It was dark," I snapped, cranky and cross and wishing part of my job included taking a snooze in the bedroom with my favorite fuzzy blanket.

"What color was his car?"

"Dark," I shrugged, stirring the soup I had boiling on the stove.

I heard Pam chuckle behind me and shot her a dirty look.

"Well, we could start by looking for a dark car with a missing window."

I saw Adam smile and fought to suppress a giggle, realizing we needed this moment with me stirring the soup and Pam stating the obvious when a picture flashed through my mind--one I had pushed far into my subconscious. I felt my body against the side of the car, felt my hand grab the back of the man's head, his fist flying up to meet my face and something else, something sharp, slicing my bottom lip.

"He was wearing a ring," I said suddenly. "On his middle finger."

"Ring?" Pam asked.

"With a clear stone in the center. A diamond."

I heard something clatter on the table behind me and turned to see what had happened. Amanda sat, her face white, a glass tipped over in front of her.

I went to her, my eyes searching for my brother.

"What's she saying?"

He shook his head.

A NAME.

"What is it?" I asked, hopeful.

HER MIND IS SO FAST... I CAN'T.

I turned to Adam, but his face had gone still, as though he were trying to hear a whisper in a busy diner.

"Who is it?" I asked again, and he looked up at me, his eyes wide with the same fear I'd seen when he handed me Butler's knife last summer.

ETHAN.

CHAPTER
TWENTY-ONE

I stood up and backed away from the table, trying to connect the man I'd seen in the hospital with the person I'd chased through the woods the night before.

I looked at Adam, touched his shoulder, and then shifted my gaze to Amanda. Her face was stiff, her lips pinched.

"We have to tell Troy," I said, suddenly hopeful he could track the asshole down, beat him to a bloody pulp, and climb atop the stallion he'd tamed to bring the snakeskin to me.

I turned to Amanda.

"Can he get to him?"

Her eyes flicked to my brother's.

ETHAN HAS AN APARTMENT ON THE ISLAND.

"She's sure it's him?"

SHE SAW HIM ON THE NEWS THIS MORNING. HE HAD A BRUISE ON HIS FOREHEAD.

The next second I had Troy on the phone.

"Justine," he said. "Is something wrong?"

"Ethan took the snakeskin."

"Ethan? How--"

"Can you find him?"

"I'll check his place," he paused. "I'm on the ferry now."

"Hurry," I said, hanging up and facing the others. "He'll call when he finds Ethan."

I saw Amanda wilt against the chair and understood her fear.

"He'll be all right," Pam spoke up. "He seems like a man who can handle himself."

That was the understatement of the day, and so we settled in for an agonizing wait. I returned to the soup, poured it out into four separate bowls, and sat down to eat in silence.

Until my brother asked a question I'd never considered before.

WHAT DO WE DO WITH THE SNAKESKIN WHEN WE FIND IT?

I looked to him quickly, wondering the same thing.

DID DAD TELL YOU ANYTHING?

NO.

My cell phone rang. One wild grasp and I had it in my hand.

"Troy," I just managed. "Did you find him?"

"No," he answered, his tone subdued. "Looks like no one's been here, either."

I stood up, ran a hand through my hair. "Does he have somewhere else he stays?"

"No."

"Another house? You said he does business downstate."

"He stays in hotels."

"His family? Where do they live?"

"I don't know," a slight pause. "This is my fault. If I'd just taken care of him at the hospital, none of this would've happened."

I shook my head, a small smile painting my lips.

"And you would've wound up in jail, pretty much completely useless."

I could feel him smile. "True story. How's Mandy?"

I threw a glance over my shoulder, saw Pam settling her into bed.

"Fine," I lied.

"I should be there."

"You're where you need to be."

"Justine--"

"Just be careful."

He paused, and I sensed his uncertainty. His vulnerability.

"Only if you do the same," he chuckled. "No more beating up rich assholes if I don't get to."

I bent my head, smiled into the phone.

"I'll do my best."

Moments later I was filling the others in, glancing at the clock, hoping I'd stalled long enough to give Dylan time to get into bed and turn out the light. And if I just wore long-sleeved shirts for the rest of the summer, he'd never know I was the next best thing to a Slim Jim.

Pam sensed my anxiety and came over to stand beside me.

"He'll understand."

I gave a weak smile and headed towards the door, never dreaming I'd dread seeing Dylan--a man I usually tripped over my own feet to get to.

The drive home seemed like a slow walk to the gallows, and when I arrived, I saw that he'd left the kitchen light on for me--his truck parked in its usual spot.

Creeping to the door, I opened it slowly, listened for any sign of movement and then shut it softly behind me. Tiptoeing across the living room I took a long time brushing my teeth before entering our darkened bedroom. I just made out his form lying in bed and stripped down to my skivvies before sliding under the covers.

I heard him draw a deep breath, felt him turn over in the darkness, and lay as still as I possibly could before reaching a hand out and placing it on his chest.

"Goodnight," I whispered, hoping my effort at reconciliation would be enough to keep him from turning on the light.

He turned toward me, and I wanted to burrow into his arms like I always did.

"I love you," I said, leaning closer, finding his lips in the dark.

He stirred, one hand cupping the side of my face.

"I couldn't sleep last night," he whispered.

"Me either," I said, not bothering to mention why.

"I'm sorry," he said, his hand still on my face, his fingers brushing my jaw and I bit the inside of my lip to keep from pulling away.

"I know," I reached up, moved his hand from my face and intertwined his fingers with my own. "And I forgive you."

I felt him relax against me, pulling me closer and I maneuvered away, so he wouldn't feel the bandage on my elbow, knowing my efforts were only delaying the inevitable but wanting this bliss to last as long as it possibly could.

"Meg called me."

I sucked in my breath, a flash of anger making me hot. "Why?"

"She wanted to apologize for what she said."

I laughed. "She already pretended to do that last night."

"She felt like she'd caused trouble between us."

I rolled onto my back and looked up at the darkened ceiling, thinking I might beat Henry Younts to the punch if she didn't lay off.

"What did you say?"

"I told her to leave me alone."

I let my breath out slowly. "How'd she take it?"

"She was drunk so who knows if she'll remember it in the morning."

"Oh, yeah?" I asked, a dark fear building. "Where was she?"

"Out with some friends on Black Lake."

I sat up quickly.

"Justine," Dylan said. "What is it?"

"Black Lake?"

I felt him shift, saw the room spring to life under the light cast by his lamp, and squinted. The next moment I put my hand to my face, trying to hide the bruise while exposing my bum bandage job at the same time.

"Baby," he whispered, frozen in place, unsure if he should touch me. "Oh, my God--"

"Dylan--"

"What happened to you?"

"It's okay," I said quickly. "I'm okay."

"No, you're not," he said, his words tumbling on top of each other as he sat up in bed, one hand reaching for my face and turning it towards the light. "Did someone hit you?"

I shook my head, not wanting to explain but knowing the moment everyone had warned me about was here.

"We need to get to Black Lake."

"Where were you last night?"

"Doesn't matter. We need to leave right now!"

He clenched his jaw; his eyes wild with a rage I didn't know he was capable of. "We're not going anywhere until you tell me where you were last night."

"Dylan--"

"And that's *after* you tell me the name of the asshole who did that to your face."

I scooted to the edge of the bed and grabbed my clothes.

"I'll explain in the truck but right now we need to find Meg."

"Shit, Justine," he said, his breath heavy as he pulled a hand over his face. "No *way*--"

I shook my head, my voice breaking. "It's a matter of life and death!"

He was silent for a moment before standing up, pulling a tee shirt over his head, and reaching for a pair of athletic shorts.

The next moment we were racing through our bungalow, running towards his truck, and he seemed torn between wanting to hold me and interrogate me.

"I saw Dad last night," I said once we were out of the driveway.

"He told me that something went wrong at the reversal, that you took me before it was finished."

He looked over, swung wide onto 23 and headed north.

"I was trying to save your life."

"I know," I said. "But something went wrong and now Henry Younts is killing people, Dylan--and the girl we dreamed about is the only one who can see who's next."

I saw his shoulders tighten.

"Her name's Amanda Bennett and Adam met her in the St. Ignace hospital. She can't talk, but he hears her, and I think," I swallowed, unable to form the words that would bring his worst fears to life. "I think Henry Younts is using death to come back to life."

"What?" he repeated, dazed. "*What?*"

"She saw an old man in the hospital die first, and then she saw," I stopped, my heart in my throat. "Then she saw Meg."

"Hold up," he said, the stupor of the moment before gone. "You told me *you* saw Meg. Not the girl in our dream."

"I know, but I was scared you'd be mad at me, but she saw Meg," I paused. "She saw her drown."

"*Drown?*" he repeated.

"Yes," I said, the implication settling between us.

"And Adam's the one who can hear her?"

I nodded.

"And he dragged you into this?"

I looked up quickly. "He needed me."

"And now Meg--" he stopped short, ignoring my last statement. "Why didn't you tell me the truth?"

I glanced over at him, saw his jaw working like it always did when he was worried and wondered how deep his feelings for her went.

"Tell me this wasn't the girl kidnapped from the hospital."

I looked down, started chipping the pink polish off my fingernails.

"Tell me you didn't have anything to do with it."

My gaze swung from my fingernails to a mysterious stain on his floor mat.

"*Shit*," he said, his cop brain going into overdrive. "They're extending the search into Presque Isle tomorrow. They caught a blue pickup on surveillance at the hospital, then another heading south on the Bridge. They could throw you in jail for felony kidnapping. Ten to fifteen if we're lucky."

I shook my head. "They're not going to do that."

"How do you know?"

"Troy said he'd take the blame."

I felt his gaze swing sharply to me. "Who's Troy?"

I swallowed. "Amanda's boyfriend."

"Her *boyfriend?*"

I bit my lip. "Yeah."

He readjusted his hold on the wheel. "The video was bad but some I.T. geek will clean it up. They'll know it's you. Adam's a minor and," he paused, "no one's going to arrest him.

"It's only until she gets better and tell Ethan to go to hell."

"Ethan?" he asked, glancing at me again. "Who *are* these people, J?"

I took a breath, wishing I'd never mentioned Troy in the first place. "Amanda's fiancé."

I saw my boyfriend's eyes widen, watched as he swallowed, obviously trying to weigh what he said carefully. "So, you kidnapped her so she could run off with her boyfriend?"

I scrunched up my face, annoyed with his appraisal of my rescue mission. "You don't know how horrible Ethan is."

"And you *do?*"

I paused, not wanting to tell him about our fistfight just yet.

"Amanda could be declared incompetent," he mumbled, more to himself than to me. "If she can't talk, they'll make it look like you were after her money. The boyfriend could be in on it."

"He's not."

He turned, his gaze hard. "You sure about that?"

"Sure, I'm sure."

"You've known the guy, what--three whole days?"

"Dylan--"

"We've gotta get you out of this. Dad's partner is still in business. I'll call him--"

"Dylan--"

"He owes us a favor, so he might take the case no questions asked. We can say the boyfriend talked you into it, that he used Adam to get to you."

"Dylan!"

He stopped, looked at me like I'd slapped him.

"Dad told me to find the snakeskin and when I went to the island. I saw someone stealing it, so I chased him, followed him to his car and--"

"He did that to your face?"

"Yes, but--"

"And your elbow?"

I tried to smile, still hopeful he might think my super strength was kinda cool.

"I broke out his window."

One look at Dylan's face and I knew "cool" was the last adjective on his mind.

"With your elbow?"

I chipped at my polish again, sure I'd missed a spot.

"That guy could've pulled a gun."

I frowned; I hadn't thought of that.

"And then one of my buddies would have to drive to our house in the middle of the night to tell me you're dead."

I sat up straighter, anger igniting my defenses. "What was I supposed to do? He *stole* the snakeskin."

He slammed his hand against the wheel, angrier than I'd ever seen him. "I don't give a fuck what he stole! You have to control this...*thing* that takes over or you're going to get yourself killed."

I felt myself shrink in the seat, knowing that he was right.

"And now Meg's involved," he stopped short, glanced at me, and I felt the accusation settle on my shoulders.

"I didn't pull her into this! You were the one who decided to get all cozy with her when you were *supposed* to be studying!"

He turned, his jaw set. "Is that why you never told me?"

I didn't answer.

"You're playing with someone's *life*, Justine."

"I know!" I cried, covering my face with my hands. "I know it and I hate her!"

He reached for his phone, unmoved by my outburst. "I'm calling her."

I tried not to think about why he had her number, and so bit my lip to keep from saying something I'd regret.

Moments later he hung up. "She didn't answer."

I looked over, saw him gripping the wheel so hard his knuckles were white and imagined he must be thinking about last summer.

And the summer before that.

"I'm sorry," I said, my voice small. "I wanted to tell you."

"But you didn't."

I gritted my teeth. "You sure as hell didn't make it easy."

He was silent for a long moment, and when he spoke again his voice was low. "I was scared, J. My dream--"

"I know," I said. "I was, too."

Something bright flashed across my peripheral vision.

"Shit!" I heard Dylan curse as he pulled the truck over.

I spun in my seat, afraid to look, knowing what I would see.

Two police cruisers flew by, sirens blaring.

I turned to Dylan; terror greater than anything I'd experienced at the hands of Henry Younts twisting my guts.

"It's Meg," he said, his voice low as he pulled back onto the road. "I know it."

"We can't be sure."

He didn't answer, just sped up as Black Lake came into view, the flashing lights of the cruisers parked in front of a small cottage halfway down a narrow lane.

Two girls about Meg's age were standing out front, talking to the officers who had just arrived. One had a towel draped around her shoulders, the other was hysterical.

Dylan pulled into the driveway, threw open the door, and jumped out. I followed close behind, feeling like an outsider in what I felt sure was about to happen.

The girls looked at me and said something to each other. Then they saw Dylan and anger slashed at their faces.

"What's going on?" Dylan asked, motioning for the deputy who had been talking to the girls to step aside. They seemed to know each other because he followed, spoke low into Dylan's ear, and I saw his face tighten.

The next moment he was in front of me, trying to explain. "They were anchored about twenty-five feet off the end of the dock. One minute she was there and the next ..." he paused. "Something hit the boat from underneath. They have a dive team on their way but I'm going in."

I gripped his arm. "Dylan--"

"*I'm going in.*"

The next second, he was rushing towards the dock, shedding whatever clothing would weigh him down as her two friends watched in terrified fascination.

"Dylan!" I screamed, running after him as one of the deputies stepped in front of me.

"Let him go," he ordered. "He knows what he's doing."

I turned, dazed, as the two friends came into view, their faces a bizarre blend of anguish and anger.

"It's the least he can do after pulling that dick move," one of them spat before bursting into tears. The other took her towel and wrapped it around the both of them as they put their heads together and began to sob.

I turned again, feeling lost for a moment in the pulsing lights and hushed cries, watching as my boyfriend sprinted towards the end of the dock. The next moment I was pushing past the girls, commotion erupting behind me as neighbors came out of their houses to see what was going on. Terrified whispers punctured the air. More vehicles pulled up as the dive team arrived.

I heard a splash as Dylan dove into the water, felt my mind spark out like a plug in a weathered socket as I raced for the dock, my feet barely touching the wood as I dove into Black Lake.

The water was cool, the weight of my clothes pulling at me when I opened my eyes and saw Dylan's body slicing the water, his strong strokes taking him towards the spot where the boat had been anchored. I felt my arms pumping like a machine as a white arm drifted into view just ahead, Meg's hair an explosion around her face.

I followed the line of her limp body, illuminated by the searchlights, and saw something grasp her ankle. A hand, bloated and gray, the fingers coming apart at the bone.

Dylan grasped her arm just as the hand pulled down, taking him with her.

I opened my mouth to scream when the black eyes came into view through the brackish water.

Miss me, Muffet?

Fear paralyzed my body, followed closely by rage as I watched Dylan struggling in the water. The next moment I was swimming straight for Henry Younts, my hands gnarled hooks as I dug them into the soft corners of the eyes I hated.

My fingers sank deep, the mealy flesh of his face splitting open against the tips.

He jerked away as Meg's ankle slipped from his grasp. The next moment she was floating upwards, Dylan's arm under hers as he broke the surface.

I turned to follow when the hand grasped my elbow, yanking me down into the water I had just released Meg from.

My lungs burst with fire, images of Mallard and our arm wrestling match flashing before my eyes. Next, I was pinning Dylan to the wall, then punching a roughneck named Stumpy in the face while Iris mouthed "Take him."

I twisted in his grasp, pulled my foot up and struck out, hitting Henry Younts in the center of his chest. Another blow to his neck, and I was able to break free, his fingers grasping my bandage as it came loose from my elbow. Eight strokes and I broke the surface, ten and I was moving towards shore as the sounds of bedlam surrounded me.

"Miss," I heard one of the deputies shouting from the end of the dock. "Are you alright?"

Another eight strokes and I reached the platform.

"Miss," he repeated. "Give me your hand."

I reached up, felt his fingers close around my wrist, and allowed him to haul me from the water where I lay panting, my hair plastered against the side of my neck and shoulders.

Moments later I looked up, searching for Dylan.

He was on shore, placing Meg on the grass with a team of medics before turning to look for me.

I staggered to my feet; my breathing coarse as I stumbled up the dock. He had me in his arms before I knew what was happening, his grip so tight I thought my bones would break.

"Why did you jump in?" he asked. "Why the hell do I even ask anymore?"

"You needed me," I whispered, my face against his chest as I shivered in my wet clothes.

He nodded, his hands rubbing my back in brisk strokes. "Something was down there."

I looked up into his bloodshot eyes. "It was Henry Younts."

"He had Meg."

"We should go," I said. "Mom...and Paul--"

"I'll call them."

I nodded.

"She can't die, Justine," he whispered, coughed hard into his fist. "She can't."

I looked down, fear beating at my rib cage like a child throwing a tantrum. "I know."

"If Henry Younts comes back--"

"We'll handle it."

He looked at me, his eyes bleary. "We will?"

I touched the side of his face.

"Bet my life on it."

CHAPTER TWENTY-TWO

We met my mother and Paul at the front entrance of the Cheboygan hospital.

"What happened?" Paul demanded. *"Where's my daughter?"*

"They're trying to stabilize her," Dylan answered. "She fell off a boat on Black Lake."

"Fell off?" Paul repeated and I saw Mom put a hand to his forearm, trying to soothe him. "How did she *fall off?*"

"Justine," Mom stepped closer, seeing my face for the first time, "What happened?"

I glanced away, hoping they would think I was injured doing something terribly heroic.

"Something hit the boat from under the water," Dylan said.

Paul stepped closer, his face mere inches from my boyfriend's. "She could swim before she could walk. No way did she just fall off and not get to shore," he paused, his eyes narrowing. "What aren't you telling me?"

I glanced at Dylan, hating that he had to do this, realizing he had done with perfect strangers hundreds of times before.

"They were drinking. I smelled it on her friends and there were empty bottles on shore."

Paul shook his head,head; rage contorting his features. "Can you blame her? She was heartbroken."

Mom put her hand on Paul's chest, said something to calm him.

"I'm sorry," Dylan said. "I never meant to hurt her."

Paul took a step closer and for a moment I thought he might hit him. "Sorry doesn't cut it right now. She's in there fighting for her life and here you stand with barely a scratch."

Dylan cleared his throat, coughed into his fist again. "I tried to get her out."

"Looks like you didn't try hard enough."

Something in his tone stoked my anger and I reached out, pushed against his chest with enough force to send him backwards. "He dove into that lake to save her drunk ass so why don't you just *shut the fuck up, Paul?*"

"Justine!" Mom gasped, her fingertips going to her lips. "Paul," she turned to him, "I'm so sorry."

"Save it, Brenda," he said, his eyes holding mine for a moment before storming past her, his shoulder hitting Dylan's as he passed.

Mom tried to follow him then pivoted on her heel. She approached me slowly, cautiously, knowing what I was capable of.

"What's going on here?" she asked, her voice shaking. "And does it have anything to do with last summer?"

I held her gaze, felt as though she were challenging me, and took a step forward.

"Yes."

I saw her lips form the thin line I remembered from childhood. "I can't, Justine...I just can't. I'm trying to move on and--"

"Don't blame her," Dylan spoke up. "She didn't ask for any of this."

"Maybe not," Mom said, her gaze traveling in a sharp line between us. "But that brother of hers and his tramp of a mother did!"

I felt myself stiffen, a blanket of fury smothering me.

"Brenda," Dylan said, trying to calm her. "You need to go sit down."

"She wasn't like this before," she pointed a finger in his face. "It's this place...this town...and *you!*"

"Calm down--"

"Stop patronizing me," she spat. "And stop acting so innocent. We both know you led Meg on."

I watched his face go slack and realized her words had hurt him. "If I did, then I'm sorry."

"Why should I believe anything you have to say?"

"It doesn't matter if you do," he said flatly. "I went into the lake because I care. Just not in the way she wanted."

Mom stood still, unable to argue, exhaustion transforming her features into someone I didn't recognize.

"Go find Paul," I said. "And stop treating us like we're the enemy. If we wanted her to die, we would've left her in the water."

She looked down, embarrassment flushing her face of the anger that had stained it moments before.

"Justine--" she stammered. "I didn't mean--"

"Just go."

She looked down, pulled her coat around her body and walked towards where Paul had disappeared not five minutes before.

"Justine," I heard Dylan's voice in my ear once she was out of sight and knew what he was going to say.

"It's okay," I assured him. "I know it isn't true."

"Meg twisted everything we talked about and made it into what she wanted to hear."

I nodded, having exhausted energy for all other options, and so he took my hand, led me to a pair of orange Formica chairs someone had placed beside a vending machine that dispensed only one brand of bottled water.

We sat in silence at first, our thoughts carrying us past what had happened at Black Lake and back to the last two weeks.

"What I told you in the truck about the person who stole the snakeskin," I paused, glanced over at him as he coughed into his fist again. "I know who it is."

He looked at me, his blue eyes questioning, and I wanted nothing more than to take him into my arms and hold his damp head against my chest.

"Who was it?" he asked, coughing again and I wondered how much water he had taken in and what would have happened if I hadn't stopped Henry Younts.

"Amanda's fiancé."

"Ethan?"

I nodded.

"The one who's looking for her? What does he want with it?"

"We don't know," I shook my head, "But Troy's keeping an eye on his apartment." I stopped short when I saw him glance at me.

"He is?"

I nodded. "Ethan lives on Mackinac and Troy works there so it makes sense that he'd--"

Dylan crossed his arms over his chest, leaned back in his chair. "When did you two figure this out?"

I sat forward on the chair, looked down at the white linoleum flecked with teal, and wondered how long it had been since someone mopped the floor.

"He's only trying to help."

"I thought that was my job."

"Dylan--"

"How long did you know about Meg?" he asked, his question intensifying the strained atmosphere we had established on our Formica chairs in the middle of a nondescript hallway.

I looked over at him. "Does it matter?"

He leaned forward, folded his hands into a steeple. "Yes."

"Since yesterday," I whispered.

"Justine--"

"I thought we could handle it."

He cleared his throat, coughed into his fist again. "You and Troy?"

I looked over at him, saw the hurt behind his bloodshot eyes and knew he had every right to be angry.

"You had no right to do that."

"I know," I said, my voice rising. "But you liked her, and I just wanted it to--"

"Go away?"

I looked down, studied the floor again.

"She might."

"Don't say that," I snapped.

He was quiet for a moment, and I wondered what he was going to say about the young woman who had taken up more than her fair share of our summer.

After some time had passed, he finally spoke. "You want to know what bothers me the most about this whole thing?"

I looked up at him.

He unfolded his hands, cupped the back of his head with one of them. "You thought I loved her."

I looked over at him, startled "No--"

"Then why didn't you tell me?"

"Dylan--"

"You thought I was in love with her."

I felt uncomfortable looking at him, and so searched the hallway for anything to catch my attention and came up short.

"I don't know how to make you understand what you mean to me."

I reached out, took his hand, and felt like I was touching a stranger.

"And I can't keep trying."

I felt the truth of his words hit me in the depths of my chest, where they reverberated against the fears I'd held since that day at the community pool. I opened my mouth to say something, felt tears coming, and swiped at my eyes with the back of my hand.

"I'm sorry I'm so messed up. I try to understand why a guy like you would want to be with someone like me--"

"Stop!" he shouted, his voice echoing down the hall. "I love you because you're beautiful and loving and kind. I love that you play those stupid video games with Adam and call Iris to check up on your cat. I love that you charmed Butt-Head Brauski into giving you a raise and that you bake cookies to take to Dad and share them with the nurses. I even love that you space out during Euchre and trump me by mistake and that you drove around town looking for that dumb coffee table I wanted and I can't stop thinking about the day we're married with kids of our own playing on that swing set I'm going to build in the backyard."

"Dylan," I whispered, my heart pounding in my ears.

"There's never been anyone else like you, J. Not for me. Not ever."

I tried to take a breath and felt my shoulders heave with a silent sob.

"And it kills that you think I'd throw it away over some kid with a crush."

I sat in stunned silence, wondering if what he said was true, knowing that my wondering was part of the problem.

Hurried footsteps down the hallway drew my attention. I lifted my head and was shocked to see the last person I expected.

"Mom," Dylan said, standing up.

I sat up straighter, prepared for combat when Dylan moved, his fluid strides intercepting Melinda Locke before she could reach me.

"What are you doing here?" he asked.

She pressed her lips together, obviously upset, and I took a moment to look at her, dressed impeccably in her standard khaki slacks and silk blouse for a seemingly random visit to the Cheboygan hospital.

"Christine called and said someone almost drowned at her neighbor's cottage. She said you were the officer who went in the lake. That you were off duty. That you were with *her*."

"Mom--" he grabbed her forearm, pulled her down the hallway, and I sat there, listening to the hatred behind her words.

"How many times do I have to tell you," she glanced at me, lowering her voice to feign courtesy. "She's nothing but trouble."

"I'm only going to ask you one time to leave," he said, but she went on as though he'd never spoken.

"What were you doing out there?"

I heard him mumble something, saw Melinda's face register shock, and something else. A knowing of sorts, a feeling that she had something on me.

"You knew that girl from your class?"

Dylan said something again, glanced back at me.

"Were you?" she stopped, her voice rising as she smiled.

I stood suddenly and started walking in the opposite direction.

"Justine!" Dylan shouted, his voice hollow in the empty hall.

"Let her go," his mother answered, loud enough for me to hear and I sped up, running now in some awful caricature of a Made-for-TV medical thriller.

I made it to the front lobby before I broke down completely.

Moments later I called the one person I knew would understand.

She answered on the second ring.

"Iris," I just managed. "Can you pick me up?

CHAPTER
TWENTY-THREE

I sat in the passenger seat of my grandmother's Oldsmobile, looking out the window as she pulled from the parking lot, the man I loved inside, trying to talk down his crazy mother while the girl he had risked his life for lay in intensive care.

"What's going on?" Iris asked, her green eyes holding the road, giving me the space I needed.

I cleared my throat, gave her the abridged version, kicking myself for not doing it sooner.

"I was afraid of this," she said while heading south on 23 and I found myself wishing we had nowhere to go on a road that stretched into forever.

"You were?"

She nodded, sighed in a way that said she had been thinking about it long before I asked her.

"When they brought you into the hospital, I wondered... Dylan was a mess and so was Adam. I knew their heads weren't screwed on straight, knew something could have gone wrong and everything had to be exactly right. But then time went on and things settled down and I thought..." she trailed off, turned to me.

"I know," I answered, "I thought so, too."

She shifted in her seat, her presence comforting me in a way no one else could.

"And now someone's stolen the snakeskin?"

I nodded. "It was Amanda's fiancé. I have no idea why he'd want it, but Troy is watching his apartment right now."

She looked at me in the same way everyone did when Troy's name was mentioned.

"And who is this gentleman?"

I felt my face heat up and looked down at my lap, wondering if it was obvious my feelings for him were conflicted, knowing Iris would see through whatever ruse I threw at her.

"Amanda's boyfriend," I stopped, looked at her again, trying to gauge her reaction.

"And this Troy works on Mackinac Island doing what, exactly?"

I blushed again, a strange tingle to my skin when I imagined him doing the task I was about to describe.

"He trains horses. Amanda's grandparents hired him. That's how they met."

She nodded, breathed in through her nostrils, so they flared a bit.

"And Amanda's fiancé, *not* her boyfriend, split your lip and gave you that god-awful bruise on your face? Not to mention your elbow looks like some toddler used it for a cut-and-paste project."

I smiled, grateful for her humor.

"You've still got it, haven't you?"

I smiled again, the tension leaving my shoulders as I sank back against the seat.

We were silent, the reality of what I'd admitted sinking in. I thought of Mom, trying to reconcile with Paul after I'd told him to fuck off. And Dylan--wandering the halls with Melinda Locke trailing behind, wondering where I was.

The last thought brought a momentary flash of guilt, but then I remembered he was with his mother--which was enough to drive any functional person insane, not to mention waiting in cramped quarters if he'd abandoned the Formica chair for the upholstered ones in the waiting room all while trying to convince Paul he hadn't led his daughter on.

Yep--his girlfriend having a tantrum might not be a blip on his radar right now.

I was pondering this thought, along with several others when we pulled into my driveway.

"You know you can come to me," Iris said, turning. "And tell me what's on your mind."

"I know," I said quickly. "I was trying to handle it but then Adam got involved, and Troy and Pam and--"

"Dylan?"

I swallowed.

"He thinks this is a load of crap, doesn't he?"

I took a quick breath. "Yes...no...maybe."

She smiled, "He reminds me of someone."

I glanced at her, my gaze sharp. "Who?"

She tapped on her chest. "Me."

At first, I wasn't sure I'd heard her right. "You? But--"

"My husband told me about his family before we got married, but I thought it was a bunch of hooey. It wasn't until later that I understood what it meant to be a Cook," she paused. "And I almost left him because of it."

I held my breath, thinking of the man who'd made my father into the person I loved.

"You did?"

"But Ben was insistent," she smiled again, and I saw a blush sweep her cheeks. "And persistent. What could a poor girl do against his charms?"

I leaned closer, intrigued. "What did he do?"

She smiled, patted the nape of her neck and the hair bunched there with a light hand.

"Damn fool took me to a place in the woods we'd heard about as kids. Folks called it the Whisper Stone. Everyone said if you stood on a certain place at a certain time of day a great wind would carry you back to your ancestors."

"A great wind?" I repeated.

"If you ask me, it was just a way for the fellas to get us girls alone in the woods."

I grinned, amused by the picture she was painting.

"There was a pool of water right next to this Whisper Stone and Ben picked up a leaf and put it in the water. Said if the wind blew it back to me then we were meant to be together."

I smiled. "Did it?"

She shook her head, "Of course not! The wind was blowing from the west! If Ben had any brains, he would have put me on the other side of the pool."

I shook my head, watching my grandmother out of the corner of my eye. "But you married him anyway?"

She nodded. "I wasn't going to let a little thing like common sense come between us."

I leaned back in my seat, wondering where the story was going, knowing it was heading somewhere, or she never would have told it.

"My fears were real, Justine. I felt overwhelmed when I thought about what Ben would face. What our *children* would face."

"Dad," I said, my heart leaping.

She nodded, her eyes downcast. "Ben said the Shaman's gifts would help our children, but I didn't buy any of it. I was too sensible. Dealt only in facts, not feelings."

I sighed, thinking she sounded an awful lot like someone I loved.

"And then your father was born, and I knew in an instant I was meant to protect him. And when Ben got sick, I knew it would be up to me to teach him what had been passed down from Calvert Cook."

"And did you?" I asked, imagining their long-ago conversations and what it must have meant to my father.

"Yes," she nodded, her eyes glassy and in that moment I realized I'd never seen her cry. "I kept right on loving him as he grew into a man and married your mother. I loved him even when he did things I didn't understand."

I felt my throat swell, thinking about the pain my father's actions had caused her.

"Iris," I asked, suddenly thoughtful. "What changed your mind? About marrying Ben?"

She smiled. "I grew a brain and realized he was a good man struggling with a legacy he'd never asked for."

I nodded, feeling my grandfather's pain as surely as my own.

"And I knew he'd do the same for me if the shoe had been on the other foot."

I swallowed.

"Give him time, Justine."

I looked out at our bungalow tucked neatly beneath a cluster of maple trees that would grow red in cool weather, warm lights melting the darkness and felt my throat swell. "Maybe I'm selfish-but I want to go back to the way things were."

"You can't go back, Muffet," she stopped me. "You can only do your best with what you have in front of you. Right here. Right now."

"But Dylan--"

"Loves you in the same way I loved Ben."

I felt a small spark of hope, believing for the first time that someone might understand us.

"How was that?"

She leaned back, softness in her face and I saw the young woman standing beside the Whisper Stone while her beau placed a leaf in a still pond at her feet.

"I loved him more than my fear. And when we started our life together, I knew he was the only man I wanted by my side."

I bent my head, overwhelmed by her words.

"Iris--"

"It's all right, Muffet."

"No," I choked, "I don't know if we can get to that place. And I want to. I want to so badly."

She paused, reached out and squeezed my hand.

"I have a good feeling about you kids. And I'm hardly ever wrong."

I felt her words light the dark places in my heart.

"Thanks for the ride."

She nodded. "Anytime."

One step, and I was climbing into the humid night, images of Black Lake mixing with the strange legend of the Whisper Stone until everything blended into an odd mixture fueled by fear and exhaustion.

My grandmother waved once, started the car, and backed slowly out of our driveway.

I turned, looked again at our bungalow, and wondered if Dylan and I would ever see our kids play in the backyard, wishing for the great wind to carry me away.

And into nothing.

I AWOKE SOMETIME in the night to the feel of our cotton sheets sliding over my skin and turned in the humid darkness. The window was open, our curtains flickering in a stale breeze, the sound of crickets needling the air.

"J--" I heard Dylan whisper, felt his warm body curl against my back and laid very still.

"Justine," he said again, and I turned, his fingers against the bare expanse of hip where my camisole met my panties.

I cleared my throat, still sleepy. "How's Meg?"

He paused, and in the darkness I saw him lean up on one elbow, a cautious hand reaching for my cheek.

"She's stable," he said, "Now it's just a waiting game."

I didn't know what to say, and so I rolled over onto my back, my breathing shallow as I tried to erase the memory of what his mother had said.

"Did Iris give you a ride?" he asked.

I drew a breath. "Yes."

"I thought so," he said, his meaning lost when he reached over and flipped on his bedside light.

I blinked, blinded for a moment as he cupped my shoulder, pulling me beneath him and I looked up into his eyes, wondering what he was doing and why he had chosen to do it now.

"I love you, J," he said.

I felt my heart lift with a fierce hope that Iris might be right. "I love you, too."

"And I don't know how things got so messed up," he paused, looking down on me before sweeping my lip with his thumb. "How we got here."

I touched his bare chest with my fingers and felt heat radiate against the tips.

"What do you mean?"

He didn't say anything at first, his fingers moving to my camisole as he took hold of the bottom and pulled it slowly over my head.

"Wait," I gasped as he tossed it aside, shrugging out of his boxer shorts, the full length of his body now against me.

"I want something that reminds me of us," he whispered, his hands on the waistband of my panties as he rolled them down my thighs. "Something that's always been so good."

I held my breath, the feel of his chest pressed to mine making me dizzy. "I do, too."

"You do?" he asked, his hands sliding up to my knees where he capped them, pushed them apart.

I nodded, unable to speak as his mouth covered mine, leaving it only to trail down my throat, his tongue leaving a trace the sticky air seemed to cool. I curled my fingers in his hair, guided his face as he feathered kisses over my breasts and down to my bellybutton.

I felt my breath stagger, anticipation of what had always come after making me arch from the bed and he braced himself, his fingers sliding to my elbow.

I drew a sharp breath. Winced.

He stopped suddenly, pulled himself back to my face.

"Please," I whispered, numb with desire. "Don't stop."

"I want you, Justine," he said, his voice low. "I always have."

"I," I just managed, feeling like a beggar. "I want you, too."

"But this," he touched my bottom lip again. "This isn't us."

"What," I gasped, still moving against him, my hands reaching for his hips to pull him down on top of me. "What do you mean?"

"This isn't you," he touched my jaw, his fingers just grazing tender flesh.

"It's *me*," I said, choking on my own voice. "I'm right here."

He shook his head, his watery eyes focusing on mine in a way that told me he might be delirious. "No..."

"Dylan--"

"I can't."

"Please--"

"*No!*"

He pulled away, and I felt him move to his side of the bed, my heart pounding in my chest, my skin still wet from his touch.

He reached over, touched my shoulder, and I stiffened.

"What do we do?" he asked.

I couldn't speak.

"What do I do?"

I groped blindly for my camisole and pulled it over my head.

"Go to bed, Dylan."

"Justine--"

"Go to sleep."

I rolled away, curled into a ball, and he hesitated before reaching over and turning off the light.

I laid still in the humid darkness, waiting until I heard his breath slide into something steady and quietly began to weep, more miserable than if he'd never touched me at all.

CHAPTER
TWENTY-FOUR

I woke up to faded sunlight and the familiar lead weight feeling in the pit of my belly. Rolling over, I saw Dylan standing in the doorway, ready for work, unsure if he should wake me.

"J--" he began. "I thought you were sleeping."

I sat up, rubbed my eyes, and propped myself against the pillows.

"About last night," he began, and I felt myself tense. "I'm sorry."

I looked down, unable to answer.

"About Mom," he began, clearly uncomfortable. "I'm going over to her house tonight." Another pause. "I'm going to tell her."

I raised an eyebrow. "Tell her what?"

He stood still, his gaze never wavering. "Everything."

I leaned forward. "Do you think that's a good idea?"

He shook his head, clearly frustrated. "I don't know what to think. I've got a girlfriend who's attacking men in the middle of the night, a classmate whose life is hanging by a thread, and a mother who wants to throw every mistake I've ever made back in my face."

My chest tightened, and I drew a quick breath.

"I didn't mean--"

"I know," I interrupted, running a hand through my hair as he touched the door frame, ready to leave. "When are you coming home?"

"Meg's mom is at the hospital," he said, the fatigue I'd noticed in his eyes marking his movements as well. "I'm going to stop by after work."

I frowned. "Well, that officially makes you a better person than me."

"Listen," he held a hand up, suddenly all cop. "I'm doing what I need to do to deal with this."

I sat, helpless.

"I'm going to talk to Mom and then I'm staying over with my sister." He touched the door frame again. "I'll see you tomorrow."

I narrowed my eyes, thinking of the night before, angrier than I'd been in a long time.

"Maybe you will. Maybe you won't."

I saw his knuckles tighten on the frame. "What's that supposed to mean?"

I crossed my arms over my chest, wanting to hide all the pieces of myself from him. "If you're gonna do what you need to do then I guess I should have the same rights."

"J," he said, his voice low. "Don't talk that way."

"Go to work, Dylan. Visit the girl you pretend you're not in love with before smoothing things over with a woman who's hated me from day one. Maybe it'll help you forget about all the mistakes you've made in the last year."

"Justine," he said softly, a simple word that carried a thousand assumptions behind it.

"Just go," I whispered.

He didn't say anything else, just turned and walked out of the room and a few moments later I heard the kitchen door close softly behind him.

I sat on the bed for a long time after he had gone, my heart numb, Iris' words from the night before hollow in my ears when my cell phone rang.

Hoping Dylan had called to apologize, I was only mildly disappointed to hear Troy's voice.

"Justine," he said. "Did you find anything out?"

I stiffened on the bed, realizing he knew nothing about what happened the night before.

"You could say that," I said, the story about Meg spilling out and I hoped he didn't blame me for not keeping a better eye on her.

"Do you think she'll make it?" he asked.

"Dylan's going to update me this afternoon," I offered, hoping it was true, wondering if I should call my mother now that Paul's ex-wife was in the mix.

He paused, and in the background, I heard carriages passing by and imagined him with his horses, doing what he had been put on earth to do. "Are you going to the cabin?"

I thought about my day, wondering what was on the agenda besides two loads of laundry and tracking down the asshole who'd stolen my snakeskin.

"I don't know," I began. "Dylan said they're extending the search into Presque Isle County."

"You told him?"

I cleared my throat. "Yeah, I mean, it was definitely time."

"You must feel better."

I didn't know whether to laugh or cry, so I lied.

"Lots."

He paused. "I meant what I said about taking the blame. I won't let anyone come after you or Adam."

I swallowed, my heart soaring. "Troy--"

"And I got ahold of Mandy's mom."

I felt a small sliver of relief slip between my ribs. "And Ethan?"

He paused. "Nothing."

I was quiet, disappointed, and he must have sensed my distress. "I should be helping you look for him."

I felt heat rise to my chest. "No--"

"I'll finish up with the horses tonight and be on the mainland tomorrow."

Something in his words made me smile into the phone.

"We'll figure it out."

"Troy," I said, feeling like my life had slipped sideways.

"See you soon," he said before hanging up, the light assurance of our meeting a stark contrast to my argument with Dylan.

Seconds later I rolled off the bed and stood up, thoughts of Troy Phillips doing an honest day's work with the animals he loved floating through my mind like sunshine through a shade tree. And at that moment I didn't care about Dylan or Meg or century old preachers who kept turning up like bad pennies.

I was simply a twenty-three-year old girl who wanted to enjoy a summer day.

Twenty minutes later I was showered, changed, and heading north in the Jeep towards Mackinac Island.

AMANDA AWOKE IN THE AFTERNOON. She'd been restless the night before when Pam and Adam stayed with her, talking on the phone with Justine and a woman named Iris about what happened at Black Lake.

The girl named Meg had fallen off a boat. Justine's boyfriend pulled her out. She was in the hospital now, the outcome uncertain and Amanda wondered where that left the rest of them.

She'd been afraid to close her eyes, afraid of the man with the rotten smile but instead she awoke to nothing more than the sun shining through the birch trees that lined Ocqueoc Lake. For an instant she was back on Mackinac Island, in Troy's bed above the stables. She would have to leave early and sneak into her grandparents' house, memories of the night before lingering on her skin.

Amanda turned her head, wondering if she would ever feel that kind of happiness again and heard voices in the kitchen.

Pam was making lunch.

And the other voice. Not Justine or Troy but...

She opened her mouth, tried to speak the name of the person she'd wanted to see since the beginning.

She tried to sit up, felt her back wither in protest, and pushed past it.

Pam was drawing the curtain back and her mother was stepping through, her face a gentle reminder that people could be different.

"Amanda," she breathed, her eyes tired, her cheeks sallow. "Troy called me."

Of course, he had.

She remembered the night she'd told her about him , hoping she would be happy. Knowing she would.

Sara Bennett sank down beside her daughter, took her hand, and brought it to her lips.

"I'm glad you got away from Ethan."

Amanda nodded.

"Are these people taking good care of you?"

She nodded again, and her mother reached out, smoothed back her hair.

"I didn't know where you were--" she began, tears shining in her eyes and Amanda knew she must have been frightened. She depended on her to take care of things, to pay for groceries and call when she needed appointments. To drive her to the store when she was having a bad day which meant today was a good one.

"And I knew that when I found you, I needed to tell you something I should have a long time ago."

Amanda looked to her mother, wondering what remained unsaid between them.

"You know I loved your father very much," Sara began, her speech sudden and sure and Amanda wondered if it had been weighing on her mind, making her sick, and steeled herself against what it might be.

"When he died, it wasn't because he was lost and took a curve too fast," she paused, touched her hair lightly. "We had a fight, and he was angry with me. He wasn't thinking straight when he took off on that motorcycle."

Amanda shifted on the bed, her heart speeding up, thinking of her father's last moments.

"When the doctor told your grandparents he was gone," she stopped again, put a hand to her face. "I wasn't surprised."

Amanda tried to move again, and her mother bent over her, took her hand lightly.

"It was my fault he died."

Amanda drew a quick breath as she shook her head fiercely, defending her mother against a man she had never met.

"Something happened to me a long time ago. Something Daniel knew nothing about and it...changed me," she paused, looked over her shoulder at Pam who was stirring something on the stove.

"The man who died that night," she put her head down, kissed Amanda's knuckles, tears wetting her skin. "Wasn't your father."

Amanda felt herself stiffen, felt her eyes widen as her breath suspended in her useless throat.

"That's why I never gave you his name," her mother said, whispering now. "Your grandparents thought I was bitter, but I wasn't. I couldn't be. And your father, your *real* father, he couldn't help us."

Amanda looked into her mother's dark eyes, the eyes they shared, and felt the room soften around the edges, felt the bed begin to liquefy as though she were sinking in a pool of water and knew what was happening.

Meg was there, standing on the shore of the lake she had been pulled from, her face a bloated mass of gray tissue that looked ready to burst. Amanda tried to look away, tried to close her eyes but knew she needed to see, knew that others were counting on her to see.

The next moment the Bad Man stepped forward and put a hand on Meg's shoulder, pushing her into the earth where she began to sink as though standing in quicksand.

Amanda opened her mouth to scream, reached out a hand to

save the girl, but she was already gone, her dark hair sprouting from the earth like weeds as another figure slowly materialized.

He was wearing a red shirt, the front stained with grease, the smell of sawdust on his shoulders and Amanda felt her heart stop beating.

"Troy!" she screamed, her voice bursting free like a corpse from its coffin.

But he didn't hear, just walked forward, watching Amanda with a look of love he sometimes wore in the gray light of morning.

The Bad Man touched his shoulder, began to push Troy into the ground as he had Meg, his black eyes never blinking and Amanda called out to Adam but felt something blocking her.

"Troy," she whispered, sobbing now, unable to process how she would live in a world that did not include him.

"She's having a nightmare," she heard Pam say as if from a great distance.

"But she was awake," her mother's voice, high and distressed.

"My son can help her," Pam answered, and Amanda felt her mind clamp on the boy, crying out to him in broken desperation but felt something smother what had seemed natural only hours before.

Amanda opened her eyes, saw her mother standing over her, and called out to the boy--over and over and over until he came running, his mother beside him.

Amanda opened her mind, spoke the name of the one person she had prayed the Bad Man would spare.

She saw Pam put her arms around her son, and knew he couldn't hear her, knew the Bad Man had found a way to take that away from them.

And Troy would pay the price for it.

CHAPTER
TWENTY-FIVE

I felt giddy as I traveled towards Mackinaw City, the wind whipping through my hair, the radio telling me to come and get my love as I slid on my sunglasses, feeling like a normal person for the first time in weeks.

I'd tried calling Mom, but her phone had gone straight to voicemail.

My message had been lame and along the lines of *I don't want to visit my boyfriend's crush in the hospital even though she's Paul's daughter. And while we're at it, I don't really feel like apologizing to him since he accused Dylan of half-assing his rescue even though he would have died trying to save Meg. Try not to hold any of this against me even though it's been your M.O. since I was twelve. Love ya. Bye.*

I tried not to obsess about what Dylan would think of me shirking my daughterly duties.

Then I remembered his face as he looked down on me the night before, the lips that promised pleasure forming the word that broke me.

No.

I glanced at my cell phone and felt a fresh tug of despair when I didn't see a "love-you-how's-your-day-going" text-- something he always did at lunch when he worked the day shift.

Maybe "doing what he needed to do" included not communicating with me.

I rolled into Mackinaw City a half hour later and parked beside a blue and white tent at the ferry docks. The harbor was bustling, the tourist season in high gear as I watched mothers dragging children while trying not to trip on their luggage.

I smiled, wondering if I would ever bring my children here and I imagined Dylan swinging our daughter onto his shoulders, pointing to things that seemed to catch her eye, bending over to kiss me when our eyes met.

I froze, my hand on the door handle of the Jeep, the image as real as the ferryboat docked at the pier and fought the urge to jump in and high tail it home before I ruined everything.

Instead, I stepped out into the melee, felt the sunshine settle across the side of my neck as I paid for my ticket and made my way to the top deck of the ferry, my heart scattering like marbles on concrete.

I sat looking out at the water as the horn blew long and loud, wondering if Troy would be happy to see me or if my sudden appearance would disrupt the routine he had established with Amanda.

Twenty minutes later the ferryboat came to a grinding halt and a wave of tourists stood, sweeping the boat clean as I sat and waited, exiting once I felt sure I wouldn't be jostled like a sock in the dryer.

Once on the docks I stood alone, feeling disoriented and wondering how I was going to find Troy when I didn't even know where he lived.

I must have looked puzzled because a dock porter with a basket full of luggage came to a screeching halt in front of me.

"Looking for someone?" he asked, and I jumped at the chance, rambled off something about a man who took care of the horses up by the West Bluff.

He shook his head, directed me towards a carriage waiting to take people to the Grand Hotel, and so I walked that way, feeling like I might never find the man I was looking for, wondering if that was for the best.

I stopped by the taxi, looked up at the driver like a teenager breaking curfew and repeated my question.

"Troy Phillips?" she asked.

"Yes," I said, and the woman gave me a knowing smile.

"He works for the Calhoun Family. They put their people above the stables on the West Bluff just past the Hotel. Big white barn. You can't miss it," she paused. "Or him."

I smiled my thanks, not daring to look at her again as I began my walk through town and up the long hill that swept past the Grand Hotel.

At once I felt the charm of the island surround me as people passed by on bikes and in horse-drawn carriages. Drivers in top hats nodded as they passed, reminding me of my favorite Jane Austen novel. Off to the right and against an expanse of lawn, a field stone church caught my eye, stained-glass windows hinting at magnificent views from within.

I heard gulls overhead, felt the breeze blowing in from Lake Huron, the sounds of laughter mingling in the air as families ate lunch on the patio of a nearby restaurant and took a deep breath.

I imagined Troy and Amanda and their secret courtship in the hidden places this island offered. I saw them sneaking off to a secluded glen, lingering on a garden bench that smelled of jasmine in the cool of the evening and envisioned myself in her place.

Once at the top of the hill, I followed a sign towards the West Bluff, my anxiety peaking when I turned a corner and saw the name "Calhoun" written on the side of the white barn the driver had described.

Moments later, Troy came into view, a beautiful Buckskin at the end of his lead rope.

I stood for a moment in the shadows of an oak tree and watched him working the horse in a circle, his strong hands gripping the rope with just enough strength to let the animal know who was boss.

And I couldn't imagine Troy Phillips had ever been anything else in his life.

I came closer, stepping from the darkness, and he turned, aware of my movement. In an instant he let the lead rope slide and the horse came to a sudden halt while his master's eyes widened.

"Justine."

"I'm sorry," I said, stumbling over the words I'd come to hate.

"Are you okay?" he stepped closer, the horse still standing in place, waiting his command.

I shook my head. "I don't know. I--"

I saw his face soften in concern. "Hang on. I'll put him up."

I nodded, watched as he took the horse into the stables behind the yard. Moments later he was back in front of me, and I stepped into his embrace as naturally as I would have Dylan's. His arms closed around me, and I stood very still, breathing the scent of horses and sawdust and sweat that had come to remind me of him.

"What is it?" he asked, and I looked up at him, feeling like he would understand everything I couldn't put into words.

"I knew you were here on the Island and I've never been here before and I just wanted to get away and see what you were doing."

He pulled back, gave me the half-smile that had impressed the taxi driver down at the docks. "You wanted to watch me lunge horses?"

I shrugged, tried to laugh.

"I get it," he said while backing away, perhaps realizing he had held me too long. "Sometimes you want to forget about how the world is falling apart just a boat ride away."

I smiled, pushed my hair behind my ear.

"Why do you think I love it here?"

I looked up into his eyes and wondered why Amanda had ever wanted to jump.

"Let me change and I can take you by Ethan's apartment."

I laughed, thinking that was the last place I wanted to be.

"Not what you had in mind?" he chuckled. "I just thought--"

"I know what you thought." I stopped, unsure if I should say more. "I'm not here for that."

He smiled again, ran a hand through his sweaty hair. "How about I show you around then. Just for fun."

I felt the soft caress of anticipation. "You can do that?"

He nodded. "I make my own hours and the horse you saw me lunging did good today."

"He did?"

He nodded again, gave me another half-smile. "Looks like I just gave myself the afternoon off."

"Lucky me," I smiled again.

"I think it's the other way around," he said, sidestepping me and I looked up, unsure if he was teasing. "Come up and see my place."

I felt my cheeks go hot. "I can wait out here."

"Uh-uh," he said, "No man leaves a lady standing in the street."

I looked down, suddenly shy as he moved ahead, leading me up a side staircase to a small door that stood directly over the arched entrance to the stables. Once inside, I couldn't help but think of Amanda. A woman's touch had added warmth to the sparse apartment, and I could imagine the happiness the task must have given her.

"You face looks better," he said, and I touched my jaw, suddenly embarrassed.

He smiled again. "I'll jump in the shower, and then we can go."

I cleared my throat and gave him a quick nod, the thought unsettling me.

"Make yourself at home. My apartment is your apartment," he said, moving off towards what I assumed was the bathroom. Moments later I heard the shower turn on and opened the fridge in a feeble attempt to distract myself.

A six-pack of Bud Light sat next to a block of cheese and some kind of leftovers he'd put in a Tupperware bowl.

Beer sounded good, and so I took a bottle, untwisted the cap and took a swig. My thoughts floated to Holly, wondering what she would do in my situation, knowing a tour of Mackinac Island wouldn't be the first item on her agenda.

And so, I started looking around.

A small living space with a couch and recliner, both worn and varying shades of brown, was just past the kitchen. I touched the back of the couch, my eyes drawn to a room off to the side. I peered through the doorway and was rewarded with a full view of where Troy Phillips laid his head at night.

Rustic pictures of white-tailed deer lined the walls, interspersed with a pine dresser and full-sized bed that had seen better days. Once again, my thoughts flew to Amanda, wondering if they had shared this space, knowing they had.

Beside the bed was a small, lopsided nightstand with a lamp and a picture. I got closer, fascinated by what the photo might tell me about the man showering in the next room.

"Caught ya!"

I jumped, something that sounded like a yak giving birth escaping my mouth.

"Sorry," Troy said, and I spun around, watched him towel dry his hair with a few brisk strokes. "Didn't mean to scare you."

I smiled while trying to pretend I wasn't checking him out and was pleased with the khaki shorts and white tee shirt he'd chosen for this semi-special occasion.

"I can start the tour here," he said. "With that picture you were looking at."

I frowned, embarrassed. "I didn't mean to snoop."

"Snoop all you want," he shrugged. "I've got no secrets."

I grinned like a fool, liking the way his words made me feel when he handed me the picture. I looked closely; saw what appeared to be an old picture of Troy's family. He was standing in front of two older boys, a man and a woman behind, their hands on the shoulders of the children in front of them.

"That's Mom and Dad and my older brothers, Mike and Steve."

I nodded, thinking how cute Troy looked as a youngster, imagining his idyllic childhood in the wilds of the Upper Peninsula. "Are you close?"

He nodded. "Mom and Dad still live in our old house. They were high school sweethearts. I get up there whenever I can."

I smiled, wishing I had an equally endearing story to accompany my own parents. "What about your brothers?"

"Steve took off for Chicago. Mike's married with two kids."

"Oh?" I asked, intrigued with how he fit into the fabric of his family.

"His wife's great. Always cooks for me when I come over."

"She does?" I asked, wondering what his favorite meal might be.

"Gives her an excuse to hassle me about settling down."

I nodded, uncomfortable with the *Leave it to Beaver*-esque feel of the moment. "That's cool. If you like being hassled, I mean."

"Don't like it a bit, but I do hope I'm as happy as them someday."

I stared at him, thinking of the life I'd have with a man whose family liked me. The idea seemed as foreign as a popcorn kernel stuck in my teeth and Troy must have noticed, because he shook his head and laughed. "Were you expecting something crazy? Sorry to disappoint you."

"No," I shook my head, the magical feeling I'd hoped for when I came here in full effect. "It's nice...I mean--"

"I know I'm lucky."

"You are," I said, my voice dropping.

"I want my kids to have the same life I did," he paused, an almost dreamy look on his face. "I'm saving up to buy some land on the Au Train River. It's a good sixty acres with low ground for hunting and a nice meadow for a cabin. Mandy wants room for a garden, so I might have to clear some trees out back and--"

He stopped short.

"Troy?" I asked.

He ran a hand over his head, tried to smile. "Sometimes I don't think about what'll happen if she doesn't get better."

I moved closer, put a hand on his arm.

"She will."

"Yeah?" he looked down, his eyes weary. "Can you see into the future, too?"

"Nope," I paused, my thoughts floating like a feather on the wind. "But I have a good feeling about you two. And I'm hardly ever wrong."

He smiled, lifted his arm, and motioned for the door. "Let's get going. My apartment is the least exciting part of this tour."

I wanted to argue but followed him out the door and down the steps instead.

Once at the bottom, he pointed to a horse that had stuck its head out of its stall.

"See that guy?" he asked. "If it wasn't for him, Mandy and I would never have met."

I waited, wanting to hear the story.

"She was feeding Walt the wrong stuff and I got pretty fired up. I'm surprised she gave me a second chance."

"Did you know about Ethan?" I asked, not sure if I should.

"No," his face hardened almost instantly. "I was head over heels by the time she got around to telling me."

I smiled to myself, imagining Troy Phillips "head over heels" and coming up with some delightful scenarios.

"I knew Ethan was working with the family and that Mandy didn't want to marry him. Something about not getting her inheritance if she didn't."

I scrunched up my face as we walked towards the paddock fence. "Really?"

"I know, right?" he nodded. "I didn't know shit like that happened in the twenty-first century."

I nodded, a strange question forming about the man I'd chased through the woods. "But if he's as rich as you say, why would he steal an old snakeskin? How would he even know where it was?"

Troy shrugged. "Nothing about Ethan makes sense. He came out of nowhere; waving his money around and three weeks later Mandy's grandparents decide to blackmail her into an arranged marriage."

"But she's a grown woman," I said, perplexed by something. "Why didn't she just say no?"

He frowned, touched Walt's neck and the white star above his nose. "Her mom's really sick and barely making ends meet. Mandy pays for everything. She needs the money."

"What's wrong with her?" I asked, wondering again if I was pushing things too far.

He looked up into the sky, shook his head. "It started after Mandy's dad died in that motorcycle accident. She started talking to people who weren't there, disappearing into the woods, and that's when the grandparents had to step in. There's a doctor who thinks he can get her on some new meds but it's expensive and," he paused. "She can't afford it."

I frowned. "You could take care of Mandy and her mom better than anyone else. She'd get a part-time job and you could build a house on that sixty acres you want to buy with the meadow," I put my hands around the topmost board and closed my eyes. "On the Au Train River."

Troy didn't answer at first, and so I opened my eyes, hoping I hadn't offended him, and was surprised to see him staring at me, his eyes full of something I couldn't put my finger on.

"That's what I told her," he said, his voice low. "But she didn't believe it."

I drew a breath, reached up to scratch Walt's ear. "When you've been on your own it's hard to believe anyone will help you."

He reached over, scratched Walt's other ear, his eyes meeting mine. "Seems like you speak from experience."

I looked down. "Maybe," a slight pause. "But things are different now...with Dylan."

Troy smiled, leaned against the stall to face me. "How'd you meet him?"

"My roommate ran him off the road, and we wound up in the ditch. He came back to see if we were alright."

"And that was it, huh?" he asked, his tone light. "Love at first sight?"

I laughed, glanced at my feet, not wanting to talk about Dylan anymore.

"Can't say I blame him."

I looked up quickly and was greeted with his lazy smile as he pushed off the fence. "Let's walk."

I followed in a sort of haze, forgetting about Ethan and the snakeskin and Meg and Amanda and everything else that seemed to be falling apart on the mainland.

We wandered away from the West Bluff and turned towards the center of the Island, down paved roads that ran along the edge of a groomed lawn, a white rampart bordering the edge.

"That's Fort Michilimackinac," Troy said, his shoulder brushing mine. "They blow off the cannon once in a while so don't freak out."

I put a hand to my chest, feigned offense. "I don't freak out. When have I ever *freaked* out?"

Troy smiled, "In my apartment when I caught you looking at that picture. You're wound pretty tight, Justine Cook."

I laughed again, liking that he might be joking with me.

"Can you blame me?"

He shook his head. "Hell, no."

We turned from the Fort and made our way into the cedar lined interior, secret paths darting left and right and I couldn't help but wonder where they led, wanting to wander these woods forever until we found ourselves standing in front of a limestone stack that looked as though it had been there since the beginning of time.

Troy stopped and shaded his eyes against the sun.

"That's Sugarloaf."

"Sugarloaf?" I repeated, shading my eyes as well.

"The Ojibwa thought it was the wigwam of the Great Spirit."

I turned to him, suddenly playful "What do you think?"

He smiled, shook his head. "The jury's still out on that one, but there's another place I want to show you. Not many people know about it."

"Oh?" I asked, the thought of wandering to a secret corner of this island with Troy Phillips casting a net of delight over me. "What is it?"

"If I told you, it wouldn't be a surprise," he said, turning, so he could jog backwards and I smiled again, quickened my pace to keep up.

We left the main trail, and after about fifteen minutes of wandering, found ourselves in a small clearing covered in myrtle and surrounded by birch, a blanket of what looked like snow on the ground before us.

"Troy?" I asked, my heart hammering in my chest. "What is this place?"

"They call it a Whisper Stone," he replied, the sun leaving dappled shadows across his back and shoulders. "There are a few in the area and legend says if you stand on a certain spot a great wind will--"

"Carry you back to your ancestors," I finished. "My grandparents went to one when they were young."

He turned, reached back and I took his hand without question.

"The rock is under the snow."

"The snow?"

He smiled. "It's just reindeer moss. But snow sounds better, doesn't it?"

I turned in a circle, convinced I'd stepped into some fantastical kingdom I never wanted to leave. "It's beautiful."

Troy smiled, his hand still in mine, guiding me further into the clearing. "There it is."

I stepped cautiously towards where the smooth dome of stone swept above the moss, giving it the appearance of an island just breaking the surface of a foamy sea.

"It doesn't seem real," I whispered, unnerved to be in this place.

He nodded, bent down, and touched the surface of the Stone. "The Ojibwa carved markings into it. They say this place isn't like anywhere else on earth."

I felt a giggle bubble up in my throat. "But that's just an excuse for the boys to get the girls alone in the woods, right?"

He smiled and looked up at me. "It worked, didn't it?"

I felt heat rise in my chest and moved to the edge of the Stone, feeling the presence of Odessa and Butler and Jonas and Esther, the folds of time that separated us only a whisper now.

"Be careful," I heard him say. "It's just a story but things aren't always what they seem. Especially here."

I turned, looked at him carefully. "Do you think there's any truth to it?"

"Can't say for sure," he didn't move. "Mandy showed me this place. Her mother knew about it."

"She did?" I asked, feeling like I could lie down in the soft moss and sleep forever.

"She was drawn to it, and I don't know why," he paused, seeming to catch his breath. "It felt right to bring you here."

I looked around, my head light as birds began to sing in the trees above, sunlight sliding between branches, making everything fluid and heavy and--

My cell phone vibrated in my back pocket.

I didn't want to answer it, didn't want the person on the other end to destroy what was happening here. Still, I knew I couldn't ignore the outside world forever and ignoring phone calls was sure to arouse suspicion.

I fished the phone out and answered it.

"J--" I heard Dylan's voice in a garble of static. "Where are you?"

I looked around, wondering the same thing as Troy's eyes held mine in a way that seemed to stop time.

"I'm..." I began, my tongue thick in my mouth. "I don't know."

"Justine," he said. "Come home now."

I felt like laughing, felt like diving beneath the surface of this snowy sea and never coming up for air again.

"Why?" I asked, watching the trees flow with the wind like reeds in a river, wondering why it mattered so much when that morning he couldn't wait to get rid of me.

"Meg," he said, the line breaking up and in that syllable, the jaw of my mind became set.

"I don't want to talk about her," I said, wondering if he heard me. Not caring if he did when the call went dead.

The next minute Troy was there, pulling me away from the Stone and whatever power seemed to be holding us there.

"It's getting late," he said, and I glanced at the light, saw that it had weakened.

"It is?" I asked.

"Are you okay?" he said, his words a strange reminder of things that could be touched and seen and tasted.

"I don't," I put a hand to my forehead. "I don't know."

He stopped walking, looked back at me.

"It's this place."

I held his gaze, felt the heaviness lift as a breeze blew from some secret valley scented with pine. "Something's different here," I whispered, my head spinning "Something--"

"I know," he interrupted, taking my hand again. "And we need to leave."

CHAPTER
TWENTY-SIX

Amanda lay in bed, unable to move or speak as Adam and Pam and her mother hovered over her.

"Something's happened," Pam said, touching her son's arm. "Do you know what she's saying?"

Amanda looked to the boy who had been her lifeline to the outside world and saw him shake his head, his large eyes reflecting his terror.

"What's happened to my daughter?" Sara Bennett asked, her hands knotted at her waist.

Seconds later they heard someone open the front door and Pam hurried out. A male voice carried in from the threshold, agitated, authoritative, and Amanda wondered who they trusted enough to let enter the tiny world they'd been sheltering.

She listened, heard Pam ask about the girl named Meg and knew it was Dylan.

Moments later he entered the room quickly and came to her bedside.

"Amanda," he said, sitting down beside her. "I'm sorry about what happened to you."

She lay there, recognizing him as the man with Meg in her vision and understood why Justine loved him.

"Was Adam able to talk to her before?" he turned to Pam.

"Yes...but," she trailed off. "Something happened."

"I think I know," he said, his voice catching. "Meg," another pause. "She's dead."

Amanda tensed on the bed, remembered the girl sinking into the earth, remembered Troy taking her place.

"What happened?" Pam gripped his arm.

Amanda watched him closely, looking for signs that he had loved her and understood that he was confused. Like she had once felt about Ethan.

"I don't know," he said, visibly upset, and Amanda saw her mother move in the corner of the room, watched her eyes flicker to Dylan for an instant before darting off in another direction. "When I left the hospital this afternoon, she was stable."

"Stable?" Pam repeated. "How?"

"Dry drowning. It can happen after a person's been pulled from the water." He stopped, blinked quickly. "Brenda called looking for Justine, said she left some kind of weird message."

"You don't know where she is?" Pam asked, her eyes widening.

"No," he answered, his voice tense. "We had a fight and I said some things I shouldn't have and now she won't talk to me."

Pam pressed her lips together and looked away, not wanting to ask more when Dylan turned to Adam, bending close, so he could look him in the eye.

"Do you know where your sister is?" he asked. "I got through to her but then the line went dead."

"Dylan--" Pam said, one hand over her mouth. "Do you think she might be next?"

Amanda looked at Adam again, willing him to hear Troy's name as she screamed it over and over in her mind.

"I don't know," Dylan answered, shaken by the thought. "But either way he's going after her."

One glance at Adam and Amanda knew he was telling the truth.

"We need to find her," Pam insisted. "I'll call Holly--"

"Already did," Dylan cut her off. "She doesn't know."

"Troy," Pam blurted, casting a sideways glance at Amanda.

Dylan came to her again, took her hand, and squeezed tightly. "Can you tell me who's next?"

She looked at him, wanting her voice more than anything else on earth.

"Is it Justine?" he asked. "Do you see her?"

Amanda tried to shake her head, tried to make her muscles move in a way they had only a few hours before and felt an invisible cord tighten around her.

"I'm calling Troy," Pam said, grabbing her phone. Moments later she hung up, frustrated. "It went straight to voicemail."

"Shit," Dylan cursed, stepping away and rubbing the back of his neck with his hand. "Where does he live?"

Pam looked to Amanda. "He logs around St. Ignace and works part-time on Mackinac Island. He has an apartment, but I don't know where it is." She turned to Sara, who had drifted into a corner. "Do you know?"

Amanda watched her mother look away.

"Sara!" Pam cried. "Where does Troy live?"

The woman started, her eyes lingering on Dylan again. "He took the curve too fast and I knew he was dead before the police told me."

"Sara," Dylan began, his voice low. "Can you tell us where Troy lives?"

She shook her head, a strange smile on her lips. "You look so much like him. So much..."

They stood watching her before Dylan pivoted on his heel, unable to stand still. "I'm going to drive around and start looking for her."

"You don't even know where to start," Pam said, hugging herself.

Amanda watched him turn, his face a blaze of anger. "Well, I'm not staying here while that asshole hunts her down."

Pam looked at the floor, and when she spoke again, her words were measured. "We need to ask Adam. If she's in danger, he'll know it."

She paused, her eyes seeking the same person Amanda had moments before.

"Adam!" Pam cried, pushing past Dylan to get to the other room. "Where is he?"

Dylan followed as she ran to the front door and pulled it open.

"Adam!" she screamed, her voice catching the breeze and carrying across the lake. "Adam!"

Dylan came up behind her, put a cautious hand on her shoulder. "He heard us talking about Justine."

She spun to face him; her eyes wild. "Do you think he's gone to help her?"

"Yes."

"What do we do?"

Dylan turned, his eyes seeking Amanda's.

"We let him."

Troy and I made it to town just as the sun began to sink across the harbor, still energized by our experience in the clearing.

"What happened up there?" I asked, questions swirling like fireflies in a mason jar.

He shook his head, motioned for us to cross the street. "I don't know, but it's never affected me that way before," he stopped once we got to the other side, touched my shoulder. "You felt it, too?"

I nodded, looked up to discover we were now standing on the sidewalk in front of The Pink Pony.

"Let's get inside," he said, motioning towards the bar and I nodded, not wanting to think about the person he'd taken here before or the guy stuck back in Presque Isle County wondering where I was.

Glancing back, he took my hand as we wove our way through people who had gathered to eat inside, soft music mixing with the deep horn of a ferryboat.

I felt my cell phone vibrate again and sped up, hoping Troy didn't notice, embarrassed when he said, "You should get that."

I nodded, pulled it out of my pocket, and answered with an annoyed, "Yeah?"

A garbled voice came through, but I knew who it was.

"I'm having dinner with a friend," I snapped. "I'll call you back later."

"Meg," Dylan said, his voice rising, "She's--"

The line went dead.

I looked at Troy, his hands shoved into his pockets, the deck lights beckoning a few steps away and thought about what I should do.

Dylan wasn't the clingy type, if he knew I needed to be by myself he always gave me the space I needed.

Which meant something was wrong.

"What's going on?" Troy asked, watching my face.

"Dylan called again," I said, the first pinpricks of fear piercing my chest. "But the line went dead."

He cocked his head, "You should call him back."

I knew he was right but hearing about Meg and Mom and Paul and how his pointless intervention with Melinda Locke had gone wasn't high on my agenda.

Still, I didn't want Troy to think I was a total jerk.

My call went straight to voicemail.

"I can't get through," I said, hanging up.

"Should I try Pam?"

I frowned, sat down on a bench just outside the deck doors, and tried to think. If something was wrong Adam would've told me, and so I decided to nip this little buzzkill right in the bud.

ADAM?

I looked to Troy, waiting for my brother's response, and he seemed to know what I was doing.

HAS SOMETHING HAPPENED TO MEG?

I waited again, disturbed by his silence.

SHE'S OKAY.

I glanced at Troy again.

DYLAN KEEPS CALLING.

HE KNOWS YOU'RE WITH TROY.

I frowned. So, he was jealous, was he? I thought back to the night before and how I had practically begged him to have sex with me only to watch him roll over and fall asleep. Memories of the phone conversations where I'd heard Meg's voice in the background came next, along with the whispered assurances that everything was fine as we lay in bed at night.

I'LL BE HOME TOMORROW.

I waited for my brother's response, wondering why he didn't try to talk sense into me and felt uneasiness settle across my shoulders.

"What'd he tell you?" Troy asked, and I glanced up at him, my discomfort rising.

"Nothing," I said, wondering if I should say that Dylan was jealous, not wanting to label what was going on for fear it would destroy the pretense. "Everything's okay."

He smiled. "Then let's have a drink."

I followed him down the steps and onto a deck that overlooked the harbor, a tiki bar situated off to the left, white lights strung above our heads in a crisscross pattern. Acoustic guitar music drifted from some dim corner, and I imagined this must be a regular gig for the musician as patrons seemed to have gathered to hear him.

Troy moved ahead, nodding to a few people who knew him before settling on a table by the water. Moments later, he pulled out a chair for me and I sank into it.

A waiter sauntered over, and soon after we had two drinks in front of us.

I leaned back in my chair, taking in the sights and smells of the harbor and the easy life it seemed to promise.

"It's nice out here."

He nodded. "One of my favorite places."

I smiled, took a drink while returning his gaze over the top of my glass as a soft breeze toyed with my hair. "How did you get here?"

Troy seemed thoughtful, as though the story of how he came to this place was one he cherished. "We had a few horses in our back pasture growing up and Dad taught me and my brothers all about them. Working here with the good ones was always his dream but Mom never wanted to leave the homestead and I thought," he paused. "I thought I'd do what he couldn't. And I wanted to make him proud."

I leaned forward on my elbows, the feel of the liquor numbing my inhibitions. "Is he?"

He shrugged. "Dad doesn't say much, but sometimes when I talk about a certain horse, he gets this look in his eye, like he wishes it were him. And then I know."

I smiled, took another slow drink, and thought about the man sitting across the table from me and his journey from the wilds of the Upper Peninsula to horse wrangler extraordinaire.

"Don't you start."

I laughed, pushed my hair behind my ear. "Start what?"

"Feeling sorry for the lumberjack who still wants Daddy's approval."

I leaned back in my chair. "Don't we all want that?"

"I guess so," he smiled, his gaze lingering as the guitarist began an acoustic version of *How Deep is Your Love*. The couple next to us stood and made their way to the makeshift dance floor in the center of the patio and I imagined what it would feel like to move slowly in his arms while the sharp world went soft around us.

"Wanna dance?" he asked, extending his hand across the table and I felt my heart gallop away like one of his horses.

The next moment he was standing, and I felt pulled by an invisible thread to follow.

"Are you okay with this?" Troy asked once we were near the others, his breath in my ear as his arms closed around me.

I nodded, unable to speak as the breeze fanned my heated cheeks.

"Sure?"

I smiled, placed my hands on his shoulders as the music carried me to a place I knew would remain seared in my memory forever.

"You're beautiful," he said, his lips just brushing my earlobe. "I hope Dylan tells you that."

The sound of his name made me hesitate, pull back.

"What is it?" he asked, and I looked up into his eyes, brought my hand to the side of his face.

Moments seemed to suspend in a continuum all their own while the guitarist told his love story through song. I closed my eyes, imagined the twinkling lights taking flight like a million stars cut loose from the thread that bound them as a boat turned slowly into the harbor. Laughter drifted over from the docks, and I felt the rough stubble of Troy's cheek against my palm, the smell of sawdust and soap lingering on his skin.

The next moment his fingers were under my chin, tilting my face towards his. I knew what he wanted, knew what I wanted, and didn't resist--just like I couldn't slow the rapid beating of my heart that told me this moment could mark the end of the life I'd created with Dylan.

I heard my name low in his throat, tilted my face as his mouth closed over mine.

A searing sensation coursed through my arms and legs, making them useless. I noticed how his touch differed from Dylan's, his large hands splayed against the small of my back in a way that made me feel safe. And while Dylan possessed the grace of a natural athlete, Troy had the primal elegance of a man who tamed the wild corners of the earth other people feared.

I reached up, ran my fingers through the thick hair at the nape of his neck, and pulled him closer, his hands traveling from my waist down to the place where my shorts met my legs.

One moment he was leaning into the kiss, his lips opening to mine and the next he was pulling away, a look of confusion on his face.

"I--I'm sorry," he stammered, his hands loosening. "I shouldn't have done that."

"It's not your fault," I said, my breath shallow. "I'm just... I'm not myself."

"Me, either."

We stood in place for several seconds, the reality of what we had done seeping past the magical veil the Island had draped around us.

"Troy," I began, unable to think, my pulse pounding in my temples.

"Don't say anything," he said, one finger lingering on the fading bruise on my jaw. "The last ferry left a half hour ago. You'll have to stay at my place tonight."

I felt a stab of panic. Dylan was home, pacing the floors of the bungalow, and I was going to spend the night with the lumberjack I'd just kissed.

"I'll sleep on the couch," he said quickly.

"No," I stammered. "You don't have to do that."

"This can't happen again."

I looked away; couples still dancing on either side of us, and felt shame stain my cheeks.

Troy paused, watching me closely. "Don't think what you're thinking."

I looked up.

"In another time and another place, I wouldn't have let you go."

I smiled, my heart unraveling as he took my hand and led me away from the deck and into the darkness.

CHAPTER
TWENTY-SEVEN

I laid on my back in Troy Phillips' bed, covers pulled up to my chin, dressed in one of his old tee shirts and tried to count sheep.

It wasn't working.

After leaving The Pink Pony we climbed the hill behind Saint Anne's Church to check on Ethan's apartment before heading back to the stables.

Since our kiss I felt uncomfortable, but not in the way I expected. Troy was a gentleman and didn't lay the blame at my feet.

What bothered me most was that it made me forget my life in Lantern Creek even existed.

I thought about Meg, remembered how her face had gone slack when she saw Dylan in our kitchen, remembered how he had gripped the door frame and understood how he felt.

Once at the apartment, Troy made up a bed for himself on the couch, telling me afterwards that we would have to catch the first ferry in the morning.

"I thought you were coming to the cabin," I asked, disturbed by my disappointment.

"I need to finish up a job on Hay Lake first. All the other guys went to the next landing but my boss needs me to finish up," he said, lingering in the doorway before turning out the lights.

I looked at the ceiling and crossed my legs at the ankles, suddenly hyper-aware of my body. I imagined Troy coming into the bedroom, imagined him pulling the tee shirt over my head and making love to me in the darkness of his bedroom, and felt a warm tingle sweep my skin.

I rolled over on my side, allowed myself to imagine what sort of lover he would be and felt my shoulders tighten.

I squeezed my eyes shut, a mixture of guilt and desire crushing me. Reaching for my phone, I dialed Dylan's number and waited, wondering what I would say if he answered and if he would ever forgive me for not telling him about Meg.

My call went straight to voicemail.

"Hey," I tried to sound nonchalant. "I just wanted you to know I'm okay and staying with a friend."

I set my phone aside, undone by how much I wanted to hear his voice, by how badly I wanted to go back to the bungalow because as nice as it felt to bunk in Troy's bed, it still wasn't home.

I closed my eyes as tears squeezed past my lids.

I wasn't sure when I began to dream.

I was standing in the clearing covered with snow when I saw Troy approaching.

"Justine," he said. "We need to leave."

I looked around, felt the heavy flow of time slide past my body, and nodded.

"Where do we go?" I asked, extending my hand, watching with fascination as Troy's fingers closed around my own.

"Anywhere," he answered, pulling lightly as we moved silently, uncertainty following as we entered a valley shadowed by pines. I looked up, unnerved by how they bent towards us, and tightened my grip.

"It's okay," he whispered. "I won't let anything happen to you."

I wanted to tell him the same thing.

Dylan and I were connected by our ancestors and the power of the medicine bag. But Troy...

He had appeared suddenly and without pretense, never representing anything other than what he was, and it made me question whether the magic surrounding me would protect him as well.

A pine tree cracked above our heads, and we looked up, watched as the top came crashing down just in front of us.

"Move!" Troy cried, pulling me behind.

Another crack, another groan, and I lost my grip, felt something separate us as a large branch fell, its dark fingers seeming to pry us apart.

"Justine!" I heard him yell, felt the ground soften as I sank into it.

I was up to my knees, the earth seeming to enfold me in a black blanket as it closed past my hips and shoulders, covering my face and I took a last breath, my lungs catching fire.

I opened my eyes, saw that I was in another part of the woods. Turning slowly, I watched as a strange fog rose from the ground up, surrounding me.

"Justine," I heard my name again, but on another man's lips.

The man I had loved without question for the last year.

The man I loved even as I lay sleeping in Troy Phillips' bed.

I moved towards the sound, saw a flash of white through the darkness, and made my way towards it, ducking down as branches swiped at my face.

"Dylan," I said, my voice barely a whisper. "Where are you?"

"I'm here," he answered, and I moved forward, afraid of what I might find. "Hurry."

That word was enough to send me scrambling through the brush, the snowy clearing in sight.

I blinked hard, blinded by the sudden light, and tried to take in my surroundings.

Dylan lay on his side, blood staining the moss just under his stomach.

I felt a scream break my throat as I dropped to my knees.

"Justine," he said again as he reached a blood-streaked hand towards me.

"Dylan," I panted, touching him with the tips of my fingers. "Oh, my God."

"I was looking for you," he whispered.

I shook my head, grabbed the hand he held out to me, and kissed it, his blood staining my lips.

"He's coming," Dylan said, "He knows where you are."

I linked his fingers with my own, looked up into the trees. "Where am I?"

"Don't you know?" I looked down, saw Dylan smile, his teeth dark with blood and recoiled from the sight. "You're in hell, Muffet."

I stood up, backed away as Henry Younts heaved himself from the ground in front of me, his teeth still stained with blood.

"I'll see you soon."

My body stiffened as a scream spilled over my lips.

An overhead light flipped on, and I blinked, covered my face.

"Justine?"

I sat up quickly, ran the back of my hand across my sweaty forehead, and tried to get my bearings. Looking around, I saw Troy sitting on the side of the bed, one hand on my shoulder.

"What the hell happened?"

I shook my head. "I don't know--"

"I heard you scream," he said. "I thought someone was in here."

I backed up against the pillows, put a shaky hand to my mouth.

"It was a nightmare," I whispered. "But I saw *you*."

"Me?" he asked, confused.

"We were running through the woods and then I lost you."

He moved closer. "I'm right here. I'm okay."

I looked up at him.

"Did you see anything else?"

I shook my head, unable to talk about Dylan bleeding to death in front of me, or Henry Younts rising from the snowy ground, his smile a smear of red.

I felt him pull back, unsure what to do, and reached for his hand.

"Stay with me."

"Justine--"

"I need you."

He leaned back, touched my shoulder, "I don't think--"

"I'm so afraid. And I need to sleep."

"It's not that," he said, unsettled.

I looked at him, my eyes questioning.

"I don't know if I can just *hold* you."

"Please," I whispered. "If you're here I know nothing bad will happen."

I saw his eyes soften, saw the protectiveness that was at the core of his being awaken with my words.

"Okay," he said as he laid down beside me.

Once settled, I turned away from him, my back against his chest as he wrapped his arms around my waist. We stayed that way until his breathing became rhythmic, and I felt my body loosen, release, and succumb to sleep.

CHAPTER
TWENTY-EIGHT

I woke up in Troy's arms the next morning, still shaken from my nightmare and felt him stir behind me, realizing that he'd been awake for some time.

"Hey, sleepyhead," he whispered in my ear. "I was just about to wake you up."

I smiled into my pillow, wondering how the happiness I felt could ever mesh with what was waiting for me in Lantern Creek.

And so, we got dressed--me in my clothes from the day before and him in canvas pants and a red shirt. He made me a bowl of Cheerios, and we sat at the table, eating in silence while considering how to explain what had happened to our significant others.

"I'm coming to the cabin tonight," he said, clearing his throat. "I need to see Mandy."

I nodded, looked down at my bowl.

"Justine."

I raised my eyes.

"I'm glad you came."

I felt my heart lift. "Me, too."

After breakfast, we walked back to the docks, watching the ferry boats that were waiting to take us in opposite directions.

I stood watching the morning light skate across the bay and wondered how many lovers had parted in this place, and in this way.

"Call when you get to the cabin," he said once my boat had pulled into its berth.

"Sure," I said, wanting to touch him one last time but knowing it would taint what we had managed to preserve.

"I asked a friend to keep an eye on Ethan's apartment."

I nodded my thanks, then boarded the ferry in silence, watching as he stood on the docks, raising his hand once before turning towards the boat that would take him to St. Ignace.

I rode across the Straits in silence, my heart heavy as I thought about all that awaited me back home. One glance at my phone told me Dylan hadn't called and a feeling of apprehension began to replace the sadness that preceded it.

My magical evening on Mackinac Island was now exposed to the harsh light of day, and as much as I wanted to see Dylan again, another part longed to stay with Troy Phillips above the stables while he lunged the horses his father dreamed of.

I thought about my restless night, thought about the dream that startled me from sleep as the Mackinac Bridge slid by the starboard window, worrying about Meg and Mom and for just a moment, Paul.

I thought all these things as I docked in Mackinaw City, climbed into the Jeep, and headed south towards Lantern Creek.

I glanced out the window, wanting to rewind the clock and go back to the snow-covered clearing where time seemed to stop.

My phone made a noise, and I glanced down, saw that I had a message.

Moments later another sound alerted me to a second one.

And then a third.

And then a fourth and a fifth.

I reached for my phone, listened to the first message.

"Justine," Mom's voice was frantic. "Call me as soon as you get this."

I bit my lip, listened to the next one.

"J," Dylan said, his voice rising. "It's Meg," a slight pause. "She's dead."

The road seemed to dissolve into tiny droplets as my vision became pinpointed on a single ball of light.

I opened my mouth, felt my breath escape in shallow spurts.

Meg was dead? It was impossible. Adam would have told me.

I looked for a place to pull over and made a wide sweep into a gas station and rolled to a stop in front of the one and only pump.

Trembling, I listened to the third message.

"Holy Moses, Squirt, pick up the friggin' phone! We need to know where the heck you are!"

The fourth was from Pam, similar to Holly's and the fifth was Dylan again, his voice breaking my heart in a way I didn't know was possible.

"Baby, I'm sorry for everything. Please, just come home to me."

All he wanted was for me to come back to the bungalow, and I'd been slamming drinks and locking lips with Troy at a Mackinac Island bar. I put my head against the steering wheel, tried to calm my breathing as I gulped in air. I had to pick up my phone, had to call Dylan but the task seemed impossible.

SIS!

My head jolted up, anger scalding my veins.

WHY DIDN'T YOU TELL ME ABOUT MEG?

I COULDN'T HEAR YOU.

BUT I TALKED TO YOU LAST NIGHT! YOU SAID EVERYTHING WAS OKAY.

IT WASN'T ME!

I thought back to last summer, thought about Dylan forgetting his cell phone at the bar and taking off for the Falls, my voice sounding in his ears.

Or what he thought was my voice.

I HAVE OUR NECKLACES.

ADAM...I paused, remembering my dream. Not wanting to remember. *WHO'S NEXT?*

My brother was silent, and it ignited a wildfire of terror within my chest.

TROY.

I felt the world swim before me as I pictured his half-smile at the docks, one hand raised in farewell, asking me to call him when I made it to the cabin.

I put my head down again, felt a sob break free from my throat as a horn honked from somewhere because a person out in the real world needed to get gas and I couldn't lift my head, couldn't do anything but cling to my brother's voice like the lifeline it was.

WHERE IS HE?

HE'S UP AT HAY LAKE. HE'S ALONE.

YOU WON'T GET THERE IN TIME.

I lifted my head, slammed my foot down on the gas.

WATCH ME.

I PULLED BACK onto the road, reached for my phone, and hit Dylan's number.

He answered on the first ring.

"Where are you?"

"I called you last night," I stammered. "I left a message."

"I never got it," he said, his voice breaking. "Are you okay?"

I fought back tears, thinking of what he'd been through the night before.

"Yes," I whispered, "I'm going to Hay Lake to find Troy."

"I'm on my way."

I thought about what I might find at the landing, thought about my nightmare, and knew Dylan Locke was the only man I wanted by my side.

Ever.

"Hurry," I barely managed. "I need you."

He hesitated, the love that had come so easily before Amanda Bennett pouring over us like spring rain.

"I'll be there."

Twenty minutes later I was crossing the Mackinac Bridge, pictures of Troy working alone while the monster who murdered my father stalked him from the forest tormenting me. I thought about Meg, thought about her life being snuffed out because of a random encounter with me and my fucked-up life.

To my surprise, I felt tears spill over my cheeks, tears for my mother and Paul, for Dylan--who'd been left alone to deal with the horror I'd avoided by running off to Mackinac Island. I thought about the totems and Butler and how his love for Odessa was more of a curse than a blessing and wished he'd never given her the medicine bag.

I gripped the wheel, my knuckles white as I sailed through the toll booth and tore up the road towards Hay Lake, praying I wasn't too late to save a man who meant more to me than I ever imagined he would.

I pictured Troy walking into the woods with his chainsaw slung over his shoulder, his red shirt slashing the forest like a walking wound.

I gripped the wheel tighter, looked at my GPS for directions to Hay Lake because no way in hell were there signs for it.

I swerved down a rutted two track, scanning the area for the landing he'd described the night before when I saw a blue pickup parked up ahead.

I slammed on the brakes, jumped out of the Jeep, and listened for the sound of his chainsaw.

"Troy!" I screamed.

Nothing.

I scrambled to his truck, looked in the bed, and saw that it was empty. A trail to the left caught my eye and I took off at a dead run, sweat running down my neck as the terrain became steep. For a split-second I thought about Rocky and wished he were here, leading me to Troy as he had Dylan the summer before.

A chainsaw screamed off to my right and I dashed towards it, crashing through the woods, aware that I was putting myself in danger. Not caring that I was.

"Troy!" I screamed again, knowing he couldn't hear me but needing to mark my presence in this dark place.

Seconds later I heard a tree snap, then fall on the other side of a hill just to the left of me. It crashed through the underbrush, branches breaking, followed by a sharp cry.

I didn't waste time, just ran with the speed Butler gave me to the top of the hill, and when I reached the crest, I saw a flash of red below.

"Troy!" I cried, my lungs sucking fire.

I raced towards him, saw that he was lying face down, his lower back pinned by the massive trunk of a white pine.

I ran to his side, skidded to my knees, and braced myself against the side of the trunk.

"Justine," he gasped. "How--"

"Don't talk," I ordered as I scanned the surroundings for any sort of advantage. "I'm getting you out of here."

"You can't--"

"Stop talking!" I yelled, trying to get my bearings. It became obvious that the tree he'd been cutting had rolled down the hillside, pinning him to a muddy patch of low ground--the only thing that had saved him from an instant death.

One look at his breathing and I knew he would suffocate in less than a minute.

I looked at the tree, thought about cutting it apart with his chainsaw but knew there wasn't time. I was strong, had pinned Dylan to the wall just two days ago but nothing had tested me like this.

"Okay," I looked into his eyes. "I'm going to lift and you're going to roll out."

"W--what?" he gasped.

"Do what I say," I whispered, my eyes holding his.

He nodded, willing to believe me and I stood, braced my back against the trunk and began to lift with my legs.

It didn't move.

Scalding terror coursed through my body, making my limbs feel weightless, but I wasn't giving up. Closing my eyes, I thought of the family he'd told me about the night before, of Butler and Odessa, of the medicine wheel and the Elk, Raven, Wolf, and Turtle. I saw the power that bound my grandmother and her child to the man she loved and beyond that, to the life force that lay beating beneath this ancient forest.

I took a deep breath and lifted again.

The tree shifted.

I clenched my teeth, heard Troy pant for air as I locked my knees against the impossible load they were bearing.

"Now!" I gasped, feeling the skin on my back rip where it pressed against the bark of the tree, hoping he had enough strength to roll from beneath before my bones shattered and the trunk came crashing down.

I saw him shimmy against the earth, the red shirt covered in mud and leaves and another dark substance I prayed wasn't blood.

"It's slipping," I gasped, my body burning from the inside out as he rolled free in one, swift motion.

I saw him clear the trunk, felt the pine give way and crash to the earth as I slid to the ground, my back a throbbing mass of agony.

"Justine," I heard Troy rasp as he crawled towards me. "My God."

I couldn't answer, couldn't open my mouth as my body seized up and began to shake.

"Justine," he repeated, at my side now and I looked at him, smeared with dirt and mud and blood--but alive.

"Troy," I reached out, put my hands on either side of his face and pulled my forehead to his.

"How?" he asked, his eyes watery. "It's not possible."

"The totems," I began, my next breath cut short by the sound of another tree breaking close by.

"Something's wrong here," Troy said while staggering to his knees, pulling me up beside him.

I looked around the valley and saw the trees casting long shadows where none should have been and remembered my dream from the night before.

"It's too quiet," Troy whispered, his arm around my waist as he rose unsteadily to his feet.

"What do you mean?"

He paused. "There's a predator nearby."

I looked into his eyes, knew what he was thinking.

"Can you move?" I asked.

He grimaced, tightened his arm around me. "I'll sure as hell try."

I braced my weight against him, remembered Dylan and I **as we escaped** the woods the summer before and knew I'd be doomed to repeat this awful scenario if I didn't kill Henry Younts for good.

"How did you know?" he asked as we staggered towards the landing. "I wouldn't have made it."

"Amanda saw it--"

"Mandy--" he said, his voice rising. "I have to get to her."

I tightened my grip, knowing it was true.

We had just descended a hill when another sound jolted us.

"Move!" Troy yelled. "It's coming down!"

I looked up, saw an oak teetering back and forth and scrambled out of the way as it crashed down behind us.

Troy bent low and I felt the muscles in his back tighten. The next second he was dragging me down the trail, propelled by adrenaline and I listened to the woods scream behind us, watched tree after tree bend forward as if pulled by an invisible rope as we zigzagged over the rough terrain.

Another oak crashed across the path in front of us, blocking our escape.

"Get over!" Troy cried, picking me up and tossing me to the other side. The next instant he was scrambling after, ducking beneath branches as another tree fell, jarring the one he was hiding beneath.

The force of the collision knocked me off my feet, sent me rolling and in that loop of earth and sky I finally caught a glimpse of the Jeep. The next second Troy was yanking me up as we tumbled into a run, the landing just ahead when a pine tree fell forward like a wounded soldier, crushing both vehicles.

We stopped so fast we almost fell.

"What do we do?" I gasped, spinning in a circle, looking up as the forest collapsed around us like a child closing a pop-up book.

"There!" Troy pointed, "Someone's coming."

I drug my eyes back to the two track and saw a familiar truck roaring towards us.

"It's Dylan," I cried, yanking on Troy's arm as another tree broke to our right, showers of leaves and dead branches falling around us.

I watched as the truck skidded to a halt, watched as Dylan jumped out, his long strides bringing him to us.

"Stay inside!" I screamed, terrified that he would be crushed.

It was only then that I saw something in his hand, something I'd been missing since Adam and I had buried it beneath the yellow trees.

He was beside me before I could breathe, looping the necklace over my head, helping Troy as he staggered towards the truck. I took a step to follow but something held me in place. Touching the silver circle as I had so many times before, I knew that Butler was with me.

Knew Dad was with me.

And that I didn't need to run anymore.

Looking up, I watched as the trees began to settle, the wind to quiet, the animals to stir.

"Justine!" Dylan grabbed my arm, his grip fierce. "Get in the truck!"

I started, my mind coming clear, and ran.

CHAPTER
TWENTY-NINE

"I'm Troy Phillips," the lumberjack I'd kissed the night before leaned forward to introduce himself to my boyfriend. "Thanks for saving my life."

Dylan shifted in his seat, glanced at me and said, "You should probably be thanking her."

I looked at my lap, every bone in my body aching, and thought back to the moment I'd first seen Troy pinned beneath the tree.

"It's okay," I said quickly, wanting to get out of the truck and at the same time cower on the floorboards with my hands over my head. "Nothing any law-abiding Michigander wouldn't do."

"Like hell," Troy said. "She lifted a 2000-pound tree off my back like she was fluffing a pillow."

I heard Dylan chuckle, a half-smile on his lips, and felt my heart catch on itself. "Nothing new."

I glanced between the two of them, wondering what to do, my eyes finally settling on Dylan, "Your Jeep--"

"It's okay," he glanced at me, his eyes lingering on what must have been a pitiful sight. "I'm just glad you weren't in it."

I felt my cheeks warm and wondered if now would be a good time to tell him what happened at The Pink Pony.

"How's Mandy?" Troy asked, his words a welcome distraction.

Dylan met his gaze in the rear view mirror. "She wants to see you."

I touched the silver circle at my throat again and the simple motion caught Dylan's eye.

"She's been wearing the other one. It's helping her."

I saw Troy move in the backseat. "What do you mean?"

"It's healing her."

"Healing," Troy repeated, leaning back against the seat and I imagined he must be thinking about the little cabin by the Au Train River.

We rode the rest of the way to Three Fires in silence, and when we reached Cabin Ten, I wasn't surprised when Troy jumped out.

We didn't follow.

Instead, we sat staring out at Ocqueoc Lake as it glittered in the noonday sun, hoping the beauty of our surroundings would shield us from a conversation we should have had last summer.

I saw Dylan glance at me out of the corner of my eye and swallowed, wondering what he would say now that we were alone.

"You look pretty banged up," he paused, emotion softening his voice into something I recognized.

"I've had better days," I said, hoping his concern would be enough to melt the ice that had begun to thaw between us. "My back is killing me."

He reached over, lifted my shirt, and gave a low whistle.

"Did you let Joey scratch it?"

I stifled a giggle, hopeful that everything would be alright again because of a bad joke.

"You should probably see a doctor."

I shook my head, memories tumbling to the moment we met. "Well, money's tight and I can't afford--"

"A trip to the E.R?"

I nodded, looking down at my lap again.

"Did you forget I have spies in this town?"

I smiled. "How could I?"

I felt him reach out, felt his fingers close around mine and was reminded of the first time he'd kissed me while the quarry lights glittered far below.

"I was looking for you all night."

I turned to him, noticed how tired he seemed, how his eyes held the weight of a thousand unanswered questions and felt the heaviness of what I'd done crush me.

I squeezed his hand, looked back at the lake. "I was with Troy."

He was silent for a moment, and when he spoke his voice was low. "I know."

I looked back at him. "You do?"

He nodded, weighing his words carefully "I was pretty sure you wanted to be with someone who appreciated what he had. And that sure as hell wasn't me."

I shifted in my seat, unsure how to respond.

"I'm sorry, J. I know you kept trying to tell me what was going on and I shot you down every time."

I shook my head, feeling some strange need to defend him. "You were scared, I get it--"

"Doesn't matter," he interrupted. "When you love someone, you have to accept the parts of them you don't understand."

I looked straight ahead, thinking of Iris and Ben and the leaf floating in the still pool at the base of their feet.

"You might even learn to appreciate it."

"Dylan--"

"I shut you out, J--and when I thought Henry Younts had gotten to you," he stopped, stroked the top of my hand. "I wouldn't have been able to live with that."

I looked over at him.

"Forgive me."

I felt a wave of relief and covered my face with my hand. "If you can forgive me about Meg."

He shifted in his seat, her name a stark reminder of what had happened.

"I know you didn't want her to die."

I shook my head, "I never wanted anything but you."

I felt his fingers tighten around my own. "Same here."

I sat quietly for a moment before asking, "What happened?"

He didn't answer at first and when I looked at him, he seemed to be struggling with what to tell me.

"Her heart stopped. I'd just left the hospital when your mom called. She couldn't get a hold of you so--"

"I'm so sorry," I interrupted.

"She was a good person," he said, his voice wavering. "And it's my fault she's dead."

"Don't say that."

"Henry Younts is picking people we're close to because he wants to break us. Why else would he go after Meg? And Troy?"

I bit my lip, terrified that he might be right.

"I need to tell you something," I whispered, my heart beating so fast I was sure he could see it. "Troy and I went out for drinks last night at The Pink Pony and there were these cool lights this guy playing this really good song and--"

"Justine--"

"When I thought you didn't want to be with me. When I thought the last year was a mistake--"

"You don't have to say anything, Baby."

"Yes, I do," I insisted, my fingers tightening around his.

"I know I was gone all night but it's," I stopped, emotion clogging my throat. "It's not what you think."

"I know," he reached up, touched the fading bruise on my jaw. "It was the same with Meg."

I smiled, wanting to believe him.

"I want to start over. No questions asked."

"Start over?" I repeated, not daring to believe he was serious.

"Right here," he smiled, and in that moment, he was bending down to look at me on a lonely road that led to the Presque Isle Lighthouse. "Right now."

"Really?" I whispered.

"I did a lot of thinking last night, and you were right," he paused. "I was making everything about last summer."

I drew a breath--a full breath--and leaned back against the seat.

"But there's still something I need to know," I said, my words measured, knowing we could never start over until we had dealt with the past.

"What?" he asked, his eyes holding mine.

"Tell me what happened at the Falls."

I saw his face tighten.

"I need to know what you went through," I paused. "What you're still going through."

"Okay," he began, pain in his eyes and I almost regretted what I'd asked him to do.

I tightened my fingers around his.

"I tried to stop the bleeding on the island," he began, his words coming slowly. "I knew if I didn't get you to the hospital you were going to die. Adam ripped off the bottom of his shirt, and we wrapped up your wrists. I'd already called an ambulance when I figured out where you were."

"When you heard the gunshots?" I asked, remembering the moment I'd killed what I thought was Karen, a grotesque wraith conjured by Red Rover to terrify me.

"Yeah," he said. "It took me almost thirty minutes to get to the trail head; I had to stop a couple of times to check your vitals."

Nausea swelled in my stomach as I imagined him searching for a pulse, hoping to feel an answering beat beneath his fingertips.

"When we got to the ambulance the EMTs took over. Adam and I rode in back."

I knew what was coming next and steeled myself for it.

"You coded twice. They had to use the AED," he paused again. "The blood was everywhere, and I think it shook a couple of the medics up because they started asking questions and I didn't know what to say. I was so messed up and I couldn't think straight, and so I made up that shitty story about us fighting and I'm so sorry, Baby. I never meant to put that on you."

I shook my head. "I don't blame you. I've *never* blamed you."

He looked down. "Watching Adam was the worst part. I've never seen anyone so scared in my life."

I drew a shallow breath, thinking of what my brother had suffered as he imagined the silent world he would inhabit without me.

"He'd be lost without you."

I looked at the lake, blinked hard.

"So would I."

"Dylan--"

"You have no idea how it felt watching them try to save your life, wondering what I'd do if they couldn't."

"Please--" I whispered, knowing now why he'd never talked about it.

"You said one word when they got your heart beating the second time."

I looked at him, startled. "What was it?"

"Dad," he whispered. "You said *'Dad.'*"

I felt a wave of sorrow wash over me, wishing for something different. *Anything* different.

"A part of me wondered if you'd seen him," he stopped, cleared his throat. "And if you were sorry you had to come back."

The tears came then, hot and quick, my heart breaking for the man sitting beside me and I knew I needed to stop living life as though it were nothing more than a series of obstacles that stood between me and my father.

"J," he said, his hand on my cheek. "I shouldn't have told you."

"No," I whispered, covering his fingers with my own. "I asked you to."

"I never left you, Baby--not until they told me you were going to be okay."

I nodded, unable to speak.

"And when you woke up, I'd already convinced myself you'd be better off without me."

"What?" I choked out. "How could you think that?"

He paused, looked out at the lake again, and I studied his profile, loving him more because of his vulnerability. "When you watch someone come that close to death you don't want them to waste a second of their life."

I sat for a moment, stunned. "And that's what you thought would happen if I stayed in Lantern Creek?"

He nodded. "I knew Mom would never accept us, never accept *you* after the story got out. And no one knows how brave you were, cutting yourself with that knife, not knowing if I'd get there in time."

"I knew you would."

He looked at me, touched the side of my face and I knew I would never question his love again.

"And I'm sorry I forgot that," I said. "Sorry I thought you'd throw everything away over a kid with a crush. Sorry that I've spent so much time chasing a ghost."

"It's not a ghost," he said softly, simply.

"Doesn't matter. It's time to end this and get back to our life. Our *real* life."

He smiled, his blue eyes holding mine. "Back to boring?"

I laughed, "No promises, Locke."

He leaned closer, his lips seeking mine.

"Good."

∼

AMANDA WAS STANDING on the porch of Cabin Ten, having walked the fifteen steps it took to get there on her own, her voice reappearing like an old friend and knew it was because of the necklace.

After Adam had disappeared into the night, she had waited with the others while Dylan went to look for Justine. Pam had paced the floor, stopping once in a while to step outside and when the boy returned shortly after daybreak, she hugged him long and hard, tears shining on her cheeks when she saw what was in his hands.

Amanda wondered what they were, wondered if they would help her and Adam came to her, placed one over her head and at once she felt her mind open and release, felt her body uncoil and told him about Troy.

Dylan returned after sunrise, his eyes bloodshot, and sat slumped in a chair with his head in his hands when his cell phone rang.

He stood up, answered it and Amanda saw his face untwist in relief and knew the caller was Justine. Then he was gone, telling them he was going to Hay Lake, assuring her he would find them and bring Troy home, and she prayed he could keep his promise.

Amanda looked out at the lake again, her heart wanting answers, and heard a diesel truck pull up outside the cabin. She turned to see Troy standing in the driveway and put a hand to her mouth, taking three hesitant steps as he closed the distance between them.

"Mandy," he breathed, his strong arms closing around her, and she felt everything inside of her slide into place. He was here. He was alive. And he was hers.

"Troy," she said, her voice rough, and he pulled her into a kiss that seemed to silence the fear that had been building for so long. When she pulled away, she looked at his shirt, saw the blood that had dried on the front of it and asked what happened.

And so, he told her how Justine had lifted the tree off his back, how they had raced through the woods, Dylan saving them just after their vehicles were crushed.

"You're okay," she said, loving the feeling of the words whispering through her throat and teeth and lips. Loving that he could hear her, understand her.

The next moment he was telling her about the night before, explaining what Justine meant to him, and she felt her heart seize up in jealousy--understanding at last how he felt about Ethan.

"I'm sorry, Mandy," he said. "I never meant to hurt you."

She nodded. She knew. And she would forgive them because Justine risked her life to bring him back to her.

"I need," she stopped, thinking carefully about what to say. "I need to thank her."

Troy nodded, stepped back to allow her entrance into the cabin and a few minutes later Justine and Dylan came through the front door. She watched as Adam ran into his sister's arms, watched as the two hugged long and hard. "T--Thank you," she finally said, taking a step forward and Justine looked at her, her large eyes widening. "For saving him."

"No," she stepped away from her brother. "You saved him."

She smiled, looked down as another, darker thought replaced it, one Pam must have been thinking about too because she whispered, "He'll go after someone else now."

Dylan looked at Justine, taking her hand when Pam's cell phone rang.

The next minute she was moving off to answer it and Amanda's eyes flew to her mother, sitting in a corner and wondered if she would ever tell her the truth about her father.

"That was Mallard," Pam said, her voice agitated as Troy and Dylan exchanged glances.

"Mallard--" Justine repeated. "What--"

"I told him what was going on with Ethan," Pam explained. "Told him to keep an eye out."

"An eye out?" Dylan asked.

"We need to get to Huffs."

"Why?" Troy asked, his gaze shifting to Dylan again.

Pam paused.

"He's got Ethan."

CHAPTER
THIRTY

"Ethan," I repeated, the word catching as I spun to face Amanda, wondering how she would take the news.

All the color that had returned to her face suddenly drained and off in the corner, her mother turned.

"We need to go!" Pam snapped, and I was reminded that Mallard might be holding the man against his will. Although I knew he was up to the challenge.

"Troy," Amanda hesitated, and he went to her, put his hands on her shoulders.

"I'll handle him."

Then I was running for the truck, climbing in while Dylan and Adam got in behind me.

Ten minutes later we were at Huffs, and I was taking the steps two at a time, terrified of what might be waiting on the other side of the door.

At first, I saw nothing but the usual mismatched combo of tables and chairs, complimented by the blinking jukebox sitting cock-eyed in the corner.

"Mallard," I called, afraid for my friend, loving him for sticking his neck out. Knowing he would do it again.

Mallard was holding Ethan on a bar stool, his wiry hands pressing him into place.

Dylan tensed beside me, took a step towards Ethan.

"So, you're the asshole who hit her?" he said, and Ethan smiled.

"Only trying to defend myself," he paused. "And besides, she had it coming."

Dylan jerked forward, his usual control gone and Mallard stepped in front, put a hand to his chest.

"Keep your fuckin' cool," he said. "And get in line because I get first crack at this shithead."

I moved forward, put my hand on Dylan's arm as if to say it was okay.

"What happened?" I asked.

"Pam told me to keep an eye out for a black car with the driver's side window busted out and damned if this prick didn't walk in, actin' all uppity an' talking about his fiancee being missing an' how he was lookin' for her. So I just happened to step outside for a smoke--saw the side of his car'd been fucked up and--"

"Where's the snakeskin?" I demanded, my hands balling up, ready to strike at the person who'd taken what was mine.

"What snakeskin?" Ethan asked, smiling slightly. "I don't know what you're talking about."

I gritted my teeth, felt Adam at my side, and wanted to push him back but knew the closer he was the more likely I was to keep a lid on the anger that was lighting me up on the inside.

HE KNOWS SOMETHING.

I nodded, my eyes never leaving Ethan's.

I heard a bang behind me, turned and saw the screen door open as Troy strode in, followed by Pam, Amanda, and Sara.

"Ethan," Amanda said, her voice rising in a way that told me she might break down completely. "What the hell is going on?"

He chuckled under his breath. "So good to see you again, my love. And in good working order."

I watched Troy tense, saw Amanda put a hand on his arm as I had Dylan.

"Where's the snakeskin?" I demanded, stepping forward, ready for round two and was pleased to see a goose egg sized lump on his forehead that must have come courtesy of his steering wheel.

His gaze shifted to me, but he remained silent.

"Answer the lady, you smug fucker," Mallard ordered, his strong hand tightening on Ethan's shoulder.

"I never took anything that wasn't mine," Ethan winced, his eyes seeking Troy's. "Unlike some people in this room."

Troy pushed forward, and Dylan moved quickly, put his hand against his chest as Mallard had only minutes before.

"You wanna go outside and settle this, you sack of shit?"

"There's a line," Dylan muttered. "I've got seconds."

"Troy," Amanda whispered, her face stiff, her hands twisting her fingers.

He turned to her. "I told you I'd handle it--"

"He'll handle it, Mandy," Ethan laughed. "But what he really wants you to do is shut the fuck up."

Troy lurched forward again but this time Dylan couldn't hold him. In two strides he was on top of Ethan, his large fists raining down on his head and shoulders.

I watched as the others stood transfixed by the scene unfolding and knew I had to stop Troy before he killed the only person who could help me.

"Stop!" I yelled, moving between them, my hands closing around Troy's wrist "You're going to kill him!"

He jerked out of my grasp, his eyes on fire as he swung around again.

"Troy!" Amanda cried, her face pinched in agony. "Please--"

He looked up at her, pausing only for an instant before he drew back and punched Ethan in the face.

"Troy!" Dylan shouted, stepping between us as Ethan tipped over on his stool, his head hitting the floor.

"Get away from him!" I screamed, pushing against Troy's chest with both hands. The next second, he was stumbling backwards, catching the corner of the table, knocking it over.

Everyone's gaze shifted to me.

"Better fuckin' listen to her," Mallard jabbed a finger at Troy while hauling Ethan to his feet.

His head seemed to roll on his neck as Mallard shoved him back onto the stool and I saw that Troy had bloodied his nose, split his lip.

"I saw you in the woods," I said. "I saw you take the snakeskin and you're going to tell me where it is."

Ethan laughed again, blood bubbling up over his lips. "Like *hell* I am."

I turned to Adam, who was standing beside me. Reaching out a hand, he touched Ethan's arm and I saw his jaw working, wondered what he was pulling from the man's mind and put my own hand on top of his.

"Tell me where it is."

"F--Fuck you," he whispered, his head rolling again. "Fuck you and this little shit."

"Justine," Dylan said, and I shut my eyes, squeezed harder.

"Tell me," I said again, felt Ethan's muscles loosen and knew we were about to break him.

"I don't have it," he whispered, his breath wheezing. "I never had it."

"What?" I opened my eyes, looked at my brother.

HE'S LYING.

"It burned," he panted, blood pooling out of his lips and landing on the front of his shirt. "It burned during the reversal."

"Then what did you take?" I asked, desperation settling like a clammy hand across the back of my neck. "What did I see?"

"You didn't see anything. I went out there because he told me to," he paused, swallowing. "The snakeskin burned but your blood never put out the fire."

I felt my grip loosen, thinking back to that night. He had been bending down, searching for something but I never actually saw anything in his hands.

White, hot terror scalded my veins as my head began to pound.

I turned to Dylan, his eyes catching mine in what seemed like a free fall.

"J--" he whispered. "I'm so sorry."

"No," I backed away from Ethan. "I don't believe it."

I felt someone beside me, looked over and saw Troy.

"Who told you to go out there?" he asked, his rage still palpable.

"Ask her," Ethan raised one shaking finger towards the woman no one had noticed, the woman who was standing in the corner, a blank look in her eye that seemed to mark her irrelevance.

"Mom?" Amanda asked. "What's he talking about?"

"Tell her, Sara," Ethan repeated. "Tell her everything."

Sara Bennett put the fingertips of her right hand against her lips, her eyes widening in fear, then narrowing in anger.

"You bastard," she hissed. "You're still taking orders from him, aren't you?"

I shifted my gaze to Troy, then Mallard, who took this as his cue to release Ethan and step away.

"Orders from whom?" Amanda asked.

Sara took a step forward, "Preacher Younts."

I felt the breath suction from my lungs.

"How?" I managed, searching for something secure and steady and the next moment Dylan was beside me. "How do you know about him?"

Ethan looked to Sara, then slumped forward on the chair. "I've known him a long spell. Longer than any of you have been alive. Longer than your grandparents have been alive."

I listened, felt my eyes slide closed, and was transported back to the afternoon I spent at Cade Lake, the sun shining through the windows as the clock chirped over my shoulder, searching for a letter Odessa's brother had written.

"J?" Dylan said.

WHAT'S GOING ON?

I opened my eyes, searched for Sara Bennett. "How do you know about him?"

She didn't answer, just came slowly to a chair, and sat down in it. At once Amanda was at her side, taking her hand.

"Mom," she began, the word breaking like autumn leaves in the hand of a child. "Does this have to do with Dad?"

Sara nodded, sadness shining in her eyes.

"Tell her," Troy ordered, his voice gruff and I moved towards the woman sitting in the chair, the woman whose face seemed to drift between shadow and sunlight.

"Esther Ebersole," she whispered, and I started, the sound of the woman's name like a prayer.

I glanced at Adam, then Dylan. "How do you know her?"

She looked down, twisted her hands, and whispered, "She was my friend."

CHAPTER
THIRTY-ONE

"Your friend?" I echoed, looking around the room, seeking the eyes of someone who would tell me I wasn't dreaming. "How--"

"Tell her, Sara," Ethan slurred, his face starting to swell and bruise from the beating Troy had given him. "Or should I?"

"Well, someone better spill their fuckin' guts because I'm tired of staring at this asshole," Mallard announced, his outburst breaking the moment and it seemed to jar Sara Bennett.

"Daniel Calhoun and I were engaged," she began, her eyes clear, her words sure. "But one night we went to the woods looking for what our friends used to call the Whisper Stone."

I stood straighter, my body snapping to attention.

"I've heard of them," Pam spoke up as she moved closer to her son. "We used to go out there as kids."

Sara nodded. "There were markings on it and Daniel seemed to understand what they meant. His grandfather taught him about them, said the Ojibwa used them in their vision quests."

I looked to Troy, remembering how the Stone had affected us on Mackinac Island, and saw the fear in his eyes. The knowing.

"We went there," he spoke up. "It was covered in--"

"Snow," Sara interrupted, a tone in her voice that said she might think fondly of the place. "I remember telling Daniel how strange it was to see snow in summer, and he laughed, told me it was just a moss that comes after a hard rain. He thought it was a joke, but I knew the Stone was special and I think...I think it helped me go back."

"Mom," Amanda said, still grasping her hand. "What do you mean?"

"I stood on the Stone, right where Daniel said and..." she trailed off.

"Tell us, Sara," Dylan prodded, his voice a steady comfort when everything else seemed misplaced. "Did something happen to you?"

Sara looked up at Dylan, her face widening into a smile I didn't know she was capable of.

SHE KNOWS HIM.

I turned to my brother.

NO.

SHE'S SEEN HIM BEFORE.

As if to prove him right, she reached a hand towards Dylan, one she barely seemed aware of. "You look just like him. Just like my Andrew."

"Andrew?" Amanda echoed. "Mom, please tell me what's going on."

Sara closed her eyes, bent her head, and I felt Dylan's hand slide into mine, felt his fingers lace with my own and knew he needed my strength as much as I needed his.

"I traveled somewhere that night, Amanda. I don't know how I got there. I don't know how long I stayed. I only know that it changed me--that I couldn't be the person Daniel wanted me to be when I came back."

"When you came *back*?" her daughter repeated.

Ethan's laughter startled us all.

"She sure as hell didn't want to come back," he said, his gaze falling hard on Sara. "Some might say she was running for her very life."

Sara held a hand up to silence him and I saw that her fingers were shaking.

"I traveled somewhere that night, but I found people to take me in, people who were kind to me. The Ebersoles had a homestead and they needed help. They let me stay upstairs and I did the chores. They thought I had no family and after some time, Esther and I became friends. I kept thinking I could get back, if I could find the Stone and do what Daniel said. But I couldn't remember. I couldn't *think*."

I tightened my fingers around Dylan's, remembering the murders at Back Forty Farm, remembered the death of Esther Ebersole, and how it had triggered the events we were still dealing with today.

"*Fuck me!*" Mallard rasped, "I've heard this story since I was a kid. There was a hired girl sleepin' upstairs the night them two was killed, and she wasn't ever seen again."

"That girl was me," Sara said. "And I know what happened."

"*What?*" Troy began, cupping the back of his head, turning in a circle. For an instant his eyes caught mine, and I was taken back to our time in the clearing. The air had felt heavy, as though time were bending backwards and if someone were to put themselves at just the right place at just the right time...

"Mom," Amanda said, taking a step back. "What are you saying? And who was Andrew?"

She smiled again. "A young man I met at the market in town. He came from a farm just past Posen. Big place on top of a hill with a little stream running along the bottom."

I felt Dylan tense beside me and turned to look at him.

"That was my family's place," he said. "The Karsten's--"

I thought of Odessa in the vegetable garden, the shadow of her friend blocking the sun from behind.

"Our grandmother's name was Odessa Cook," I spoke up. "She had a friend...with a baby--"

"Andrew's sister," Sara smiled again, a perfectly lovely thing that seemed at odds with the woman she had been fifteen minutes before. "She introduced us and before long we were in love. I knew Daniel was waiting for me but the longer I stayed in that place, the more my old life seemed like a dream. The more I *wanted* it to be a dream."

"How did you get back?" Troy asked, his eyes grazing over Amanda's, meeting mine.

Sara turned to him, the shadows settling around her face and I felt panic begin to rise again.

"I wasn't sleeping when the Ebersoles were murdered," she began. "It was a mild night, and I had my window open when I heard a noise in the barnyard. I looked outside, saw Jonas and Esther and Abraham arguing. I saw Abraham come at Jonas with his gun. Saw Esther jump between them," she paused, swallowing past the grief that still seemed present. "I saw everything, and I knew Preacher would kill me for it."

"And we would've," Ethan spoke from his chair. "If she hadn't lit out like a scared rabbit."

Sara turned, fury in her face again. "You were a terrible man then and you're a terrible man now. I saw you hiding in that big locust tree and knew you were up to no good. Esther knew you wanted the gold Abraham kept in the safe. Knew you wanted *her*--"

"Damn right I did," Ethan spat back. "That bastard built his lumber business up with *my* inheritance. Took the woman *I* was supposed to marry."

"Your father knew you couldn't be trusted. That's why he left the farm to your brother. Abraham knew it, too--"

"Then he should've known I'd come after it."

The room was silent, Ethan Ebersole's words settling like a cold wind when I turned to him.

"You and Henry Younts went out there that night to kill your brother, steal his gold, and make it look like a robbery. But you discovered Esther and Jonas in the barn instead. And when Abraham came outside to confront them--"

"*He* killed Esther," Ethan interrupted, his face twisted. "That wasn't part of the plan. I just wanted the gold, but it seems my brother caught wind and hid it someplace because that safe was empty when Henry blew it open."

"So, you took off after Sara," I whispered. "Thinking she might know where it was because the only other people who knew about it were dead."

Ethan smiled, his mouth a bloody mess. "Henry had me keeping watch in that big locust tree when I saw Sara here peek out the upstairs window. I knew she'd run right to that fella she was sweet on and then to the sheriff, so I took my gun inside to finish the job, but she ran out the back door. I chased her all the way through the woods to that Stone but when I got there she was gone," he paused, his eyes on Sara. "Just up and vanished."

"I knew you'd hurt Andrew if I went to him, knew you wouldn't stop until you killed me, so I went to the Stone, stood where Daniel had shown me and I remembered. I remembered everything."

"And it brought you back?" Dylan asked.

"Yes," she answered. "But being there changed me. After I met Andrew--after we fell in love--"

"You didn't *want* to come back," her daughter whispered.

"Don't be upset, Mandy. I can go back and *find* him again. If I can just remember. If I can *think*."

"Mom," Amanda repeated, helpless. "*Please*--"

"When I came back, Daniel was standing in the same place I'd left him. I'd only been gone a moment and he didn't understand, thought I was playing a trick. I told him what had happened, told him about Andrew, and he took off on the motorcycle, ran that curve too fast and when he died, he took everything with him and now I can't *think*, can't remember and every time I go back to the Stone it gets worse."

"Mom," Amanda said, exchanging looks with Troy. "Why would you want to go back? Your life is here. *I'm* here."

Silence descended on the room as we waited for her response.

"Because," Sara whispered. "Your father is there."

CHAPTER
THIRTY-TWO

"My father," Amanda repeated, backing away and I looked at the necklace she was wearing, Adam's necklace, and knew it was the only thing keeping her sane. "Was some man from over a hundred years ago? A man I've never met. A man I'll *never* meet--"

"Don't say that!" Sara snapped. "You'll see him."

"No, I won't!" Amanda shot back. "And what makes you think I'd even *want* to go back? Everything is here. My life is *here.*"

"Of course, you want to go back," her mother said, softly now. "Of course you want to know your father, know your family."

"Mom--" Amanda said helplessly, her eyes searching the room. Catching mine.

"I wanted to tell you a long time ago, Mandy. But then time passed, and Ethan found you. And your grandparents insisted you marry him. He had money, after all. Too bad it belonged to Abraham."

"Abraham," Amanda said, the realization slowly dawning on her.

"Turns out Sara did know where Abraham buried that gold,"

Ethan spoke up. "It came in real handy when I dug it up over a hundred years later."

"What?" Amanda began. "What do you mean?"

"I did take a shine to you, Mandy--but you were just a means to an end. All I wanted was that gold, and I knew Sara would help me find it if I promised her one little thing."

Sara shook her head, the shadows long and dark under her eyes. "I just wanted to see Andrew again. He promised me he'd take me back, take *us* back if I told him where Abraham hid the gold."

"But you said you dug it up," I spoke up. "Why didn't you kill her then?"

Ethan smiled. "Seems Sara here was smarter than I thought because she dug up that gold and hid half of it-"

"I knew you wouldn't stop looking for me, for the gold-" she said. "And I needed something to keep me safe. To keep us safe," she looked to her daughter.

"So we struck a deal," Ethan explained.

"Deal?" Amanda asked, her face hard. "What deal?"

"She gets Andrew. I get the gold plus a nice, fat inheritance. After the wedding, of course."

I saw Troy tense again and turned to him, my eyes begging him to keep his cool.

"That's not true," Sara spoke up, her voice cracking. "I never wanted you to marry my daughter. It was her grandparents.... And *you*...all you ever cared about was money and Esther knew it."

"Esther knew I wanted to take care of her. Knew I loved her."

"She knew all right," Sara spat. "And it made her *sick!*"

I watched Ethan move on the stool, his eyes darkening. "How 'bout I finish that piece of business I started at the farm that night? Only this time you won't have any Injun magic to save you."

"Stop," I ordered, and to my surprise he obeyed. "How did you get through on the Stone when you didn't know how to use it?"

Ethan shook his head, a strange look in his eyes that told us he might not be in his right mind. "I helped the Younts boys track that shaman down. We got the answers out of him right before Henry finished him off."

"Butler," I gasped, my gaze moving to Adam. "He *told* you?"

"He told me enough," Ethan said. "And I had time to figure it out, time to gather all the pieces I needed from folks who had heard about it and when I finally got through I knew I needed to find my girl Sara again. Had to find that gold. But she was out of her mind, wouldn't talk to me no matter how nice I asked, so I had to make her believe I could take her back to Andrew."

"And you believed him?" Amanda asked, her eyes narrowing as she looked to her mother. "Why--"

"What choice did she have, Mandy?" Ethan smiled, swiping at his lip again. "I was the only one who knew how to use the Stone. She was the only one who knew where the rest of the gold was. It was business, plain and simple."

I saw Troy tense out of the corner of my eye.

"Go ahead and hit me again," Ethan looked up at him. "I won't be answering any questions and you all seem real interested in what I have to say."

I met Troy's gaze, and he nodded, his jaw set as Ethan continued.

"I knew the Injun's magic had done something unnatural to Henry and Jonas, but they were gone when I got here. Then, late at night, I started hearing Preacher's voice in my head, telling me what I needed to do to bring him back."

"Bring him back?" I repeated, my voice weak.

"You never finished the job, Muffet," Ethan smiled, his voice sounding more and more like the one I had come to fear above all others. "An' that left me jest enough room to squeeze through the door. With a little help, that is."

The others seemed to be floating in water as the familiar silence filled my ears. I felt a hand on my arm, knew it was Dylan, and then the sensation dissolved into nothing.

DON'T FIGHT IT.

I saw Sara Bennett running through the woods, her white nightgown tearing on the low branches of a cedar tree. Ethan was behind, crashing through the woods, half-drunk with the whiskey he'd been sipping since noon and it slowed him down, made him sloppy as the girl found the Stone. Stepping across the white moss, she found her mark, her lips moving silently, and vanished.

I sat in stunned silence at the base of the Stone while the light grew stronger, then weaker, watched as deer and squirrel broke the stillness into soft pieces, watched as a man came out of the woods, a piece of white fabric in his hand, and felt my heart stop.

Dylan.

He had the same build to his body, the same hair and eyes, and he was looking for someone, calling Sara's name and I knew he wanted to make a life with her and the baby she was carrying.

Something moved in the shadows behind the Stone. I watched as Ethan stepped from the woods, watched as Andrew Karsten turned, watched as they spoke, their words melting into an argument.

Andrew pulled a gun from his coat as Ethan drew out a long knife he had hidden in his waistcoat. Then they were wrestling for the weapons as Andrew's gun went flying into the underbrush. I tried to look away but stood stunned as Ethan plunged his knife into the heart of the man Sara loved. The man he had promised to reunite her with.

I felt a scream set fire to my throat. The sight was too awful, the resemblance too jarring, and so I covered my face, my breath making a heated tent until I dared to look again.

Andrew was dead, killed by the man who was now sitting in the chair at Huffs and I knew I could never tell Sara, knew she would never survive it.

And so, I crawled towards the man, touched his face and felt like I was touching Dylan. Bile rose in my throat and I turned quickly, my heart racing, and knew I had to get out of this place before it twisted my mind like Sara's.

Heavy footsteps crunching in the dried moss startled me, brought me to my feet and in that instant I knew who it was.

"Hello, Muffet."

I took a deep breath, weighing my words carefully.

"I'd say it's nice to see you but," I paused. "It isn't."

He laughed, took a step closer.

"That was some fancy work out at Hay Lake. You almost got us." Henry Younts laughed. "I won't miss again."

I stood for a moment, watching him. "Your boy Ethan just spilled

his guts. Told us how you were going to Back Forty Farm to steal Abraham's gold."

"Did he now?" Henry Younts chuckled. "Well, what's another sin to a damned man?"

I held his gaze, wondering if I'd shaken him. Knowing I had.

"We know about Sara Bennett and the Stone, and we're going to find a way to fix what went wrong last summer."

"That so?" he stopped, stood very still, his black eyes moving between my own. "I'll tell you one thing, Muffet--I'm clawin' my way back from that little piece o' purgatory you sent me to and when I git back you ain't ever gettin' rid o' me. Although I jest might git rid o' you. An' sweet baby brother."

I paused, desperate to keep my emotions in check as I took a step backwards, my foot sliding against the edge of the Stone.

"Mayhap I'll take him first, make you watch while I cut those pretty brown eyes right out o' his head."

I clenched my teeth so hard my jaw hurt. Regaining my footing, I moved towards him, my hands extended as though rage alone could kill him.

My sudden movement caught him off guard, and he stepped back, stumbled over the moss that seemed to tangle at his feet before planting his stance, his hands reaching for the shotgun that was always strapped to his back.

"Why don't you fight like a man," I spat, my eyes narrowing. "Or in this case, like a woman."

"You prissy bitch," he hissed. "I could squeeze your neck 'til your face turned black and there ain't nothin' your law dog could do about it."

I stopped moving, watched him closely.

"Try it, then," I said, fury steaming my veins. "I've never been more ready to send you straight to hell."

He paused, one hand slung over his shoulder, touching the butt of his shotgun. For an instant he glanced away towards a shadowy glen where voices could be heard and I saw something in his black eyes I'd never seen before.

Fear.

I listened closely, heard Dylan say my name and knew the vision was releasing me.

"See you soon, Muffet," he touched the brim of his hat, backed up one step at a time, his large form blending into the shadows until it seemed to blow away with the wind. "Real soon."

Voices from deep in the woods pulled me from the vision, tied me to the material world in which I lived, and I took a deep breath, gasped, and heard my brother's voice.

YOU'RE OKAY... YOU'RE BACK.

I blinked hard, felt hands slide beneath my shoulders.

I swallowed, looked at Troy as he helped Dylan ease me into a seated position.

"What did you see?" Pam asked, bending close.

"I went to the Stone," I said, searching for Sara. "You were running away."

"Running away?" she repeated, her eyes glassy.

I shifted on the floor, thinking back to the moment Ethan had pulled a knife and stabbed Andrew through the chest. They were arguing. Had it been about the gold?

"Justine," Dylan said, his voice soothing over the picture of his lookalike bleeding to death. "What else did you see?"

I shook my head, wishing I could tell him everything, so he could fix it, and we could go back to watching *Casablanca* on our sofa.

I remembered Henry Younts' black eyes, felt the sharp edge of his threat against Adam and hoped my brother couldn't hear my thoughts.

"Henry Younts was there," I whispered, and I felt Dylan's hand tighten against my shoulder.

"What did he say?" he asked.

I was questioning what to reveal when Amanda's scream split the air.

Dylan jumped to his feet beside me as Troy lifted me from the floor and turned.

Ethan was standing, the long knife he'd used to kill Andrew Karsten in his hand, and I knew he must have hidden it as he had that day in the snow-covered clearing.

"Put the knife down," Dylan ordered, and I saw Ethan jab at him as Troy and Mallard moved in a slow circle, trying to disarm him.

"Stop," I begged, pushing forward, Andrew's blood on the white moss flashing before my eyes.

"Justine!" Dylan called over his shoulder, one hand on his gun. "Troy--keep her back!"

Troy turned, caught me in his arms as my eyes locked with Ethan's and I felt myself being pulled backwards to the night he'd chased Sara through the woods, back to the moment he'd stabbed Andrew and further yet, to the first time he'd seen Esther in the parlor of his home, hoping he would be the one chosen to marry her.

I saw the hatred that had consumed him and knew it had melded his soul to Henry Younts.

Another series of wild stabs and Ethan was stumbling backwards across the floor. One hand groping behind him, he pushed the screen door open and plunged down the porch steps.

"He's getting away," Troy said, moving forward and I clutched at his arm, not wanting to see that knife hit its mark again.

"Keep an eye on him," Dylan said, drawing his gun. "I need to call for back-up."

Troy nodded, his hand on the screen door as Ethan staggered in a loose, zigzag pattern across the street towards a hay field, his lips moving as though speaking to a person we couldn't see.

"What's he doing?" Amanda whispered and I turned, motioned for Adam to stay where he was.

The next moment Ethan stopped, pivoted toward us while readjusting his grip on the long knife.

"No!" Amanda screamed, and I saw Troy grab her, suddenly aware of what was happening as Ethan drew the blade across his throat in one, swift motion.

CHAPTER
THIRTY-THREE

I lay curled up in a ball on one of the beds in Cabin Ten, drifting in and out of a fitful sleep, the image of Ethan slitting his throat marking the moment as the most horrific of my life.

Dylan was lying behind me, one hand around my waist, his eyes worn and worried and I knew he was thinking the same thing I was.

I remembered Ethan's lips moving and wondered who he was talking to. And then the knife had flashed, and Ethan's knees had folded, and he had fallen into the grass like a marionette, his body jerking as I covered my face and screamed.

"Baby," Dylan's voice brought me back to the present. "You can't keep thinking about it."

But I *was* thinking about it. I was thinking about Amanda, numb with shock as Pam drove her and Troy and Adam and Sara back to Three Fires before we called the police.

I thought of Dylan--stepping forward, taking control like he always did, smoothing things over with the men he worked with.

We had just stopped by to talk to Mallard, walked in on a bar fight, and tried to break it up.

The next minute Ethan stumbled outside and did the unthinkable.

Statements were taken, Mallard promised to come down to the station and talk to the detective and I had no idea how a simple dream had turned my summer into a full-blown nightmare.

I thought all these things as I lay in Dylan's arms, hoping his strength would seep into my bones and erase the image of Ethan falling into the grass.

"Are those the kinds of things you see?" I asked, turning to look at him. "When you tell me to call when I get home and lock the front door and make sure my phone is charged. Is it because of *that?*"

He nodded.

I shook my head, a strange chill causing me to shiver, and Dylan reached down to the foot of the bed and pulled a blanket over me.

I thought about what Ethan had said, thought about Butler and how Henry and Jonas had tracked him down, forced him to perform bad medicine so Esther Ebersole could live again.

"I have an idea," I said, my voice a whisper and I felt Dylan's arms tighten.

"Baby--"

"We need to find Jamie Stoddard. He's the only one who might know how to fix this. He talked to Butler. He was there when--"

"We don't know where he is."

I stiffened in his arms. "We never looked! We never even *thought* about looking."

"You won't find him."

"How do you know?" I asked, my voice rising.

"I just do," he said, his fingers at my cheek. "I want you to close your eyes and get some sleep. I'm not going to let anything happen to you."

I took a slow breath. Released it.

"Henry Younts said he'd see me real soon and I bet he's going to make good on that promise. In fact, he was probably talking to

Ethan, telling him to cut his throat, so he could come back and finish us off and I don't understand why you don't want to find the one person who could help us? Jamie Stoddard might be *alive,* Dylan! He might *still* be alive!"

"You need to stop."

"Why?" I asked, heat flushing my face. "*Why--*"

"Because he's dead."

"*What?*" I gasped, sitting up quickly. "How?"

"I kept track of him. He used an alias until he got out of the state. Then he settled in Indiana and tried to find work and," he paused, watching me closely. "He died last winter."

"Last winter?" I echoed, my voice trailing off. "Why didn't you tell me?"

"I'm sorry." He glanced down. "I knew you cared about him, knew it would upset you."

I looked at him, touched his face softly to let him know I wasn't angry--that I could never be angry after what I'd seen in the hay field that afternoon.

"What do we do?" I asked, sliding back down beside him, my head a ball of static that seemed to be drowning me. "I don't know what to do."

"Close your eyes," he said softly. "I'll get in touch with your mom and Holly. Mallard's gone to the station and Rocky's up at the house with Pam and Adam."

I took a deep breath, knowing the dog would protect my brother with his life.

"Amanda's asleep out on the couch and Troy's here, too."

"Dylan--"

"He'll have to go through us to get to you."

I frowned. "That doesn't make me feel any better."

"Sleep," he whispered. "So you can think."

He was right, and so I closed my eyes, exhaustion carrying me to a place where everything was dark and silent and gone.

I don't know how long I'd been sleeping before I felt Dad enter the room and sit down on the edge of the bed.

"Muffet," he said, and I opened my eyes, saw that we were alone.

"Dad," I whispered, the pain fresh and raw. "It was so awful."

"I know," he said.

"What do we do?" I asked. "The snakeskin burned. The totems are gone. I don't know why my strength hasn't gone with it."

"The medicine is a gift that lasts forever. It comes when it's needed."

Something in his words stoked my anger, and I sat up in bed. "Well, what if I don't want it to last forever? What if I want to take that shitty medicine bag and burn it to a crisp? Then Odessa would just have to figure out how to fend for herself!"

Dad nodded. "Maybe you should."

"Yeah," I said, wiping at my nose. "Maybe I should--and while I'm at it I'll give Butler a piece of my mind."

"You should do that, too."

I narrowed my eyes, suddenly suspicious. "Is that why you wanted me to find Amanda Bennett? So we could stay ahead of Henry Younts while he's trying to kill the people we love? Well, I've got news for you, we never saw that last one coming. Or at least Amanda didn't. And she was supposed to have the inside scoop."

"I'm sorry, Muffet."

"Why are you talking to me this way?" I asked, watching his face for signs of anger. Finding none. "Why don't you give me some sage advice--or at least a fucking clue, so I can be happy like you wanted."

"I should, shouldn't I?"

I stopped, unnerved by his reactions, turned, and saw Dylan slumped in a chair past the bedroom, his gun in his lap, his head in one hand, exhausted.

"He doesn't deserve this, you know," I whispered.

"I know."

"All he wants to do is teach history up at the high school, maybe coach some basketball on the side, so we can buy that bungalow."

"I know."

"And instead, he's spent the last year thinking I love you more than him."

My father looked at me.

"Do you understand what I'm saying to you?"

He nodded.

"Then maybe you can tell me how to give my brother his childhood back. Or how to let the man in the next room know I'll fight for us instead of the ghost sitting next to me."

"You already know what to do, Muffet."

"No, *Dad,*" I spat, angrier than I'd ever been. "I don't know because I don't fucking understand what you want me to do! Why do you keep coming back if you're just going to let me watch a man slit his throat? What's the point of Butler's medicine if I can't use it to protect the people I love?"

"You can, Muffet."

I sighed, fatigue making my skin prickle.

"You don't need me. You've never needed me."

"Dad--" I said, suddenly afraid. "Of course, I need you."

"No," he said, standing up. "You want me--and I'm glad. But you don't need me."

"Wait--"

"It's time for my little bird to fly."

"Fly?" I asked, thinking of the robin that hit our front window-- the red bird I followed through the forest to Back Forty Farm.

"You've found the bridge."

"What," I said, desperate now, reaching for him. "No--"

"Your mom used to let you wander around the woods all day long. Sometimes I'd ask her why, she was always so protective, and do you know what she said?"

I looked at him, wondering why she had never told me this story.

"She trusted you, said you could sniff out a trail with nothing more than a broken branch to go on," he paused, smiled in a way my mother must have loved. "She called you her little path finder."

I smiled, liking the person my mother had been.

"But she was wrong," he said, standing now, and I looked at him, feeling like this moment was more important than any other we had shared.

"What do you mean?" I asked.

"You weren't meant to find the path," he said. "You were meant to make it."

I SLEPT SOUNDLY the rest of the night even as strange, whimsical dreams surrounded me. I stood in a wide field, closed my hand around a firefly only to find it empty moments later.

I thought about Iris, thought about Holly and Mallard and Meg, of Adam and Pam and Troy. I thought about my mom and Paul and Amanda and the strange circumstances that had brought her into my life. I thought about Andrew Karsten, killed in the mossy clearing over a century ago with a piece of Sara Bennett's nightgown in his hand.

I thought of Jamie Stoddard and was surprised at the depth of my grief.

I wanted him now, wanted to see his crooked smile and amber eyes, wanted to watch him push his brown hair out of his face. Wanted to take hold of his strong hands and ask him what to do.

Wanted to follow.

Like I'd done before.

But I couldn't.

A hummingbird darted past my face, and I turned, saw the Stone in the distance and walked towards it. Dropping to my knees, I traced the strange symbols with my fingers, felt the power of the medicine bag draw me back to the moment Butler had first placed the totems inside of it.

I saw Sara Bennett standing here as Daniel Calhoun leaned

against his motorcycle, hoping she would grow tired of the game, so they could go home.

I saw her learning how to work the earth at Back Forty Farm, her footsteps taking her to the homestead of Odessa Cook and her son, Calvert.

I looked down, saw myself standing barefoot in the forest of my childhood, saw the trail I had always followed and the long row of pines that narrowed into blackness.

Moving closer, I saw a person standing at the end of the row, a person in a nightgown not unlike the one Sara Bennett had torn as she fled Back Forty Farm.

"Justine," the voice came, carried on the wind like so many others before it.

I nodded, knowing who she was, what she was, and felt sleep release me.

"Dylan," I gasped, sitting up in bed, bright light blinding me.

The cabin was quiet as I swung my legs off the bed and jammed my feet into my tennis shoes.

"Dylan," I called again, wondering where he was--knowing he wouldn't have gone far.

I made my way through the living room, saw movement outside the window.

Troy opened the door, saw the look in my eye and came to me quickly.

"What is it?" he asked.

I reached out, touched his arm. "I know what to do."

"You do?" he asked, hopeful.

"We need to find the Stone. And we need Sara."

"J," I heard Dylan's voice behind me, spun to see him coming in from the porch, Amanda behind. "What's going on?"

"Where's Sara?"

I saw Amanda glance at Troy. "Up at the house."

"We need to take her to the Stone."

"The Stone?" Dylan echoed, coming closer. "What are you talking about?"

"We've only got so much time before Henry Younts comes back. And I can't let him hurt you," I paused, my thoughts darkening. "Or Adam."

"He's not going to hurt us," Dylan said, his eyes cutting to Troy.

I turned to Amanda. "Have you seen anyone else die?"

She pressed her lips together, looked at Troy, and shook her head.

"That's because there *aren't* any more."

"No," Amanda said, her voice rising. "I would have seen it if Ethan were one of them. I would have seen it and I would have *stopped* him."

"But you didn't," I said. "And now we're sitting ducks."

"Maybe it's the necklace," Troy offered. "It healed her injuries so maybe it took her visions away, too."

"No," I said, my mind set. "I can't cross my fingers and hope another person doesn't end up like Meg. Or Ethan."

"Justine," Dylan said, the fear starting to build behind his eyes, and I hated that it had anything to do with me. "Why are you talking about the Stone? Why do you want to see Sara?"

I looked at him, praying he would understand.

"The night Esther was killed, Jonas went to Odessa's house and stole the medicine bag. Then he tracked Butler down, forced him to perform bad medicine."

"I know this," he said, clearly frustrated. "We *know* all of this."

"But what if it never happened? What if Jonas and Esther never snuck off to the barn and Henry and Ethan never tried to steal Abraham's gold? Esther would be alive and everyone would die of natural causes."

He stepped closer, his eyes clouded with worry.

"No."

"I have to do this."

"*No!*"

I reached for his hand, and he grasped it so tightly my knuckles blanched.

"Dad came to me and told me I needed to make the path, told me I'd already found the bridge and I think I know what he meant."

"Justine," Troy said, and I turned to him. "What the hell are you talking about?"

I took a deep breath, steeled myself for what I was about to say. "The only way to kill Henry Younts is to stop him from becoming immortal in the first place, and the only way to do that is to use the Stone."

"*Use the Stone*," Troy repeated, his face going slack. "Is this some kind of sick joke?"

"I wish," Dylan said under his breath.

"Don't you get it?" I said. "The bridge isn't a thing or a place or even the Stone itself, it's a *person*."

I watched Amanda's eyes widen and knew she understood.

"Sara said it was her belief in the Stone that helped her go back. She was meant to meet Andrew, meant to fall in love and have a baby," I paused, my eyes darting between the three of them before settling on the young woman who had jumped from Robinson's Folly.

"No," she raised her hands as though trying to push me away. "I can't--"

"Dad wanted me to find you because you belong to both worlds. *You're* the bridge, Amanda."

"No," she gasped again, turning to Dylan. "Is she crazy?"

"Like a fox," he sighed.

"We can't risk it," Troy interrupted. "Anything could happen. Just look at Sara, for Christ's sake."

I was silent, my gaze shifting to Dylan, remembering the night we had watched an old movie in the dim light of our living room.

"Do you trust me?"

He paused, his eyes reflecting the pain he'd hidden for the past year.

"Yes."

"Then let me do the thinking for both of us."

He touched my cheek, his eyes darkening. "I can't lose you again."

I covered his hand with my own.

"Then come with me."

CHAPTER
THIRTY-FOUR

I was sitting in the middle of Pam's living room, Adam by my side, wondering how a woman who seemed lost in her own world would ever be able to help me enter a new one.

Amanda took a seat beside her mother, Troy standing over her shoulder, his eyes seeking mine and I imagined he was remembering our time at the Stone, wondering if the unseen power we'd felt then would help us now.

"What is it?" Sara asked, her gaze flicking to her daughter. "What does she want?"

"She needs your help, Mom," Amanda answered, taking hold of her hand. "*We* need your help."

I leaned closer, "I need you to try and remember what Daniel told you about the Stone."

I didn't want to look at Pam when I said it. Or her son.

ARE YOU GOING BACK?

ADAM--

I'M COMING, TOO--

YOU CAN'T.

SAYS WHO?

SAYS ME.

"I don't know," Sara said, her face pinched.

"Sara," Dylan stepped in. "He told you something that helped you go back in time. Something that took you to Andrew."

"No," she insisted. "Daniel's gone. Andrew's gone."

"Sara," I said again, touching the top of her hand. "He took you to the Whisper Stone, and he told you a story. Do you remember what it was?"

She looked down, pushed a strand of hair behind her ear. "It was my fault."

I took a deep breath, my patience crumbling, and looked at Dylan--really looked at him. I took in his strong jaw line and mouth, his straight nose and thick hair lost for a moment in the blue eyes that seemed to change color with his mood.

I imagined myself in the clearing again, felt my cheek against the cushion of white moss and remembered the moment Ethan plunged the knife into Andrew's chest. I remembered the horror I'd felt as Andrew bled to death and knew why Sara had lost her mind.

"Sara," I began again. "Daniel's gone but there's someone here who wants you to remember. Someone who wants you to come back to him."

"Justine--" Dylan said, and I glanced at him, hoping he would understand.

"It's Andrew," I swallowed past my guilt. "And he wants you to remember so you can be together."

"Andrew?" she asked, her head lifting, and I hated myself for lying to her.

"Yes," I said, moving over to allow Dylan room. "He wants you to remember."

"Is it really you?" she whispered, her eyes on Dylan, and he shifted on his knees, shot me a look that said he wasn't happy.

He cleared his throat, muttered, "Yes."

"How?" she asked, her face spilling into a smile. "I don't understand."

"I can't stay long," he said slowly, his words strained. "But if you tell me what you remember then maybe we can be together."

I glanced at Dylan, gave him a little nod.

"I can?" Sara asked, her eyes softening, and she turned, touched Amanda's arm. "What do you think of our girl?"

Dylan nodded, and I marveled at how completely he was beginning to immerse himself.

"She's beautiful, Sara. And I'm sorry you had to raise her alone. I should have been there."

Sara shook her head. "That was my doing. I got scared and ran off. I was so afraid Ethan and Henry would kill you."

"You did the right thing."

"I did?" she asked, almost childlike.

"Yes. But now you need to tell us how you went back," Dylan continued. "So we can spend the rest of our lives together."

She pushed her hair behind her ear again, and I noticed her hands had stopped shaking.

"It's okay, Mom," Amanda said, squeezing her shoulder.

I HOPE YOU KNOW WHAT YOU'RE DOING.

I glanced at Adam, saw Sara do the same.

"And this must be Calvert Cook," she said.

"Calvert Cook?" Dylan looked at me, caught off guard.

"You were always so fond of him, Andrew. Did you bring him back, too?"

Dylan paused. "He misses you. Remembers how nice you were to him."

Sara nodded again. "Poor boy. Growing up without a pa was hard on him and his gran was a hard woman. Come here, Cal and let me look at you."

I watched the color drain from my brother's face.

WHAT DO I DO?

"He caught a cold in the night air and lost his voice," Dylan said quickly. "He's not feeling well."

Sara smiled, wagged a finger at him. "You took sick doing that once before. But did you listen to what Doc said?"

PLAY ALONG WITH HER.

I looked at my brother, saw him shake his head.

"Naughty boy. Your ma will have to take you to the shaman for some of his tonic," she paused, her face shining. "Now, come closer so I can see you."

I looked at Adam, saw him take a faltering step forward.

"Cal?" she asked again, cocking her head to the side. "Is it really you?"

"It's him," I said quickly.

"His hair is darker," Sara said, her eyes narrowing. "Who is this boy, Andrew?"

"It's Cal, Sara," Troy spoke up from behind.

"No," she said, her hands shaking again. "No...he's *not*. And you," she turned to Dylan, looked at him closely. "Who *are* you?"

"I'm Andrew," Dylan said, placing one hand on her cheek.

Sara shook her head, her eyes clouding over as her speech became agitated. "You don't have that scar on your chin, the one you got when your pa's fishing hook caught you down by the creek."

"Sara," he whispered. "It's me."

She looked at him again, her eyes watery as Dylan leaned forward, his lips seeking hers.

I watched Sara's eyes slide closed, watched the bliss that seemed to eclipse her face and promised myself I would do everything in my power to save the man she loved.

"Andrew," she sighed, pulling back.

"Yes," he answered, all pretense gone.

"I love you," she breathed, her eyes clear. "And I remember."

CHAPTER
THIRTY-FIVE

I was seated in the passenger seat of Dylan's truck, watching the woods fly by in a verdant blur, praying the man sitting beside me would still be there after all was said and done.

Sara had, true to her word, explained everything she remembered, everything her weary mind could recall, and I still didn't feel strong enough to stand on the Whisper Stone with any measure of assurance I would return.

"You should call your mom," Dylan broke the silence, his eyes cutting to me in numbed terror as he turned off 23 and onto a side road. Glancing in the rear view mirror, I saw Pam's car do the same.

"And tell her what? That I'm planning to use an old Ojibwa petroglyph to travel back in time and kill the man I was supposed to have finished off last summer?" I paused, drew a shaky breath. "If everything goes okay no one will miss us."

"This is bat shit crazy," he said, his eyes back on the road, his hands kneading the steering wheel. "I can't believe I'm doing this. I can't believe I'm letting *you* do this."

I glanced at him. "It's the only way."

He shook his head. "I wish I could argue with you."

"I wish we were on our way to that Mexican restaurant in Cheboygan for three dollar margaritas."

His laughter was soft, low. "Me, too."

"And after this is over that's the first thing we're gonna do."

He chuckled. "Really?"

I felt heat splash my cheeks.

"Well...maybe the *second* thing."

He reached over, took my hand. "I'm sorry about what happened back there. With Sara--"

I shook my head. "It had to be done."

He looked back at the road.

"Henry Younts said he was going to kill Adam," I whispered.

"*What?*"

"Said he was going to make me watch."

"Shit," he muttered. "No wonder you're hell-bent on this."

I swallowed hard. Nodded.

"But we have to be careful. Anything could change the future. Could change *us*. Could change Adam."

"I know."

"Do you?" he asked. "Because I might not get through."

I glanced at him sharply. "Don't say that."

"You have to be prepared. Sara said she believed in the power of the Stone, that believing was the most important part, and we both know that I--"

"Can be kind of a meathead?"

He laughed, but the sound held no joy, only a short spurt of breath that told me he wanted it to be over.

"What if I can't do it?"

"Stop talking that way."

"You'll be alone."

"You said you'd come after me."

His fingers tightened around my own.

"Every damn time."

I smiled, took a deep breath as we turned onto a two track that led into dense woodland. Minutes later we saw a cluster of evergreen and cedar, a flash of white at their base and knew we had found the Whisper Stone.

Dylan parked the truck and I stepped out, feeling a reverence for this place that had first manifested itself on Mackinac Island. I walked around the perimeter of the clearing, listened to the birds singing in the trees above us, and bent to touch the Stone with my fingertips.

"Justine," Dylan said, and I turned, saw him standing behind me and went to him, pressing my lips to his for a long moment. I felt his breath catch, felt his hand cup the back of my head, and prayed the power we were about to engage would allow us to be together.

A rumbling noise caught our attention and I pulled away as Pam's car came into view. We turned, watching as the others climbed out.

At once my brother came to me.

SARA DOESN'T KNOW WHERE SHE IS...DOESN'T KNOW WHY WE'RE HERE.

I glanced at Amanda.

TAKE ME.

"I'd never forgive myself if you got hurt."

DAD SAID WE'RE STRONGER TOGETHER.

I thought about his words, realizing he was right but knowing our chances of getting four people to the same place via an old Ojibwa petroglyph were slim to none. And I needed him safe with Mallard and Pam and Rocky and Troy while I took care of unfinished business in 1889.

"If something goes wrong you still have a shot at ending this."

DON'T SAY THAT

"There's a reason Butler divided the medicine between us."

He looked at me, his eyes holding.

"Sometimes strength comes from being apart."

I watched his eyes flicker away, watched him cover his ear with his hand, and then he was stepping into my embrace and I felt my heart burst with a fierce, primal love.

Stepping towards the stone, I looked from Amanda to Troy, my eyes lingering on the latter.

"Are you sure you want to do this?" he asked.

I nodded. "Take care of Adam."

"I will," he said, his eyes telling me he would protect my brother.

Then I was walking towards the Whisper Stone, watching the light slant through the trees as Amanda stepped into Troy's arms.

Looking back, I held my hand out to Dylan as Adam went to his mother.

"You need to hurry," Pam said. "The sun's starting to set."

I nodded. Sara had said that was important.

But we had a bridge, a living person whose father had searched for her until he stumbled upon the same clearing we were in now.

I looked to my feet, remembered the snowy moss covered in blood and prayed we weren't too late to save Andrew Karsten.

"Let's go," Amanda said, her eyes on Troy, and he nodded, his jaw tight and I knew it took all his strength to let her go.

We stepped onto the stone, linked hands.

My heart hammered in my chest, wondering if this crazy idea would work or if I'd end up looking like a fool.

Or worse.

I remembered my father's words and turned my face to the west, feeling the air moved around me and prayed for the great wind to show itself. I thought about Butler and Odessa in the vegetable garden, their fingers touching as he dug his hands in the earth. I thought of Esther's cameo and how Jamie's had stared at the face shining above it, feeling like he'd stepped into a dream.

I took a breath, smelled sweet pine on the air and felt myself shift, felt my body lift.

Everything was draped in a silver veil that touched the trees as they bent in a climbing breeze. I turned to Dylan, his hand laced in mine and willed him to believe in what I was seeing.

I closed my eyes, the wind whispering my name like a bell.

"Justine."

I drew a breath and knew it was happening.

"I said I'd see you soon."

My eyes flew open as I struggled against the force that surrounded me.

"He's mine."

Dylan's hand loosened, his feet sliding against the stone as if pushed by an invisible wind.

"No," I cried as Amanda skidded backwards, pulled by the same thing Dylan was fighting and tightened my grip.

HE'S HERE!

My body froze from the toes up as a large figure emerged from a dark grove of cedars.

"Stop!" I screamed, feeling my body lift again, not wanting to leave.

I watched, helpless, as Henry Younts lumbered towards the stone, watched as Troy ran at him from behind but knew it was useless. He was too large, too powerful, and in one motion Troy was thrown to the ground.

Amanda screamed and my throat seized up as Henry Younts pulled the shotgun from his shoulder.

Two blasts rang out.

Droplets of scalding water sprayed my side and I cried out in pain. Looking down, I saw a peppering of read against my white shirt and knew I'd been hit.

I went down on one knee, my fingers seeking the wound as Dylan's hand was pulled from mine.

"Justine!" he cried as he slid away from me, coming to rest at the base of the stone.

At once the figures on the other side of the veil seemed to scatter as Henry Younts came forward in three, huge strides.

"Dylan," I gasped, watching as he tried to stand, tried to crawl towards me.

Then Henry Younts was standing over him, the butt-end of his shotgun raised high.

GO!

The voice jolted me.

HE WANTS TO KEEP YOU HERE!

Dylan--

GO!

"Adam," I gasped as he broke free from his mother and sprinted between Dylan and Henry Younts.

I screamed as the weapon swung downwards, the veil clouding my vision.

I closed my eyes.

Let go.

And felt the great wind carry me away.

AMANDA BENNETT FELT her feet slide from the stone as though it were covered in ice as Henry Younts lumbered from the forest, the largest man she had ever seen.

She watched as Troy ran at him from behind, watched him throw the entire weight of his body against their attacker.

A shot rang out.

And then another.

Justine winced as the buckshot hit her, the strange, silvery veil absorbing what should have killed her.

Dylan cried out, crawling on his knees to get to her as Henry Younts raised his shotgun.

She watched Dylan crouch, waiting for the blow when Adam ran between, giving him just enough time to fire thirteen rounds into the man who never seemed to die.

Henry Younts dropped his weapon and staggered backwards, his wounds oozing black smoke instead of blood. He grabbed the low branch of a cedar, the light erasing his features as he stepped backwards again, vanishing.

Amanda stood slowly as Troy rose to his feet and wiped a bloody lip with the back of his hand.

He took a step towards her when Pam's scream jolted them.

At once Dylan knelt over Adam, who lay motionless, a gash on his forehead that was beginning to ooze blood.

"Adam," he said, his voice laced with panic. "Can you hear me?"

Troy knelt beside him and felt for a pulse.

"He's alive," he said. "But we need to get him out of here."

Dylan stood up slowly, turned back to the stone.

"She was hit," Troy said, and Dylan glanced at him, his jaw working.

"I know."

"You have to go," Amanda said, her eyes moving to Pam, sitting beside her son in mute shock. "And you need to take this."

She removed her necklace. Placed it in his hand.

"You're not coming?" he asked, dazed.

She shook her head, glanced at Troy. "I need to stay."

"But--"

"She loves you. That's all the bridge you need."

Dylan looked down, cleared his throat. "If something happens--"

"We'll take care of him," Troy swiped at his lip again, bent to take Adam into his arms as Pam rose slowly to her feet.

"Troy--"

"Go!"

Silence as the two men stood motionless, the trees making a noise that said the wind was ready, the time right.

"Don't come back without her."

Dylan paused, his eyes locking with Troy's in a way that spoke to all that remained unsaid between them.

"I won't."

EPILOGUE

I lay on the ground, the smell of well-worked earth beneath my cheek and coughed. My body was heavy, my arms useless as I tried to lift them.

I thought about what I had seen, thought about my brother and felt a primal cry rip past my lips.

Rustling in the leaves startled me and I moved my hand and felt a wet substance on my fingertips. I took a breath--the chilled wind smelling of autumn--and raised my head.

A field stretched away to the horizon, heavy with corn and ready for harvest.

A boy stood a few feet away, watching me, his bare feet coarse and brown from a season spent outdoors.

I gritted my teeth against the searing pain and tried to sit up.

He moved away, afraid.

"Please," I gasped, breathless. "Can you help me?"

He took another step back.

"Where am I?" I asked, knowing the sight of my bloodied shirt had frightened him.

"Who're you?" he asked, his voice high. "How'd you get hurt?"

I couldn't answer, couldn't imagine where the others were but I knew where I was, knew what I had to do even as my heart collapsed in grief.

"Ain't no one supposed to be out here in my Uncle Johnny's field."

"Uncle Johnny?" I managed as the boy came closer, his face illuminated by the setting sun.

"*Adam?*"

He cocked his head to the side. "Who's that?"

I swallowed.

"My brother," I whispered, knowing it was useless, wanting to say it anyway.

"I ain't seen your brother."

"I know," I whispered, tears needling to the surface.

He took a skittish step towards me, ready to run at any moment.

"What're you doin' out here?"

"I--" I tried to steady my voice. "I think I'm lost."

He tilted his head to the other side, mashed his face into a semblance of pity.

"I'm Justine," I managed, pulling myself into a seated position.

"I'll take you up to the house," he said, wiping his forehead with the cuff of his shirt. "My ma will tend to you."

Gritting my teeth, I extended my hand and allowed him to help me to my feet.

"What's your name?"

The boy hesitated before wrapping an arm around me, the house he spoke of sitting on top of a hill, light shining from inside.

"I'm Calvert Cook," he said. "But folks just call me Cal."

ACKNOWLEDGMENTS

I am forever indebted to the people who have supported me. Nola Nash, thank you for your friendship and your wisdom and for being the BEST BFF and tour guide ever. Kiersten Modglin, you have such a great sense of this business and I appreciate your help and friendship. Denise Birt, I so appreciate your guidance and grace and eternal kindness. Rob Samborn and Shanessa Gluhm,- I'm glad to know both of you and so glad one lead me to the other... and Renea Winchester and Nancy Johnson- glad to lead YOU to each other, and glad to call you both friends.Thank you to my author friends: Wade Rouse, Gary Edwards, Christina MacDonald, Hannah Mary McKinnon, Claire Fullerton, Kellie Coates Gilbert, Lori Rader-Day, Alison Ragsdale, Jennifer Laird, Tina Hogan Grant, Ward Parker, Sharon Gloger Friedman, Renea Winchester, Kathy Ramsperger, Joanna Evans, Benny Sims, Jessica Reino, and Seth Augustein.

To Terry Shepherd and Ramirez and Clark Publishing, you ROCK!

To the readers who have embraced my books and turned into a mini army on their behalf and to all the library and book store staff who have set up events for me and supported me in my efforts: Tamara Tomac, Tom Lowry, Becky Koetje, Judy Broadworth, Perri Saunders, Bobbi Jo Schoon, Julie Censke, Kim Foghino, Christine Nofsinger, Michelle Johnson, Diana Heimstra Anne Berenger, and everyone at the Presque Isle District Library!

To my family- Mom, Dad, Scott and kiddos- I love you more...

ABOUT THE AUTHOR

Laura is a teacher who loves to write about her home state of Michigan. She has a B.A. in Creative Writing from Western Michigan University where she studied under Stuart Dybek, and has had her short fiction and poetry published in Chicken Soup for the Soul, Word Riot, Tonopalah Review, SaLit and SLAB: Sound and Literary Art Book. "The Pursuit of Happiness," a short story she wrote while at WMU, was chosen as a finalist in the Trial Balloon Fiction Contest. Her debut novel, Evening in the Yellow Wood, was a National Indie Excellence Winner for Cross Genre Fiction. It has also received a Readers Favorite Bronze Medal, an IPPY Silver Medal in Regional Fiction, and was a Finalist in the American Book Awards.

When not writing, Laura enjoys musical theatre, hiking, swimming, reading, and performing with her Celtic band--Si Bhaeg Si Mohr. She also enjoys spending time with her husband and children as well as her many animals.

Laura loves to connect with readers on her blog: laurakempbooks.com/blog (Sea Legs on Land), as well as on Facebook (Kemp Camp), Twitter (@LKempWrites) and Instagram. (lkempwrites) (woodys_book_tour_).

Made in United States
Orlando, FL
25 August 2024